Tragically BEAUTIFUL

TORI ALVAREZ

TRAGICALLY BEAUTIFUL

GRAFFITI HEARTS
BOOK TWO

TORI ALVAREZ

ETERNAL DAYDREAMER PUBLISHING

ISBN-13: 978-1-7343363-3-7 (Paperback edition)
ISBN-13: 978-1-7343363-4-4 (Ebook edition)

Cover Design: Eternal Daydreamer Publishing
Editor: Jacqueline Hritz
Formatting: Eternal Daydreamer Publishing

❀ Created with Vellum

Always to my mom. I think of you everyday.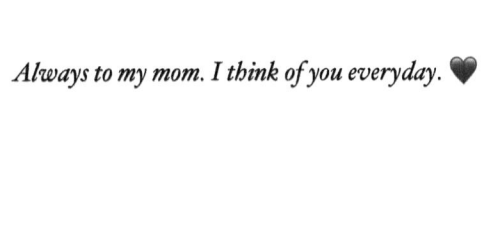

CONTENTS

PROLOGUE

ALEJANDRO
17 Years Ago

LISTENING AND BEING QUIET WAS THE EASIEST WAY TO FIND out the secrets our parents kept from us. They were always so focused on their discussion, they didn't pay attention to their surroundings. Things have never been easy, and I'm only ten. I listen because I like to know what struggle is coming my way so I can plan for it.

Like when my dad loses his job again. Or when mom stays out too late with her friends. Or when we don't have money to pay rent. I know this is when he gets drunk and mean. It is best for Javie and I to stay away. I've taken one too many beatings for being in the wrong place at the wrong time or jumping in for Javie, but he was too little to take it. It's my job as his big brother to protect him.

Javie and I are on the couch, watching TV as Dad walks into the apartment, stumbling around drunk. As soon as I see him, I tell Javie to go to our room and close the door. Mom isn't home, and that will set him off.

"Where's your bitch of a mother?" he yells after coming back into the living room from his bedroom.

I shake my head and raise my shoulders, not knowing where she went. Any words leaving my mouth will be used against me.

"She didn't have work today. Shouldn't she be taking care of her damn kids?" he spits out angrily.

I always wonder why he calls us "her" kids. Aren't we his kids too? I stand slowly to make myself scarce while he is looking in the fridge. Just as I enter our bedroom, the front door opens. I close the door quickly and crouch in the corner hidden out of their view to listen.

"Where the hell have you been? Out whoring?" Dad starts in right away.

"Out. Why the hell do you care anyway?" She responds casually.

I know this is going to get bad. I hope I can make it into the room quickly enough to hide Javie if he comes this way. I just can't move yet, I need to know what is going to happen. Güela will need to come pick us up if this was going to be one of their explosions.

"Because you're my fuckin' *vieja*. You should be home when I get home. Have a fuckin' meal ready and take care of the damn kids." He shouts.

"You can make yourself something to eat," she calmly states. Today is different. She usually gives it back just as hard as he dishes.

"What the fuck, puta." He goes straight to calling her bitch, the one name he knows sets her off.

"I'm leaving. Just thought I would let you know." Her voice is flat, uncaring. I want to peek around the corner to look at her, but I can't risk being seen.

"What do you mean you're leaving?" Her statement catches him off guard; he sounds confused.

"Leaving you. I'm done." I hear her take a deep breath. "I thought it would be different. You said it was going to be different. We were going to make things happen. But here we are, still stuck. Getting evicted every year. No money. Having to move in with your mom or my parents. Stuck with two kids."

Stuck with two kids? Did she not want us?

My dad is silent. All the fight he just had in him was let out with her words.

"I don't understand."

And he didn't. I don't know if they loved each other really. They got pregnant with me in high school. And like any good Mexican family in the hood, you kept the baby and got married. My parents dropped out of high school to start working.

"*No puedo*. It's too hard."

A few seconds later I hear the front door open and close. I crawl to our bedroom door and sneak in. I wasn't sure if his anger would show soon, so I put Javie in the closet, and I laid on the bed. Best he finds me, not him.

CHAPTER 1

ALEJANDRO (ALEX)
November

HOSPITALS ARE FOREIGN TO ME. I HAVE NEVER HAD TO SET foot in one until today. That's a strange thought. A twenty-seven-year-old man who has never been in a hospital must not be normal. But here I am. In an uncomfortable seat, waiting patiently for news about my grandmother. My cousin Antonia is leaning against me, and my brother Javier is on her other side. I don't know how long we've been sitting here like statues, waiting to hear anything. Inside me the panic is raging, but I will never show this to either of them. I promised myself a long time ago I would take care of them, and I have done just that.

The waiting room door opens, and I'm greeted by the most beautiful blue eyes. A girl followed by Garrett walks in looking directly at Antonia, but I'm sure she only knows her as Toni.

"How is she?" The girl, who I can only assume is a friend

of Toni's from college, asks. There is a sadness in her eyes as she inquires.

Toni straightens up and grabs her hand, squeezing. "We still don't know much." She then walks into the arms of Garrett. In spite of Toni's efforts to push him away, he is here, worry written across his face.

Blue Eyes takes the seat Toni just vacated and extends her hand to me, "I'm Lola. And which cousin are you?"

I'm mesmerized by her. Her smile is soft and caring and her eyes welcoming. I need to stop staring and answer.

"Alex. And that is my brother, Javie, over there." I point to the corner of the room where he'd moved when they walked in. She turns to him, lifting her hand in a small wave.

"Have you heard anything?" She turns back to me asking.

"They are running tests, but they think it was a stroke. She still hasn't woken up." Toni answers before I have a chance to open my mouth.

"Can we get you anything?" Lola offers, her eyes full of worry.

"I'm good," Toni answers, "but I need a few minutes."

I watch as Toni walks out with Garrett in tow. She needs to try and make that relationship work. I know she doesn't want to trust him, but she needs people in her life who are not tethered to the hood.

Lola stays in the seat next to me. She's fiddling with her hands nervously. I'm probably not the type of guy she's accustomed to being around. I stand up to give her space. She looks up at me as I do. I force myself to turn away because it feels like I could get lost in her eyes.

"We're good here if you have to go," I tell her, giving her an out. She probably didn't plan on being in a room with a couple of thugs.

"I'm fine. I want to be here for Toni," she answers, her voice soft.

Silence surrounds us. Javie is pacing now, making circles around the room, and I have taken up residence in a corner.

After several long, tense minutes of trying to avoid looking in Lola's direction, I hear her ask, "Are y'all okay with me being here? I can wait for Toni out in the hall if you'd rather."

"It's fine. Sorry, am I making you nervous pacing?" Javie goes to sit by her.

Lola gives him a genuine smile that makes her eyes dance.

"You didn't make me nervous. Y'all were just so quiet, I wasn't sure if I was the reason."

A twinge of hate bubbles knowing he's close to her and I'm not. I shake my head. What the fuck? Caring whether Javie is by some chick I just met? I drop my head side to side, cracking my neck to let the frustration out. There's too much going on right now. That's all that is.

"My brother is not one for many words." There is a teasing to his voice. He's flirting with her.

"Oh."

"You'll get used to it." He shrugs his shoulders.

Why in the hell would she need to? I think to myself. It's not like she will be spending any time with us.

It's been a month since Güela passed away, and there has already been so much change. Charity is not a word or action I humbly accept. The whole concept makes me feel weak. Out of control. Incapable. Those are feelings I avoid at all cost. I take care of my family, end of story. Until I can't. While I'm grateful Garrett has accepted Toni and all she hid from him, including us and the hood life we were brought up in, I hate knowing he and his family took care of so many things when Güela passed. He has the monetary resources to jump in and resolve any and all of the obstacles we came across.

Güela's house is now ours, Toni's, Javie's, and mine, thanks to his lawyer. My alcoholic deadbeat dad and Toni's money-hungry mother were circling like vultures, ready to swoop in and sell. They would have blown through the money in record time.

I feel obligated to him now, and I hate owing people. You never know when they are going to cash in and what you will be expected to do. I like to be the one in power. I like to be the one owed.

This neighborhood has taught me how to survive. I may not have much money, but I sure do hold power status with the connections I have made. I listened and learned the ways. I never pushed for more, letting my work speak for itself. Too bad my dumbass dad ruined it for me and I had to give up the business. Asshole is probably going to prison for his last fuckup, getting busted for selling weed at a bar.

Now I don't know what I'm going to do. Toni is insistent I don't go back to selling. But if I don't sell, how in the hell is a high-school dropout supposed to make money?

The front door opens, interrupting my thoughts. Toni walks in with Lola close behind.

"Hey," Toni says casually, walking toward the hallway to the back room. She came home last Friday too. She goes into Güela's room with Lola, and they spend time in there. I haven't asked why, but I figure it's her way of coping.

Lola looks at me as her lips pull in a small smile. She lifts her hand up giving me a quick wave. I nod in return, acknowledging her. I have not really spoken to her. What's the point? I'm still mesmerized by her beauty, but that's all it is. Pure physical attraction, and I can get that anywhere.

LOLA

THE PAST FEW weeks have been hard on Toni. Her family dysfunction has surprised me a couple of times, but I think I was able to hide my reactions. I don't want my naivety to jeopardize our friendship. I'm glad she finally began to trust Garrett. He's been her rock and helped carry her burden. He has more knowledge in terms of what needed to be done.

"Pizza tonight?" Toni asks. We are laying in her grandmother's bed. This has become our new normal for Friday nights. The grief of losing her grandmother still heavy, she copes by coming to her house on the southside to spend time with her cousins.

Meeting Toni's cousins was a shock. I don't know what I expected, but they were not it. It is not fair to have that much beauty in one family. She's gorgeous and the guys...wow. Speechless. It is strange how different they each are. Javie is unassuming and caring. He is easy to talk to and makes you feel welcome. Toni is strong-willed and speaks her mind freely and often. Alex...he's...breathtaking. Since meeting him, I have not seen him show any emotion. When he walks into the room, he owns it. During all the turmoil they have had to endure, I have not seen him cry once. Not lose his temper. Not break down. He is a rock.

"Sure," I answer her. I always want tacos from the taqueria down the street, but everyone told me last weekend they were done with Taco Fridays. "Is your boyfriend leaving for the ranch tomorrow?"

I love to call Garrett her boyfriend since she tried to avoid it for so long. It took a bit for her to adjust to his status. His family owns the biggest cattle ranch in Texas, so they are wealthy. It is hard for Toni to trust him because she feels less-than since she grew up in poverty. He keeps reminding her she is more than enough.

"Not this weekend. I have to go to his stupid fraternity party tomorrow." She also hates the fraternity parties.

"But I'll be there." I prop myself up to look down at her. She's still laying on her back, staring at the ceiling. The usual when we arrive, she spends several quiet minutes becoming extremely acquainted with the ceiling. I know she's letting herself drown in grief since I was there a few years ago when my mother passed. I just lend my silent presence. She always asks about dinner when she's ready to move on.

She rolls her eyes, sits up, and makes her way out of bed, so I follow her.

"Pizza night," she announces to the room, where Alex, Javie, and Garrett are watching TV.

"Really?" Javie questions.

"Yes," I answer moodily. "I'll give up one Friday since it seems everyone voted behind my back." I couldn't hold the smile back.

It's strange, but this tiny home has quickly become my favorite place to be. But it's not really the home; it's the people inside that make it a safe space.

"I'll call it in. What do y'all want?" Garrett says.

"Nah. I'll go get it," Alex announces.

Once Alex makes a decision, no one ever questions it. He rarely lets anyone take the lead. I saw how hard it was for him to accept all the help Garrett and his parents gave. He wanted to be able to handle everything that came at them after his grandmother's passing. But all of it required money. Money that they didn't have. His posture changed around Garrett when he was having to accept money. His presence wasn't quite as large. It was a miniscule change, but watching him constantly, I've picked up on a few things.

Now that things have settled and the three of them own their grandmother's house, I have watched him step up more. His demeanor stronger, more powerful.

"Make sure you add jalapenos to it," Toni chimes in.

I go into the kitchen for a water as Alex walks in behind me. He begins rummaging through a drawer filled with junk.

"What are you looking for?" I ask as I watch him taking all kinds of papers out.

He doesn't answer, so I take the couple of steps to him and look up at his face. "Need help finding something?"

"I'm fine. You can go to the living room with everyone." He seems to always dismiss me. I can't remember a time that we were in the same room alone.

"You look frazzled. If you tell me what you are looking for, I can help. You know girls are better finders than guys are, right?" My mom said that often. My dad would complain about a lost item, and my mom would find it in seconds.

He finally looks down at me, glaring. "I've got it."

"Fine." I spin around, mad that he has dismissed me again.

As much as I want to get close to him, he keeps me at a distance. I walk back out into the living room and take a seat on the couch by Javie. Unlike his brother, Javie has welcomed me with open arms. I thought he was flirting with me when we first met, but it has quickly turned into a comfortable platonic relationship. He's easy to talk to.

"Are you going to the fraternity party Toni's been complaining about?" Javie asks me.

"Yup. Wanna go?" I ask him. I'm part of Greek life, but I'm not happy in that environment. I go through the motions because that's what's expected, I guess.

"To a fraternity party?" Javie releases a booming laugh. "Nah. I don't think I would be welcome there." His smile is kind.

I don't know why I invited him. He would probably stick out, but not as much as his brother. They are both ruggedly good-looking, but Javie's personality is friendly. Alex somehow announces sex and danger. And as much as his body language silently yells to stay away, I just want to get closer.

"I don't know about 'not welcome,' but most of them are a bunch of conceited a-holes," I agree.

Alex walks out of the kitchen to the front door, announcing, "I'll be back."

I wonder if he's this cold all the time or only in front of me.

CHAPTER 2

ALEX
February

I'M CRAWLING OUT OF A BED I SHOULDN'T BE IN TO MAKE my way home. I refuse to spend the night with any girl because I don't want anyone to get false hope for a potential relationship. I've never been in an exclusive relationship. No one has ever excited me enough to want to be.

I sit on the bed, sliding on my boots on, when Cara walks out of the bathroom and stands in front of me. She pushes my knees open to slide herself closer to me. My gaze travels up her nude body.

"Where are you going?" She is trying to act nonchalant, but I can clearly hear the hurt. Fuck.

"I gotta get home." I grab her hips and pull her closer letting my face fall between her round, large breasts, kissing softly. Her head falls back as she relishes the attention.

"Stay here," she says, in a slightly whiny voice.

"Not today. Maybe next time." I try and soften the blow. I nibble up to her mouth.

Her arms wrap tightly around my neck. She's trying her best to keep me here. I grab the backs of her thighs, picking her up, and she wraps her legs around my waist. I can't deny she is hot. Her kisses move down to my neck, and I feel the sucking. She is trying to mark me to keep others away.

Hickeys. The mark of the neighborhood. If someone has one, they are taken. The last one I gave and received was before I dropped out of high school. I haven't been interested in anyone enough to give one, and I sure as hell won't get one. I turn around, quickly laying her down so I can separate us.

I place one last kiss on her lips picking my shirt up off the bed to slide it on.

"Fine." She quickly pulls the sheet to cover her naked body.

"I'll see you later." If I would have known she was going to stick so quickly, I would have avoided her like the damn plague. I have no time for this shit in my life.

The drive home is quick. A small neighborhood tucked away, hidden from the rest of the city. A dirty secret never to be revealed. Burglar bars, graffiti, frequent bus stops, run-down buildings—that's my life. What has always been my life and what will always be my life.

I park on the street in front of a small, old house. The only home that has provided stability in this shit place.

I fall into bed, my head spinning from the alcohol as a memory of Güela hits. I know I can't keep this shit up indefinitely; I just don't have a way out.

"WHO WERE YOU WITH LAST NIGHT?" Toni asks.

"No one important." Which is the truth.

"Who is no one?" She will continue until I answer. She may be my cousin, but after growing up together she is more like a baby sister.

Güela took us all in when our piece-of-shit parents didn't grow up and threw us on her doorstep.

"Does it matter?" I take the seat across the table from her.

She finally looks up from her laptop, the one I bought her so she would have her own for college, closes it, and stares at me. She is the only one who will bust my balls on my life decisions.

Javie and I have been living with Güela since I was ten and he was eight. Toni's mom had already left her at Güela's. So it's been us three with a grandmother since then.

"Yes."

"April. New to the hood." *I lean back waiting for her to start.*

"April..." *She lets the name hang.* "So what is April like, and when can I meet her?"

Since I won't be seeing her again, I answer, "You won't be meeting her."

"Why not?"

"Because I'm not dating her."

"But you'll have sex with her? What does she need to do to keep your attention?" *She shakes her head in disapproval.*

"Why not?" *I shrug not in the mood for this conversation.* "And as for my attention...I guess no one is interesting enough to keep it..."

"No tienes verguenza?" *Güela turns on me, disappointed in my lack of shame.*

"Si ellas la van a dar, la tomaré. (If they are going to give it, I'll take it.)" *I answer Güela.*

In return she slaps the back of my head with her hand. "Y cuando te vengan embarazadas? Qué vas a hacer? (And when they come to you pregnant? What are you going to do?)" *she questions. I know she worries. We shouldn't be having this conversation now.*

"Condoms. Always use condoms." *There is no other answer I have for her.*

Toni and Javie bust out laughing at the bluntness I just displayed. Güela, not so much, because she gives my head another slap with a dish towel this time.

"But for real, Toni. I don't know what will keep my attention. I just know no one has."

I DON'T KNOW what I was thinking, but having sex with Cara did not erase Lola from my thoughts like I thought it would. She has become a permanent fixture around the house the past few months, and the more she's around, the harder it's getting to control thinking about her and keep her at a distance. It seems like she wants to get close, but I can't let her. She deserves a man who can take care of her, and I have nothing to offer. Life isn't passing out options in my direction.

LOLA

TONI, Javie, and Alex have finally decided to clean out their grandmother's room. With Toni staying at the house more often, they thought it was time. Their home is located between the university and Garrett's ranch. It makes it easier for Garrett when he's coming back into town from ranch. Toni is going to take over her grandmother's room, so we are going through her closet and drawers to separate things the family will keep or donate.

I am watching her as she looks at every item she holds. Her eyes close, and I can imagine a memory flooding her mind. She is incredibly strong. It took a couple of years for me to build the courage and go through my mother's belongings. My dad had everything boxed up until we were ready to sit together.

Toni and I are alone in the room. The guys wanted to give Toni some time alone. They said they had each already come in and had their moment. I wonder how Alex handled his time. Did he finally let himself break down? I wish I could see behind his tough exterior. He is always cool and collected; life never seems to rattle him.

Toni and Javie follow his lead in all matters. They work together, but nothing is done until Alex gives the final approval. He is head of this household. Envy has creeped up on me a couple of times watching how Garrett fawns over Toni and Alex is her protector. But I want Alex as so much more than my protector.

"OMG," Toni exclaims happily. "Maybe Alex did act like a kid once upon a time."

She hands me an old photo of a young Alex jumping on a couch laughing while their grandmother watched him from a distance. My eyes are glued to his young, happy, carefree face. I know life wasn't easy for them, but I wonder why he feels he can show no one his true self. This mask of a man can't be the whole person.

She snatches the picture out of my hands and stands up before leaving the room. I follow her to see what she's going to do. Alex is in the kitchen, drinking a cup of black coffee, something I will never understand, and reading something on his phone.

"I found something that proves you can smile," she teases.

"And what is that?" He responds back, sounding bored and not looking in her direction.

She places the picture in front of his phone.

He glances at it. "Huh." Grabs it from her hands and tosses it on the table, going back to whatever was on his phone.

"That's it?" She's confused.

"I was a kid." He shrugs his shoulders.

Toni shakes her head, turning around walking out. I don't think he realizes I am close enough to see and hear their conversation or lack thereof. I stay frozen in my spot right outside the kitchen, watching him. He waits a couple of seconds then picks the picture up again, staring at it. I wish I could see his face, but I notice his shoulders slump just a fraction. I don't know what prompts me, but I walk up behind him and wrap my arms around him. I feel him stiffen.

A couple of seconds pass, then he pats my hand on his chest. I let him go as he stands up and turns to me. His lip pulls up on one side, a peace offering I suppose, and he walks away, leaving his coffee and the picture on the table.

It is in this moment I realize my feelings for him are growing. I knew I was physically attracted to him. My body hummed when I watched him. I was attracted to how protective he was over those he cared for. Toni and Javie had his devotion. But now I know he feels things; he just doesn't allow others to see that part of him.

CHAPTER 3

ALEX
April

I PARK IN FRONT OF OUR HOUSE AFTER ANOTHER LONG week on the ranch. As much as I appreciate the opportunity Garrett and his family have given me, I hate being away all week. I somehow continue to owe their family over and over. First for everything that happened when Güela passed and now for giving me a job and helping me earn my GED. Not so long ago, I had no idea what I was going to do with my life. Where it was heading. A high-school dropout doesn't usually get second chances like this.

As the phone rings all I can think is, 'It's too early for phone calls'.

"Hello."

"May I speak to the parent or guardian of Alejandro Martinez?" A gruff man asks.

It's the school again because I haven't attended classes in several weeks. I guess they finally noticed.

"He's not here." I answer honestly. My dad hasn't been home in several days, and I really don't know when he'll decide to come back. He does that. Disappears for days, sometimes weeks, on end, and then he appears again needing money. Luckily for us, he's only an alcoholic. I can support that habit.

"Is there a number I can reach him?"

"Look sir, you're taking to Alejandro. It's me. You're calling because I haven't been in school, right?" Might as well get this over with and he won't have to call and wake me again.

"Alejandro?" The way he pronounces my name is annoying. If he can't pronounce Alejandro, he might as well just call me Alex like everyone else does. "Why haven't you been in school?"

"I need to work. My grandmother can't afford all of us without help." Again, no reason to pussyfoot around the truth.

"And your dad?"

"He's a piece of shit that takes and contributes nothing." The quicker I can get him off the phone and off my back, the better.

"Oh..." He sounds confused. "But you need to be in school."

"Yeah, well, we also need to eat and pay bills. So when my dad decides to make an appearance again, I'll have him withdraw me, and you won't need to worry about me."

"What will you do?" What's with all the questions? I won't be his problem once I withdraw.

"I heard about a part-time program. I'll do that so I can also work," I lie.

"Okay. Well it seems like you have a plan. I'll let you go. Bye."

THAT WAS the last time I heard from the school. I think they were thrilled to get rid of a troublemaker. I was known for fights and disruptions. They weren't my fault since I don't start crap, I just finish it.

This job and Garrett's mom helping me to earn my GED in the evenings has given me some direction. Javie and I quit selling for good. I'm keeping clean at Toni's request. She freaked out when my dad was sentenced to five years. He, of course, won't serve them all, but she doesn't want that for Javie and I.

Now I just need to figure out my next steps. I can hear music coming through the front door, which means Javie already has people over. Not really what I want to deal with right now, but a cold one would hit the spot.

I open the door, and my gaze lands on the blue eyes that bring me to my knees every time I look at them. She is sitting on the chair, sipping a drink with Javie and a few of his friends. She is the only girl in the room.

"Javie!" I say his name just a bit louder than I'd intended. I tilt my head a bit towards the bedrooms.

I walk back, expecting him to follow.

Once I am in the furthest room from the living room, I turn around closing the door as soon as he walks through.

"What the fuck is Lola doing here?" I start in on him right away.

"What do you mean, why is she here? She called, and I went to pick her up," he answers, confused.

Of course he's confused. No one knows she is the one girl who has been starring in every dream I've had recently. Running my hands all over her creamy, soft skin. Letting her long, blonde hair fall just covering her perky breasts as she rides me. Her crystal-blue eyes boring into me, searching my soul.

But that is all it will ever be. A poor man's fantasy. She is too good for me. She is going to be a college graduate. She comes from money. She really shouldn't be slumming it in the ghetto. She needs a man who can take care of her. I have zero to offer a girl like her.

"Just because she calls doesn't mean you have to go get her," I argue.

"True, but if I didn't go and get her, you know as well as I do she would have just driven over here. She would have let herself in too. Toni gave her a key."

"What the fuck? Why the hell did Toni give her a key?" This is getting worse.

"How would I know? You know Toni does whatever the hell she pleases. Those two are like two peas in a pod. Both of them are too stubborn for their own good." He shrugs his shoulders in resignation.

I breathe in long and slow, holding it a bit before I release, trying to calm myself. There is no way in hell anyone will ever know how I feel about that girl.

"I know. Sorry." I shake my head in disapproval for his benefit. "I didn't shower before I left the ranch. I'll be out in a bit."

He turns around and walks out, leaving me trying to figure out how I will be able to be around the woman who takes my very breath from me during another long night of drinking. She is a goddess and doesn't even know it. She is sweet and thoughtful but doesn't listen to anyone when she has her mind set on something.

I have caught myself being mean to her on a few occasions. Being mean to her is so much better than what would happen if I let my defenses down. The cards have been dealt, and she is a queen while I'm only a joker.

The shower has given me some time to get my head on straight. At least thinking of Lola has given my overworked mind a break from what my next step should be. As much as I love the ranch, I don't see myself working there forever.

Wrapping a towel around my waist, I open the door to get dressed in my room and walk right into her in the hall. She stops in front of me with a gleam in her eyes.

"Hey," she begins. A small smirk forms on her beautiful,

full lips. Her eyes glide down my bare chest before slowly coming back up to meet my gaze.

"Hey yourself." I lean on the wall behind me, getting a little excited about her checking me out before I come to my senses. "Why are you here?" I ask a bit forcefully.

"Hanging out, just like everyone else." She crosses her arms in front of her in defiance.

"Sure, everyone else belongs here. You don't, college girl. You need to go do what you college kids do." I need to make her feel unwelcome.

"Toni said I'm welcome, so I'm staying."

"Are you done in there?" A voice I didn't want to hear tonight chimes in.

"Yes." I turn to face Cara.

She walks between Lola and I, running her long, fake fingernails across my chest as she passes. There is no denying what she wants tonight. But she will not be joining me in my bedroom. If she comes in, she will never want to come out.

The look of disgust on Lola's face is unmistakable. Cara closes the bathroom door behind her.

"Don't let me keep you from *that*?" she whispers with sarcasm dripping. She turns and heads to Toni's room.

I don't know how she ended up here, and as much as I don't want Cara, she may be useful tonight to keep Lola at a distance.

In my room, I dress quickly, needing a beer to calm my mind.

I walk straight to the kitchen, getting two beers out of the fridge. I open the first, chugging the entire can in under a minute. I toss it and open the next, ready to face her. I take a seat in an empty chair, away from where they have a card game going on the coffee table, not wanting to participate. I just need to keep my distance and watch over her.

She doesn't know the fools in this neighborhood. She

didn't grow up with this type of necessary selfishness. If she trusts the wrong person, she could get burned. Not that they are bad or anything, but she is not one of us. Some don't take kindly to outsiders coming in. Especially perky little true-blonde chicks with money coming out their asses. Not that any of these fools need to know that.

Of course, Cara doesn't know how to keep her distance, and she comes right up to me after a few minutes.

"You haven't called lately," she begins quietly.

She is stretching the truth. I haven't called at all in months.

"Busy at the ranch and tired when I get home."

"We don't have to go out. I can take care of you. Make you a good meal." She is pushing. Strike the idea of using her to keep Lola at a distance. I may need Lola to help me keep Cara away.

"Thanks, but I actually eat really good on the ranch." I look up at her, hoping she gets the hint.

Cara bends over, giving me full view of her cleavage; her hand on my shoulder grips firmly before she whispers, "But I can give you a meal no one at the ranch can." She kisses my neck. I look past her shoulder, and Lola is staring at me, her lips pulled down. As soon as I catch her watching, she looks away, back at the cards on the table.

I lift my empty hand, pushing Cara back a bit because she is about to get carried away again. She is face to face with me, and my mind blanks with what I can say to let her down.

Luckily, I don't have to say anything. She squints her eyes at me in question before standing up and heading to the kitchen.

I stand, taking a couple of steps closer to the game, as Jesse gets up from the couch, leaving the only available spot next to Lola. I move around a couple of people sitting on the floor to take his vacated spot.

"Joining in?" Lola asks as she turns to look at me.

"No." I don't have anything else to say.

Lola comes in closer to me, then whispers, "Then why sit over here. She looks like she wants you." Her eyes go to Cara briefly.

She pulls back, looking me in the eyes, searching. But for what? I'm so blinded by her, nothing else matters. But she can never know that. We stay in this stare-off for several moments until someone calls Lola's name for her turn. She turns quickly to join back in.

I order people to grab beers for me, not wanting to vacate this seat, not wanting to let go of this time with her. As time goes by, Lola manages to move her body closer to mine. The warmth of her body is soothing the beast I fear I have become. But, of course, the consumption of many beers means I need to relieve my bladder.

I make my way to the bathroom, fearing that, with how much everyone has had to drink, one of those assholes will try to move in on Lola. Either they don't realize or don't care that she is out of their league. I speed through my business, not wanting to leave her alone for too long. Javie, who orchestrated this damn get-together, has been outside with others all evening.

Lucky for me, no one tried to move into my spot. Yes, I've claimed that spot. I can't believe Lola has drank as much as she has playing game after game with the others. I can tell she is getting tired as her upper body is now leaning into me, and when she blinks her eyes, they take a moment longer to open.

"Okay, party's over. Everyone out." I raise my voice above the music.

Lola is startled by my announcement as she tries to stand. I grab her waist and sit her back down.

"Not you." I whisper in her ear as I stand and chase every person out.

Cara frowns and stands from the chair she had been sitting in across from us, where she'd been watching my every movement. I yell at Javie through the back door to wrap it up.

I return to a sleeping Lola. Her head lolled to the side uncomfortably. I sit down grabbing her legs and swinging them over my thighs. She adjusts herself a bit, tucking herself into my side. A starving man would never turn down this small morsel. I keep us on the couch until Javie finishes escorting everyone out.

He closes the front door, locking it before coming to take a seat in the side chair.

"Why did her being here get your panties in a wad?" Javie speaks quietly and juts his chin at Lola enclosed in my arms.

"They weren't in a wad. She doesn't belong here. Just like I forced Toni to stay away. They are too good to be tethered to the ghetto. They need to be as far away from this place as possible." I try and keep my voice as low as possible, not wanting to wake her.

"They don't think so. Toni has been coming back more than ever now. Only difference between Toni coming back around now and then is she's bringing along that one and Garrett."

"I know. But Toni isn't looking for the parties over here anymore. She is coming home." I take a deep breath, looking down at the beauty I'm holding. "Why would she want to party over here anyways? Doesn't she have friends at school?"

Javie lifts his shoulders and drops them. "I'm done. I'll see you in the morning." He stands then looks back again. "Need help getting her into Toni's room?"

I shake my head. He turns around, leaving me with a passed-out Lola.

Looking down, I realize she is even beautiful sleeping drunk. Her hair has fallen slightly in front of her face, so I trace the side taking the few strands and tucking them behind her ear. I've only had a few brief moments of physical contact with her. A small tease, wrapping her arms around me or tucking herself in my lap, offering her strength. I never understood what prompted them though. But now here she is. I could stay here all night holding her. Protecting her.

But that isn't my job and never will be. I snap myself out of those thoughts. Getting her to bed is all I need to do. I tuck my arm under her legs, standing. She stirs a bit, mumbling. I don't understand the first gibberish she mumbles. But then my heart stops.

"Why don't you like me?" she mumbles as she wraps her arm tighter around my neck, tucking her head in.

I freeze, not knowing if she is awake or not. After a few moments of silence, I know she is asleep again.

I carry her down the hall to Toni's room placing her gently in bed. I slide off her shoes before bringing the blankets over her.

I let my hand brush the side of her face. "*Ya tienes mi corazon, amor.*" (You already have my heart, love.) I place a soft kiss on her forehead. This will be the only time I will allow my lips to touch her.

LOLA

COFFEE AND BACON. That's what I smell as I try and open my eyes after a late night of drinking. My mind drifts to last night. I wouldn't usually have drunk so much, but having Alex next to me all night made me nervous. He's beautiful and strong and protective, and oh-so very sexy. And he's still keeping me at a distance.

And that's the reason I kept drinking beer after beer, even when I knew I shouldn't. I must have passed out last night because I don't remember getting into bed. I lift the covers and realize I am still in my clothes from yesterday. Great! I wonder who had to bring me to bed. I search my mind for any memories and see Alex over me. I must have been dreaming because he said something about *amor*. Even I know that word. Everyone does. And it would not be coming out of his mouth.

I wonder if that skank stayed the night with him. Ugh... thinking about him is useless. I need to get up and join the voices I hear in the kitchen.

Stripping out of yesterday's clothes I put on the pajamas I should have been wearing and make my way to the bathroom.

I take a long look at myself in the mirror. Hungover green is not a good look. But who am I trying to impress anyway? I quickly finish up because the coffee is calling my name.

Garrett and Javie are sitting in the living room playing a video game.

"Morning," I tell them on the way to the kitchen.

Javie snorts, "That's it? Morning? Hangover much?"

I turn around raising my middle finger flicking him off while smiling.

"Good morning, sleeping beauty." Toni jumps at the chance to tease me.

"Good morning!" I smile sweetly at her while glancing at Alex at the stove, his back to me.

Grabbing my coffee, I sit with Toni at the table. I choose the chair facing Alex. While I have no chance with him there is nothing wrong with enjoying the view. I look down, studying my coffee, not wanting to make it obvious I'm enjoying the scenery.

He can't be ignored. He is in some athletic shorts and a wife-beater tank exposing most of his tattoos. He's not a pretty boy. He has an animalistic magnetism. His broad shoulders, the lines and curves of the muscles he works hard for, his constant five o'clock shadow, his dark, almost black hair, and his eyes are panty melting. He rarely smiles, but when he does...my heart skips a beat. He's always so serious. I want to be the person to make him smile more.

He is somewhat of an anomaly. This guy, who one might find intimidating if they found themselves caught in an empty alley with him, is the most caring individual I have met. After all the stories Toni has been sharing with me over the past few months, I have come to see Alex as so much more. Those stories and watching him interact with Toni and Javie have led to me fall utterly and deeply for him.

But no one could ever know. Toni is my best friend, and I don't want to screw up our friendship because I'm crushing like a schoolgirl on her cousin. Well, that, and because Alex still does not like me much. He's always so short with me. Like last night, he didn't want me around. I was able to talk Javie into picking me up because Garrett and Toni had date night before he leaves for the ranch today.

Consumed by my own thoughts, I'm startled by Alex next to me waving a piece of bacon.

"My version of a white flag," Alex tells me with a small genuine smile.

"Why do you always have to be an ass? Don't you know not everyone enjoys your temperamental attitude as much as I do?" Toni quips quickly catching on he may have been rude again last night.

His eyes leave me and find Toni. "I'm not an ass. I'm just trying to keep y'all away from here. You are coming back again and bringing someone with you." He brings his attention back to me waving the bacon again.

I grab it. "Thank you." I can't keep my lips from spreading into a huge grin.

"What did he do?" Toni looks at me, raising her brow in question.

Not wanting to answer, I stay quiet and just lift my shoulders before taking a bite out of the perfectly crispy bacon.

When I refuse to answer, she turns in Alex's direction and repeats herself. "What did you do?"

Just then, Garrett and Javie walk in. Perfect, now everyone is going to jump in on this conversation. A conversation I don't want to have. I don't want to know why he doesn't want me around. I want to stay in my bubble of ignorance so I can continue being close to him any way I can.

Alex raises the spatula he's holding out to Garrett. Garrett takes it, walking closer to the stove.

"You sure you trust me with breakfast?" Garrett asks Alex before standing in front of the stove.

"Just don't burn them, " Alex answers him before turning back to Toni.

Those two are so stubborn. Poor Javie is always the mediator, calming situations down.

"What did I do?" He stands across from Toni. And a stare-off has begun. Battle of the wills with those two.

"Yes. What did you do if you are apologizing?" she asks again.

They watch each other for a few moments. I wonder if Alex is hesitating, trying to come up with a reason he didn't want me here, instead of "I just don't like her."

"I wasn't exactly rude. I just asked why she would be here. Just like you, she does not belong here. But her even more so. The only reason I haven't been chasing you away is because I know we are all still dealing with Güela's passing. But I wish you wouldn't come back either." His face falls as he speaks, a sadness brewing in his eyes.

"But I do belong here. It's my home just as much as it's y'alls'." A single tear falls and rolls down her cheek.

Garrett and I have learned over the past few months not to get involved in their family dynamics. We may be friends, but we always stay quiet and *never* take sides in their frequent squabbles.

"Yes. It's your home, but you are destined to be so much more. You aren't stuck here." Alex places his hands on the table in front of him, lowering himself to Toni's height. "I'm here. No matter what. I have a GED and no real career options. You? You have your pick for your future, and I'm just making sure you make the right choice. Like that one." He points in Garrett's direction. "That was a good choice. And this one." He nods his head in my direction. "Another good choice."

Alex then turns to me. "Like I said last night, you are too good for this place. You need to go and hang with your college crowd. Not some deadbeats who will never amount to shit. Don't follow my damn cousin over here anymore. Got it, blondie?" He stands quickly, returning to the stove, relieving Garrett of the duty, not really wanting an answer.

It is quiet except for the scraping sound as Javie pulls a chair out. Alex and Garrett bring everything to the table before sitting themselves.

Alex's words are playing over and over in my mind. They aren't sitting well with me. I don't agree with them. Toni didn't even put up an argument after it.

The only sound is the clanking of dishes as everyone serves themselves. I haven't made a move yet.

"I don't agree" comes out of my mouth before I have a chance to think things through.

Everyone stops what they were doing, facing me.

"What don't you agree with?" Javie jumps in quickly.

"With Alex," I state, looking at Alex. He is sitting next to me.

"Care to tell me what exactly you don't agree with?" Alex watches me as I sit up straighter, giving myself the courage to speak.

"First of all, the deadbeat comment. I'm not sure who you were speaking about, yourselves or your friends. But if you were speaking of yourselves, you are wrong. Yeah, you weren't born into privilege, but you are the furthest thing from deadbeats."

Alex opens his mouth, but I'm not done. I raise my finger up to him. "If you were speaking about your friends, well then I have no argument because I don't know them well enough. But I came to spend time with you and Javie because I feel safe with y'all. Toni was busy, so I couldn't hang with her last night. Some other friends were going clubbing, and I wasn't in the mood. So my option was you guys."

"Fine, we're not deadbeats, but you still don't belong over here." Alex stands his ground.

"Look, if you don't want me over here because I'm going to mess up your ," I quote with my fingers, "'game,' or you just don't like me, then tell me. I'll stay away." I look down at the coffee in my hands, scared of his answer.

"That's enough." Toni jumps into the conversation. "Let's just eat, and this conversation is done. Lola," Toni speaks in my direction, "You are welcome here because you are my bestie." She uses the word "bestie" to make me feel better because I know she cringes when I use the word.

"Alex," she pauses, but I am too nervous to look up to see their facial expressions, "I know you are looking out, but give it a rest for a bit. Please."

I can't remember a time when I have felt as embarrassed as I do in this moment. The need to flee is overwhelming, so I stand quickly, the chair falling behind me; I walk quickly out of the kitchen and into Toni's room.

"Can't you just be nice for once?" Toni yells at Alex as I scramble out.

Terrified someone is going to follow me, I close the door behind me and lock it. I would rather not face anyone right now. I find my phone and pull up the Uber app to find a ride home. This isn't the part of town where Ubers frequent, so I will have several minutes before one arrives. I change out of my pajamas, gather my things, and sit on the bed to track the car. Fifteen minutes. What am I going to do for fifteen minutes?

A soft tap on the door announces company. I know that tap is not Toni. She would have just tried to walk in.

"What?" I yell through the door.

"Can I come in?" Javie asks.

Do I want to talk to him? Not really. I know he cares about me. He is the sweetest guy. He and Alex resemble each other, but Javie does not have Alex's muscle bulk. Javie is lean and muscular. And while they both have the dark hair and eyes, Javie's are welcoming.

"I'm changing," I lie. "I'll be out in a bit."

I'll come out when the Uber arrives.

"Okay," he responds sadly.

This is just as bad as waiting for water to boil. The time is moving so slowly. Each time I glance at my phone, only one freaking minute has passed, and sometimes not even. Finally, the car is down the street, and I can make my escape.

I walk out of the room, my bag slung over my shoulder. I contemplate saying bye, but my red face just wants to leave. I'll text Toni later, maybe. I make my way to the front door and open it before anyone realizes I'm walking out.

"Hey! Where are you going?" Javie chases me outside.

"Home." And right on time, the Uber pulls up in front of the house. I walk away as fast as I can without actually running.

CHAPTER 4

ALEX

IT'S BEEN TWO WEEKS. TWO WEEKS SINCE I HAVE SEEN those piercing blue eyes. I know I wanted her to stay away, but I didn't realize how painful it would be not having her around. I thought I just wanted to be home on the weekends, but it turns out it wasn't home I wanted. It was her. In the back of my mind, I knew she would be there. She had become a fixture around the house. Stopping by to eat, hanging out to watch movies, studying at the table with Toni all kept her coming by. Now I have scared her away, just like I wanted, and all I can think about is seeing her.

It's for the best, though. Last weekend at home wasn't all that exciting. Same old shit. Drinks with the same lame people who are stuck in the hellhole with me. Do I really want to continue to do the same thing for the rest of my life? That thought is more depressing than wondering what I'm going to do with my life.

"Hey, *guey*!" Juan calls out to me. "Aren't you leaving?"

Am I leaving? Since starting this job at the ranch, I have

always gone home on the weekends, but what am I really going home to? What I really want isn't there, and I could never have it anyway.

"Not this weekend. I think I'll stick around," I answer. The house for workers is always stocked with food and beer. I can eat and drink here just as easily as I could at home. And at least here, there's better company. Juan and some of the other guys are actually pretty cool.

"You were always leaving like a bat out of hell every Friday. Why stay now?" He comes into the large kitchen area where I'm sitting at the banquet-style table.

He's right. I would practically run through the door, grab my things, and be in my car, heading home. Tonight, I strolled in and sat down. Watching the guys coming in and either settling in for the weekend or getting their things to leave is something I've never witnessed with always being the first one out the door. I don't even know who stays and who goes. Maybe it changes each weekend. I guess I will be finding out soon enough if I continue to stay.

"No reason." I shrug my shoulders casually, not wanting to admit the real reason.

"Like I believe you, *pendejo*." His booming laugh fills the room.

I wasn't sure how the house worked on the weekend. During the week, we each take turns cooking and cleaning up the kitchen.

"What do we do for dinner?" I decide to ask, hunger beginning. I usually pick something up on the road into town because, after working all day, I'm always starving.

"Manny took some meat out to barbecue," he answers, downing a bottle of water in one chug.

"Great. What can I do?" If I'm going to stay, I might as well help.

"Go start the fire." He nods his head toward the patio

door where the large pit is. "Manny went to make some calls, and he'll be out in a bit."

I step outside, taking in a view I had only seen on TV until I began working here. My cards had been dealt. I was stuck in the ghetto with no real options to leave. Then life got turned around, and here I am.

I get the charcoal and wood in the pit, ready to start the fire. Lighting it, I watch the flames, getting lost in my thoughts of her. She is all I think about. I am in desperate need of someone to break the spell she has on me.

"Catch," Juan says, walking out the door.

I turn around to watch him toss a beer in my direction.

"Thanks." I pop it open while grabbing a koozie from a bucket on the table.

We both sit down at the table, waiting for the fire to be ready and for Manny to come out with the meat. We drink in comfortable silence, except for the sounds of the ranch. Tonight is different. More relaxed than the busy, quick weekday dinners.

"Where are you?" Juan asks.

"What do you mean?" I answer.

"Your mind. You stayed here for a reason. No use in trying to deny it." A knowing smirk appears.

"No reason." What is this? A chicks' gossip session?

"Okay. If you want to keep it to yourself, I get it." He takes a long draw from his beer before continuing, "But I would bet money it's about a girl. No guy avoids places unless there is a girl involved."

He's right, but I won't admit it. I never want to admit it. Not to anyone. If I do, then it becomes more real than I want to allow. I miss her but need to move on. She will be around. Realistically, I know this. We will cross paths time and again because she is best friends with my cousin. It would be stupid for me to think otherwise. I just need to get over her.

I need something to snack on, too hungry to wait for dinner to be ready. I also need to figure out how to get my head on straight. No use in drowning in thoughts of a girl I never had and will never have.

"I'm gonna get some chips and salsa. Want anything else?" I ask before going inside.

"Get a couple more." He lifts his beer up to me.

I nod my head in agreement.

Manny is in the kitchen, seasoning some steaks to throw on.

"We can heat up some of the sides we have in the fridge from this week," Manny lets me know. "It's just us three here this weekend. I'm surprised you decided to stay. I took out three steaks thinking Juan and I could have steak and eggs in the morning. No more since we have to feed you." The smile that's stretching across his face lets me know he's teasing. But I am glad they took out extra meat. I would have been shit out of luck, with no dinner, if they hadn't.

"Thanks, man. I know I decided late to stick around."

I grab everything and head back outside, following Manny.

He looks at the fire as I set everything down on the table.

"Fire needs a few more." He places the meat down on the side of the grill and covers it. He sits at the table with us and takes one of the beers I brought.

"What keeps you here?" Manny questions.

"He won't say." Juan answers before I have the chance. "But if you want to start placing bets, I think it's because of a girl."

"No reason. I just didn't feel like driving back into town." I try and figure out what to say to these guys who I have worked alongside for months now.

In spite of being with them day in and out, I realize I don't know much about them. I'm sure they figured I have some sort of connection to the family because they have seen me with Garrett when he's here, and I would head up to the Anders's home in the evenings. No one knew what I was doing at the house. Those were the nights Mrs. Anders was tutoring me for the GED test I was getting ready to take.

"How long have you been working on the ranch?" I ask whoever wants to answer. If I decide to avoid home for a while, I should get to know my housemates.

"I've worked here since I was in high school," Manny begins. "It was summer of my junior year when I started. I spent the summer working. I was in 4-H and had raised pigs since I was little. I wanted to learn about raising a steer. My parents weren't sure how that would go, but my dad has a friend who is friends with Mr. Anders. Mr. Anders gave me the chance to start learning about the ranch. I stayed all summer here at the house, working." He smiles as he tells his story. "Five years now. When Julio decides to retire, I want to be the ranch manager."

"Really. This is what you want to do?" I'm surprised by his answer. While I'm grateful for the opportunity, I don't think this is for me. It is *hard* work. You are always working against all the elements.

"Absolutely."

"And you, Juan?" I ask, not understanding the drive to want to make this place long-term. Summer just began, and it's already hot as hell out here.

"Too many years to count and many more to come." Juan begins. "There isn't much for me but this place. I never finished school when I moved here from Mexico. But I have it good here."

He was right about that. The Anders took care of their employees. While the house could sleep many more, only a handful stayed. I'm guessing they are small-town folk who head on home.

"I just finished high school a month ago," I admit to the guys. "I took classes and passed the test for my GED. I didn't finish when I was supposed to either."

"What's your story?" Manny asks.

"Same old sad story, I guess. Worthless parents. A grandmother that raised us. I dropped out of high school to work and help pay the bills." This was really the first time I had spoken about my life. Not sure what else to say. Never one to expose too much, I stop. Manny gets up and checks the fire before placing the steaks on.

"So how did you end up here?" Manny questions, breaking the silence I left.

"Garrett is dating my cousin. She has a worthless mom too. She, my brother, and I were raised by Güela. When my grandmother passed, the Anders helped us. I had no direction and no diploma, so Mrs. Anders tutored me, and I was able to get my GED. Toni, she's the one with the brains. Just graduated college."

"Ah! So you *are* related to the girl who Garrett was crying over months ago." Juan's smile is large. "I had to pull him away from the bottle a few times because of her."

"I'm sure you did." I laugh at that thought.

"Are you going to start drowning yourself in the bottle like Garrett did?"

"Huh?" I act dumb, knowing full well he is referring to the girl who has me here.

"Sure, act like you don't know what I mean, *pendejo*, but we know," he persists.

I consider telling them, but this shit is so convoluted. Garrett is dating my cousin, who is best friends with the girl who has my heart. I can't risk Garrett finding out anything, because Toni will have pretty boy confessing everything he knows. I die with this secret.

"You know," I nod in confirmation, "but not one I want to talk about," I admit.

"In love with another man's chick?" he teases, trying to get me to admit something.

"No. She's just out of my league." I'm hoping this will pacify him and end the conversation but is vague enough, even if it does get back to Garrett.

"No such thing." Manny decides to jump in. "She's only too good for you if you let her be. I'm tired of all that crap. Who the hell gets to decide who's better than who?"

"You're right, Manny." Not knowing how I hit a nerve, I try to calm him anyway. "But this time I decided. I know. She needs someone better than me."

"Why?"

"She just does. I don't want to talk about her."

He nods his head in understanding before checking on the steaks.

LOLA

HIDING out at my dad's seems like the way to spend my weekend. It was too hard last weekend coming up with excuses why I was avoiding Toni. Even Javie called and asked if I was coming over. I couldn't. I can't see Alex until my embarrassment wears off. I know it's irrational embarrassment because I didn't do anything, but fighting with Alex, and the thought that he hates me or doesn't want me around, has my stomach in knots.

For me, he projects a calm presence, which is in contrast to the arrogance he exudes. He knows the power he holds, and he uses it. I've seen his friends cower when he walks into the room. There is no questioning what he says. The only ones who get away with it are Toni and Javie. And the only reason he allows it is because he loves them fiercely. I swear he would lay down and die if either of them needed him to.

I did it. I went head-to-head with him, and I lost. I don't know why I couldn't get my mouth to stop. Words just kept escaping. Now I don't know where I stand. I don't want to face him. I can't. At least he was somewhat cordial with me, even though he said I didn't belong. How will he treat me now? He made it perfectly clear I was not to come around.

"What do you want for dinner?" my dad asks through my bedroom door.

"Whatever you want," I answer. "Let me get dressed, and we can go out."

I can't stay inside wallowing all weekend.

"WHILE I LOVE HAVING you at home, what has you here all weekend?" My dad begins questioning after we get our drinks and appetizer.

"No reason." I shrug my shoulders, shoving a potato skin in my mouth.

"Want to try again?"

"No."

He takes a drink, watching me. His knowing eyes waiting for me to come clean. Picking up a mozzarella stick, he points it at me. "Are you going to make me wait? Really."

A giggle comes up as tears begin to form thinking of Alex again.

"I just need to avoid Toni for a bit. And this is the best place to do it." I start slowly, knowing I won't be able to hold the sad tears at bay. "I crushed on her cousin, and he can't stand me." I bite my lip to stop the quiver.

"I'm sorry, honey, but I'm going to need a little more. I know I'm biased, but I don't see how anyone could dislike you."

"Well, he does. He's always going on and on about how I don't belong at their place. 'Go hang with your college friends. Hang with your kind.'" I use a deep voice to try and mimic his. At least with the frustration of Alex pushing me away, the tears stop.

"Well, maybe he has a point. You told me yourself that Toni and her cousins aren't from the best part of town."

"I know. But where they are from doesn't mean they are bad people," I instantly defend them.

"I'm not saying they are. Don't misconstrue what I'm saying. But is he saying he doesn't like you, or is he just trying to keep you away from his hard life? There is a difference."

The question makes me pause. I can't answer that. Alex is guarded, so I don't know how to answer. At times he can be so sweet and protective, but the next minute he makes me feel unwelcome. And now that I have my head out of my ass, I can see how he does the same thing to Toni too. He doesn't want her around the neighborhood. He keeps Toni away because he wants her to be more than where she is from. But why keep me away? I'm not from there. I never will be. I'm a visitor to their world. Why try so hard to push me away?

"What are you thinking?" my dad continues, bringing me back to the conversation.

"I hadn't thought about that. I guess I was so blinded by the crush, I hadn't considered whether he hates me or is just pushing me away from the life they grew up with." My mind still spins with the unanswered question.

"Now that you have figured some things out, does that mean you are going back to your apartment?" His knowing smile appears.

"Tomorrow. You still owe me a brunch." While I may have new things to consider, and the embarrassment has eased with this new revelation, I will always stay for my dad's French toast.

"Deal." He grabs his beer clinking it against mine. "Back to Toni's cousin. What's his name?"

Some people might find it weird to have these conversations with a dad, but since my mom passed, he is all I have. He has been incredible. These conversations were strange at first, but his acceptance without judgment and steady advice have helped make them natural.

"Alex. He's the older of her two cousins. It's Alex and Javie."

"How much older?"

"Four years."

"What's he like, other than trying to keep you away? Is the crush only physical or is it more?"

"He's easy on the eyes," my cheeks burn thinking of him, "but it's more. All I've been able to do is watch him from afar. He is closed off to everyone. I don't even know if he has true friends that he trusts. It's just him, his brother, and Toni. They have this circle that can't be broken or penetrated. He protects them. Watches over them."

"How so?"

We are interrupted briefly as our waiter brings us our food. We settle in before I continue.

"It's hard to explain. He just never seems out of control. Ever. He's probably one of those people that sleeps with one eye open. He has a bigger-than-life presence. It's almost like nothing bad could happen if he's around."

"Huh. Not the answer I was expecting. Well, you won't ever know how he feels about you if you keep hiding away." He gives me a good-natured kick-in-the-butt wink before noticing a baseball game on the TV above me, and the conversation turns to sports.

CHAPTER 5

ALEX

ANOTHER WEEK DOWN. ANOTHER WEEKEND AVOIDING home. I'm still not ready to be around her. I need to keep my distance until I can shake her. Pulling into the ranch house, I see Garrett's truck parked outside. I didn't realize he was coming up this weekend.

Stepping inside, I am assaulted by her laugh. She's here. It's her uninhibited, relaxed-and-having-a-good-time laugh. She doesn't have to be in front of me for me to envision her lips pulled back and eyes dancing. A smile that lights up a dull room. The one I am rarely privy to since I am a dick. I pause where I'm standing, not wanting to disturb her.

"Hey, *guey*," Juan says as he bumps into my frozen body.

"Sorry." I begin walking again.

"Surprise!" Toni says enthusiastically, throwing her hands up in the air. "Since you have been refusing to come home, we decided to come to you." She winks at me.

"Great, my peace and quiet is obliterated now, huh?" I tease walking towards the large table in the kitchen to find Lola, Garrett, and Javie. Garrett and Javie nod their heads hello while Lola continues to stare at her clutched hands on the table.

My chest tightens, knowing I'm causing her to cower, to become so unlike the girl I just heard.

"Seriously, y'all didn't need to come. I like it out here." Not untrue. "I'm just trying to figure out what is in store for me. Wasn't in the mood to deal with shit in the hood. Go on home."

I don't want Lola to look or feel the way I'm seeing her right now.

"We're staying." Toni walks up to me, standing in front of me then pushing my chest, making me move backward. I continue moving until she stops. Whispering, she continues, "You better play nice. I mean it."

Wanting Lola happy, I nod in agreement. I hate that I have caused her to shrink when she is meant to shine. Toni continues to look at me. She's studying me, so I walk around her, back to the kitchen.

"What are we making?" I ask the room.

"Let Garrett do the cooking," Juan chimes in, laughing, "It's time for pretty boy to get busy while we relax." He pats my shoulder as he walks past me to the fridge pulling out a soda.

"I was going to, *culero*." Garrett stands.

Javie stands with him, going to the counter, where there are several bags filled with food. They begin taking things out as Toni sits down with Lola, Juan, and Manny.

Unsure of myself, I announce, "I'm going to take a shower." This will give me a few to regroup.

The Texas summer heat is beginning to rear its ugly head, so I keep the water lukewarm, cooling off from the outside. The water feels good, but my mind continues to swirl with thoughts of Lola. Being nice to her is not the problem. I would fuckin' give her the world if I could.

I dry myself off, wrapping a towel around my waist to walk to the room I've been occupying for the past couple of weeks. And then suddenly, a déjà vu moment. Lola is in the hall, leaning on the wall across from me, like she had been waiting. Her features serious, she starts right away.

"Look, I know the last time we spoke, it wasn't pretty. My bad, so I'm sor—"

I open my mouth to argue, but she lifts her hand to stop me.

"I'm sorry. I won't get in your business again. Toni and Garrett insisted I come."

Disappointed at her statement, wanting so much for this encounter to be slightly flirtatious like the last time, before it crashed and burned, I'm quiet.

She watches me for a second, and when I say nothing, she takes a deep breath, "That's all I wanted to say." She turns to walk away.

I move quickly, not wanting it to end like this. I place my hand on her shoulder, halting her. She faces me, our bodies close, my hand burning to touch so much more than her bare shoulder.

"You have nothing to be sorry for. It was me. I was the asshole. I should be the one apologizing." My hand squeezes her shoulder, not wanting to break this small connection. "You are too good for our neighborhood. There is no reason for you to be there. I didn't do a good job of explaining that. You," I bring my other hand to cup her chin, making sure her gaze stays on me, "deserve everything. And everything is not where we are." But what I really meant to say was "Everything is not who I am," and I'm really pissed at life for it.

"I come to spend time with y'all because y'all are my safe space." And before I could do or say anything, her arms come around my waist, hugging me close, her head on my chest. My arms automatically wrap around her, wanting to protect this golden-haired, pure-hearted beauty from any and all heartbreak.

In this moment, everything is perfect, and I wish it could stay that way. But since I know it can't, I'll cherish it before the spell is broken.

"Lola, what do you want to drink?" Toni's voice breaks through as she yells from the kitchen.

Lola pulls away, looking up at me with a slight smile. She places her hand on my bare chest, the warmth searing me as her smiles broadens, before turning and yelling, "I don't know. I'm coming."

My heart leaves with her as she makes her way back to the kitchen. How I will ever handle seeing her with another guy is beyond me.

The kitchen is empty when I enter, voices coming through the door that leads the patio. Lighthearted conversation and laughter fills the empty room. If only I could figure out a way to become someone who deserves her. To have those eyes see into my soul. Lost in my own thoughts, I didn't realize the door opened.

"Not joining us outside?" Javie asks, opening the fridge and pulling out sausage links.

"Yeah, I'm coming. Just taking a breather after the long day."

"Are you okay with Lola here? I know last time we were all together, shit hit the fan." His question is somewhat timid.

"It's fine. She came to find me already. I was being a dick trying to keep her away like I'm doing with Toni. I forget she's not used to my asshole behavior." I shrug, dismissing all the feelings I have about it.

"Sure?" he probes.

I have protected Javie his whole life. He rarely experienced the beatings Dad liked to inflict when he was drunk. I would hide him away and take them for us. He did not handle them well. He's a sensitive fool, but he's my brother. I've toughened him up over the years, making sure he can handle shit if it comes his way. But everyone knows he's my brother, and it has yet to be an issue. Too many are scared of me to even risk messing with him. That, and there is no reason to unless you want to get to me. He is nice to a fault. I guess one of us has to be.

"Really." I follow him out so he can stop worrying about keeping the peace and enjoy himself.

Juan, Manny, Toni, and Lola are sitting at the table, playing Uno. Now I understand all the laughter. It's funny how that card game can turn grown adults into kids, laughing and teasing the shit out of each other as they torture those next to them with the worst cards.

I keep my distance, enjoying watching her relaxed. At the grill, Garrett is placing burgers down.

"How has it been out here?" Garrett asks me.

"It's been great."

"But?" he probes.

"No 'but.' It is great. I just don't think it's for me for the rest of my life." I answer him honestly. His family has done so much for us; I owe him the truth.

"I understand. This is an adjustment from city life. It is temporary, if you want it to be, or permanent, if you want. It's up to you."

"I know. I just don't know what else is out there."

"You'll never know until you look." He claps my shoulder. "Watch the grill." He walks away.

"Need another, darlin'?" He raises his drink to Toni to see if she's ready for a refill. She shakes her head, but Lola pipes in, "Bring me a water. Thanks for asking." Her sassy attitude showing.

"If you are trying to hide it, you are doing a piss-poor job, you know." Javie stands near me.

"Huh?"

"You haven't taken your eyes off of her." His voice lowers as he nods his head in Lola's direction.

I'm stunned silent. I thought I hid my feelings better, but it seems Javie is figuring out there is something there.

"Your business, not mine. But I would be more careful about the googly eyes you get around her." One side of his lips pull up in a smirk.

LOLA

IT IS TOO hard to sit in such close proximity to Alex and not stare at him. Or want to be closer to him. Especially after that hug. Oh, gosh! I didn't think before I acted. His apology got me, and I reacted before I could think. It is a good thing he hugged me back because I might have been mortified again. I was so turned on by just a hug. It took everything not to run my hands up his back. He may play the part of a bad boy, but I know he has the biggest heart inside. Now if only his heart would let me in.

Pay attention to the cards. Pay attention to the cards. Glancing out of the corner of my eye, I catch him looking at me. I wish I could get in his head. Why does he have to be so darn quiet? Crap, I lose my focus, and here I am having to pick *all* the dang cards, one after another until I finally have a card to throw down. I can't help but laugh at myself.

"Doesn't look good for you, *guera*." Juan jokes. Thanks to Garrett, I know the nickname he just bestowed on me.

"I know. I know." I laugh, not knowing how else to respond.

Manny places a blue five down, and we keep going. The

casualness and comfort out here, not having to keep up pretenses, is refreshing. It brings me back to my time in Italy on my semester abroad. It is where I felt most comfortable, until recently. Tonight is the perfect type of night. I can just be.

I have been placed in a box for so many years, the list of expectations growing long. "Sorority sister," "cute," "bubbly," "agreeable" are just a few words I needed to be. When I wasn't, the judgment that came was instant. I thought sorority life was for me. I followed in my mom's footsteps. But it was not how she described. I didn't fit in, or I didn't *want* to fit in. I'm not sure which.

The game continues, and as relaxed as the evening is, I am also hyperaware of Alex and where he is. He has moved around the patio but has yet to sit down.

"This game can continue all night, and I'm hungry, so wrap it up," Garrett declares and places a plate of burger patties in the middle of the table on the stack of cards as Javie comes out with bags of chips and burger fixings.

"Thank you," I announce.

Garrett and Javie grab chairs to sit as Alex stays leaning against the wall closest to the grill, watching us. I don't dare say anything or look directly at him. Our moment earlier was just how I want to keep things. I don't need to open my mouth and ruin our truce.

"Eating?" Juan calls over to Alex.

I glance around the table and realize the only open space is next to me.

"Coming," he says casually.

My whole body comes alive when her is near. It's like my nerve endings are reaching out to him. He may project danger, but I feel safest when he is near.

As we are grabbing for things in the middle of the table to fix our plates, my arm brushes past his several times. Instant sparks. How I will ever get over these feelings if he never returns them? My chest tightens at the thought of not being with him. I don't think I've wanted anything so badly and not been able to have it.

I can't just turn on my bubbly, flirtatious self and expect him to fall for it. He will see through it. And besides, I don't want it to be that fake, superficial, "I think you're hot" start. We are way past that. I want him to let me in. I want to share my life with him. If only he would stop trying to push me away.

"Lola!" Toni's voice breaks through my inner dialogue, and I look up to see her snapping her fingers at me. "Earth to Lola." She laughs. "Where did you go?"

Shaking my head, "Nowhere. Sorry." I won't ever share what I was thinking. "Just lost in my head. It was nothing." I smile, hoping to cover my bruised heart. "What are we doing after we eat?" I try to change the subject.

"Not much. Relaxing, since we are waking early if you want to go riding and watch the sunrise," Garrett answers.

"What time do we have to be up if we go out? And can we drive instead?" Never ridden in my life—I don't want to ruin everyone's time with me not knowing what to do.

"I'll be up at five to saddle the horses. We should get out by quarter 'til so we aren't rushing." Garrett looks at me. "You don't want to ride?"

"Not that I don't want to, just never have. Don't want to put a damper on anything that early in the morning," I admit.

By the look in his eyes, I know he's thinking.

"I just learned myself, and I'm no expert. You will be fine," Toni chimes in happily.

"I'll drive you out to the pond if you want," Alex offers quietly.

My eyes leave Garrett and turn toward Alex. "Really?" I'm surprised by his offer.

"Sure." He nods slightly. "I'm not the best rider yet either."

"Well, I'm staying the third wheel. I want to ride." Javie says out loud, then adds, "Sorry, Toni." He shrugs his shoulders while smiling.

"Better for me, then. I only have to saddle three horses." Garrett finds the silver lining.

"You fools can go on out. Too many early mornings here. I'm staying in bed," Manny chimes in as Juan nods his head in agreement.

The rest of dinner is filled with conversation and laughter, but Alex, is quiet throughout, only offering quick responses when asked something directly. I wonder why he offered. I would imagine he may want to sleep in since he's up early too.

TUCKED IN BED, covers drawn high, I'm swimming in thoughts of Alex. Trying to keep them PG-rated, but my mind insists on going back to him, bare-chested with only a towel hanging low on his hips. His strong chest, the *V* pointing downward, one quick pull and down the towel would go.

"You and Alex call a truce?" Toni's voice breaks my thoughts. She decided to share a room with me this weekend.

"Yeah. I think so. I apologized." I admit to her.

"Why would you do that? You have nothing to be sorry for."

"I pushed. I know better." My lungs fill with air in a long intake.

"That's what he needs. Push back. Because he always thinks he knows best."

I exhale slowly. "Maybe from you and Javie, but not from me. Not from an outsider who should know better than to inject herself into someone else's life."

"You are welcome in our lives." The sincerity in the tone of her voice fills me with warmth. I need her as much as she needs me.

"Thank you. And yes, I love to be welcome in *your* life. But being in your life does not create a seat for me in Alex's. That's his life." A small thud in my chest reminds me of my bruised heart. With no response from her, I know she understands.

CHAPTER 6

ALEX

I TOSS AND TURN MOST OF THE NIGHT KNOWING SHE IS IN bed down the hall. How can I possibly make a girl like that happy? My thoughts continue to play tricks on my mind all evening, considering the possibility of making her mine. Being able to hold her small frame close to me. Stroking her long, golden locks. Kissing those reddish, full lips. Running my hands over her soft skin. Those images were enough to get little man to stand at attention most of the night. How fucking pathetic! I wouldn't even be able to hold my load if I were to get her underneath me.

The alarm I set on my phone goes off, but it was not necessary since I am already up, lost in my dreams of her. I stay in bed a bit longer, needing to think of the most unsexy thoughts possible so others don't see a morning woody before coffee. Stepping in cow shit. Raking a dirty stall.

After changing and brushing my teeth, I make my way to the kitchen, where I find Lola and Toni busy. Tired after a long week, running on no sleep, and now starting a very early morning, I make my way to the coffee pot.

"Since you are taking the truck, Garrett thought we could make a picnic of it. We're fixing some snacks while they are saddling the horses," Toni fills me in.

"Sounds good," I answer truthfully, sitting at the table wanting to help, but much too tired. The weeks away from Lola, missing her, now have me not wanting to leave her side.

I start sipping the black, bitter liquid I hope will give me enough energy to last through today. Lola is gliding back and forth from the fridge to the counter, a smile perched upon her lips, even this early. Her hair pulled up in one of those buns girls place atop their heads. I'm not a big fan of it, except that it gives me full view of her neck and shoulders. She's in some jean shorts and a tight tank. I let my gaze drop down her round ass and slide down her toned legs, and a familiar twitch brings me back to any thoughts to calm him. Loose athletic shorts are not the best cover-up.

"Ready?" Javie comes into the kitchen through the patio door. "Horses are ready."

"Yup. We just need to load the truck," Toni informs him.

"I got it. Go," I announce to Toni.

"Sure?" She turns, facing me.

"Yeah. Get going. Lola can tell me what to bring." I try to ease her mind. She is probably worried about leaving Lola here with an asshole. The asshole being me.

"Okay." She turns to Lola. "You got the rest?"

"I got it. Go." Lola gives her a little push in the direction of the door. Toni gets the hint and pulls a hoodie over her head, walking out following Javie.

"Do I need to help you get anything else ready?" I ask, not wanting Lola to have to do the rest on her own.

"Nope, it's all done. We were just bagging everything up. If you want to start taking those bags out and the blankets

Garrett left on the couch, that would be great." Her eyes light up as she looks at me.

I mock salute her, and she rolls her eyes at me playfully. This. This is the interaction I should be having with her. Only problem is, if she were to start dating someone, I would not be able to be around them. Not without a scene.

I grab the bags she pointed to as I glance at her placing cut up fruit in a plastic bowl. I begin loading the truck as she finishes up what she was doing.

"Anything else?" I ask her for direction.

"Just the cooler. Let me get my hoodie on, and I'll help you carry it out." She offers to help.

"I got it." I bend over picking it up and walking out.

She follows behind me, making her way to the passenger side and getting in.

Turning the key, the radio blasts the rock music we were listening to on the way back from the field. I move quickly to turn it down, not wanting to mess up this tranquil morning with her.

"Sorry. We need that at the end of a long day," I explain.

She just smiles, "Listening to music in the car is the best. I know there are windows and people can see me, but I swear, I love to dance and sing in the car like nobody can see me."

"Now you have me curious." I put the truck in drive.

The pond isn't far, but I have to follow the roadless, narrow, worn-down path. We drive in comfortable silence for a bit until she asks, "You know your way around well now?"

"Somewhat. It's still weird not following roads or having landmarks to guide you." The ease in which we are existing right now is how I want to feel around her all the time.

"I'm lost, so I'm trusting you to get us there." A short giggle bubbles up.

"Almost there."

I place the truck in park, looking around for the others.

Figuring they took a more scenic route, I start pulling the blankets from the truck and laying them out. When she sees what I'm doing, she comes up to help.

"Take a seat, shouldn't be long now." I tell her, grabbing the last couple of blankets and placing them near the ones I'd spread.

I lower myself near her but put a little distance in between, not wanting to crowd her or, more truthfully, not wanting to be tempted to lose my resolve.

Except for a few birds announcing the sun's arrival, all we hear is the still of the morning.

"It's so peaceful," Lola whispers.

She has her legs pulled in to her chest and her head leaning on her knees, taking it all in.

"It is," I answer, not wanting to break this perfect moment away from our real lives that keep us apart.

She begins adjusting her hoodie over her legs, stretching it out. "Are you cold?" I ask, just now noticing the early-morning chill before the sun heats everything up.

"I'm fine." She's back to hugging her legs, but now they are covered.

The sound of horses trotting has us both turning around to see the others coming in our direction. They get near and dismount before Garrett ties each of the horses to a nearby tree. More blankets are spread, and a few minutes later, light is appearing over the horizon. Everyone is quiet, each lost in our own thoughts, appreciating the beauty before us. It is one of those perfect sunrises that project shades orange, pink, and purple, blending seamlessly. I sneak a glance at Lola as a tear escapes her eye.

Not thinking, I cup her cheek, swiping it with my thumb. Her eyes widen in surprise, then soften before she leans into my hand slightly. The rustle of movement reminds me we are not alone, and I quickly pull my hand back. She turns her face away from me.

The still of the morning comes to an end when Garrett announces his hunger. He and Javie begin unloading the bags and the cooler so we can set out the food the girls packed.

With a full stomach and feeling relaxed for the first time with Lola around, I lay down. I place the hoodie Toni took off behind my head as a pillow and close my eyes.

LOLA

AFTER ENJOYING THE QUIET MORNING, everyone is ready to head back. Garrett wants to check on the herd and head up to his parents' house. I help clean everything up as Garrett and Javie load the truck back up.

"Alex," Toni says as she goes in to shake him.

"Don't." I get her attention. "Let him sleep. I'll stay here until he wakes up."

I had been enjoying watching him sleep. His usually hard look has been replaced with a calm I have never seen before.

"Why?" Her brows pull together in confusion.

I shrug my shoulders, not knowing how to answer exactly. Because I want to watch him sleep. Because I am trying to spend more time alone with him, even if he isn't aware he's spending time with me.

"Sure?" she asks again.

"Yes. Now go. I'll be fine." I smile, easing her concern. Javie is standing by his horse, watching our exchange.

"See you at the house." She waves as she walks towards the horses.

I watch as they begin to ride away. Once I can't see them anymore, I pull out the book I was reading from my bag and lay down on my stomach, close to him but far enough so that we are not touching. His long, deep breaths signal a deep sleep.

I begin reading where I left off yesterday on the drive to the ranch, getting lost in the love story blossoming on the pages. The insta-love story I'm reading is not helping with my unrequited love. Wanting so much for him to notice me as something other than a nuisance around his home, I daydream of him returning my affection.

Not sure how much time has passed, but I'm startled when I hear him clear his throat. I turn to face him as he rolls to his side propping his head on his hand. He looks around, blinking his eyes a couple of times before he asks, "Where did everyone go?"

"Back to the house." I sit myself up, my arm numb where I had been laying on it. I shake it to get the blood flowing again as the painful tingles prick.

"Arm asleep?" His knowing smile so different from what I'm used to.

"Yes." I continue to shake it.

"Why didn't you wake me? I could have driven you back." He sits up, moving his body, probably stiff from the hard ground.

I shrug my shoulders again because I don't have an answer I'm willing to share. The shrug seems to be my answer for everything today.

He picks up the water bottle next to him, taking a long drink. "I'm surprised I didn't wake up when they left. I'm usually a light sleeper." I stay quiet, not wanting to ruin this moment by saying the wrong thing. "Living in the hood, you have to be a light sleeper. You never know what can happen."

I'm floored by this small nugget of information he just offered. He never speaks of himself or what he has been through.

"Was it hard?" I ask just above a whisper, scared of pushing but wanting the conversation to continue.

"Was what hard?" he counters, looking at me.

"Not sleeping peacefully?" I turn to face him completely, hoping I didn't overstep.

He looks at me pensively for a few moments before answering. "I hadn't really thought about it 'til now. I needed to be a light sleeper when we were little because my dad was a dumb fuck that liked to beat us. I woke when I heard him come in drunk so I had enough time to hide Javie. I guess it just stayed with me. That's why I'm surprised I didn't wake up when they packed up and left."

I was holding my breath through his statement, not wanting to break this spell. I have heard through Toni what he has done for her, and overheard Javie and his admiration for his older brother. Even Garrett told me that he needed Alex's approval to date Toni because of the power he commands in his family. But never once anything from the horse's mouth.

I was speechless at the end of his admission. I had never been through anything remotely similar. Never once had to worry about my safety. I had no words.

"Yeah, well. We better get going." He starts to stand, but I place my hand on his arm, halting him.

He pauses, his gaze wanting to be anywhere but on me. I bring my other arm and brush his chin gently in my direction, not leaving it there, but bringing it back safely to my lap.

"I don't know what to say, or even if there is a right thing to say, because I have never been through the things you have had to endure. But..." I bring my hand up again stroking his cheek, "I will always be a shoulder if you want or need it."

A fraction of a smile pulls at his lips before our moment ends.

"Thank you. But it really isn't necessary. I've handled shit all my life and don't expect that will change anytime soon."

He makes his way to get up again, and my panic sets in, not wanting it to end this way. I close my hand gripping the arm I was holding. He pauses, looking at me.

"I uh..." What do I want to say? So much and nothing is swirling around my mind at the same time.

"You don't have to worry about me. I'm a big boy, and I'll be fine. Land on my feet each time." His lips pull into a smile, but I would bet money he's plastering it on for my benefit.

"I know. I just want to be there. If you want it. Even if you don't need it." My heart is breaking for this man who has carried the responsibility of a family on his shoulders since he was a child. He wasn't afforded his childhood innocence.

He nods his head just a fraction. I know this will be the only acknowledgement I'll receive, and before I have time to think about what I am doing, I crawl into his lap, straddling him and wrapping my arms around him. My face is tucked into his neck, and I'm filled with a scent that is uniquely him. It takes a second for my mind to catch up to what my body was doing, but once they're both on the same page, I am embarrassed once again and scared to move.

And just like that, I feel his arms come around me. One hand comes around, landing on my hip, and the other is cupping the back of my head, and now I'm the safest I've ever felt.

Seconds pass by before he says my name, getting my attention. He loosens his arms, placing his hands on my shoulders and pushing me back slightly. His usual stern look is back on his face. "I can't have you or anyone taking pity me."

He is strong and prideful; this I have learned. "I don't pity you. Not in the least. You are strong and capable." I pause, hoping I articulate the next statement correctly. "But I am sad you lost your childhood, having to take care of everyone."

His hand strokes my cheek, "Don't be. It is what it is. No reason to focus on crap we can't change."

"Okay." I give in to him.

"Ready to go?"

No. Not at all. I want to stay right here. Feeling you this close always. But I answer, "Sure."

BACK AT THE HOUSE, Alex retreats to his room after we unload the truck, and he stays there until they call him out to watch a movie. Except for a few words here or there about inconsequential things, he says no more to me. The time by the pond, by ourselves, will be the fluke I will hold on to.

CHAPTER 7

ALEX

HOLDING LOLA IN MY ARMS, HER CLINGING TO ME, HAS been on replay all week. I want so much to say "fuck it" and go for her. And it may be hot for a little while... no... it *would* be *hot* for a while, but the reality of who I am and what I can't offer will come crashing down around us. I can't have some girl trying to save me. I don't have the means for a girl like her.

It took everything I had to break that moment. It would have been too easy to take her lips and kiss her senseless. I wanted to change the sadness in her eyes that she had thinking of my shitty childhood. But kissing her would have just opened another can of worms I can't deal with.

I CAN'T BELIEVE I let Garrett talk me into going two-stepping. It's not like I don't know how, but it's not really my scene. Although, not sure what my scene is these days because I don't want to hang in the neighborhood bar either. Javie and I walk in, not sure if Toni and Garrett have arrived.

"This way." Javie grabs my attention before walking away.

I follow him, scanning the crowd around me. Always, and I mean always, know your surroundings. You never know when trouble may come. Especially for a guy who looks like me in this club. I'm not the typical country bar type of guy.

"Hey!" Toni yells over the music, smiling. Garrett waves at us and hands us each a beer from the bucket on the table.

There a several people I don't know standing and sitting around three bar tables pushed together.

Garrett proceeds to point at people and yell names. I'm not really listening; I have no reason to remember them. This is their world, not mine. I'm not sure why they insisted we meet them.

"Javie!" Her voice comes through loud and clear above the music. And it's saying my brother's name, not mine. I refuse to turn around and look at her.

From the corner of my eye, I can see her tucked safely under his arm. Her small frame engulfed in his, with her arms wrapped around his mid-section.

"Hi, Alex," Lola sends my way. I catch the change in enthusiasm as she says it.

"Hi, Lola," I respond facing her but quickly turn back to everyone else. I can't get lost in her eyes. I take a long pull from my beer, emptying half the bottle.

"I'll be back." I wave my bottle to the crowd before making my way to the bar. I need to step away and get my head on straight. I assumed she would be here and thought I'd prepared myself, but seeing her...seeing her wrapped in Javie's arms almost undid me.

Leaning against the bar, I wave down a bartender, placing my order. He sets a tequila shot and beer in front of me. I need something to take the edge off.

Taking my time before heading back over, I watch the people around me. Mostly cowboys and a few odd ones out like myself. I try and avoid eye contact with a couple of girls who are trying desperately to get my attention. Getting female attention has never been a problem.

I walk slowly back to the table, regretting my decision to come instead of hiding out at the ranch again. I watch as Lola laughs and talks to the people at the table around her. She is on a stool, and Javie is by her side. Her protector. He's going to need to watch it because he can't get caught up with her either.

I stand at the opposite side of the tables from them, listening but contributing nothing. Seems like it is going to be a long evening. Toni and Garrett are off dancing, along with half the table.

"How are you liking working on the ranch?" one of the guys asks me.

It takes me a second to come out of the bored stupor I was in. "It's good. Hard, but good."

I keep it vague but positive. These are Garrett's friends, and I don't need to cause any trouble for Toni. It's the truth. It's hard work, but it's honest, so I can't complain.

"I love it out there. School keeps me busy, so I don't get to go out there like I would like to."

Surprised by his answer, I ask, "You like working out at the ranch?"

"Sure do. Not many can say that. I grew up out there. The Anders' ranch is where every teenage boy made their summer money."

"Ah! Makes sense. I didn't know where all those new kids came from this week. I guess school must have just let out. Huh?"

"School usually lets out and they take a week or two to

fuck around before parents kick them out to go to work." He laughs. "Or at least that's what my parents did to me."

I guess not all Garrett's friends are silver-spoon kids.

I see Lola swaying with the music from the corner of my eye. Anyone who looks at her would know she wants to dance, but no one is asking her. How could anyone leave a beauty alone and wanting? What are these idiots thinking?

And just like that, some stranger comes up to her, and she's up and walking to the dance floor. Again, I want her to be happy, but watching someone else doing what I want to do is bullshit. I give them a moment to walk away before following and standing by the dance floor to keep an eye on her.

I watch them as they make their way around the floor. He's guiding her, and she looks happy to be out there. This is her world, and I need to make sure she stays here. I need another beer to calm the frustration rising. While I know I can't have her, wanting her is still a problem.

I make my way back to the dance floor to check on her, and her face has fallen. The fucker's hand is sliding down her back, over her butt, and back up again. She looks uncomfortable.

No guy has the right to take liberties unless the girl approves them, and Lola sure as hell does not look like she has given him the go.

Walking up to them, I get his attention. "I'll take over from here." Posturing to ensure he knows I'm not in the mood to fuck around.

"Alex." Lola's eyes widen, and her body relaxes when he lets her go.

He sizes me up. It takes a second for him to nod his head and walk away. I turn to Lola extending my hand to her, my heart in my throat, wondering if she will walk away from me.

She places her hand in mine, I pull her close, still holding my beer, placing it on her lower back.

My body relaxes with her so close. I begin to move, and she follows my lead. A slow country song is playing, so I can keep her body flush with mine. I can feel her hand gripping my shirt in the back. She's so close, I can smell the sweetness of her shampoo.

After a few moments of this relaxing calm, she pulls away slightly, looking me in the eyes. I can see a question stirring, but no words are leaving her mouth. What is going through her head?

"Uh..." She pauses, clearing her throat. "Thanks for saving me."

"Of course. I saw him trying to cop a feel."

"You saw him?" She seems confused.

I nod.

"You were watching me?"

Shit...What is she going to think when she realizes I was following her like a fucking stalker?

"I noticed you having trouble on my way back from the bar," I try and explain, bringing my almost full beer up, showing her.

Her brows pull in, creasing the skin in between. Again, she is holding something in.

"Never mind." She drops her gaze down to my chest.

"Hey." I let go of her hand, cupping her chin and lifting her face to look back up at me. "Say it or ask it."

"It's nothing really." Her lips pull into a fake smile.

"It's something." I'm losing all control having her look so pained. I want to do everything in my power to make her happy again.

"I just thought you were watching out for me."

Confused, I ask, "What do you mean watching out for you?"

Her gaze goes around the dance floor as she takes a long breath in. She exhales and says, "The way you watch over those you care about. The way you protect Toni. It's stupid. I just thought you were looking out for me, but you just happened to notice. It's fine. Thank you, still, for cutting in." Her words come out fast and a bit jumbled with embarrassment. She looks down at our moving feet.

My heart was about to thump right out of my chest now knowing she wants me to be her protector. The song ends as another, more fast-paced one begins. She pulls back with a weak smile, but I can still feel her hand with a fistful of my shirt. I can't let her continue believing I don't give a damn. Her hand releases my shirt, and she takes a step back about to turn away from me. I tighten the grip I have on the hand I'm still holding, pulling her back to me. She looks up at me, confused.

"I was watching you. I can't help but watch you." I hope these words ease her mind.

Her eyes widen in surprise. Her hand comes up to my neck as she lifts up on tip toes pulling my face down to hers, our lips meeting. It happens so quickly. I am lost in all that is Lola. I have been dreaming of a moment like this for far too long; I'm not going to let it go now that it is here.

Her arms wrap around my neck as I pull her body flush against mine deepening the kiss she began. I lick across her lips, and she opens, welcoming, as our tongues dance together. The intensity too much, too fast, so I slow us down, pulling back placing my forehead on hers and catching my breath.

LOLA

STARING INTO HIS DARK EYES, I begin to wonder whether this is it or whether he will think it was a mistake. He's not pulling away, and I'm lacking the right words. We are bumped by a couple dancing by. He turns around, grabbing my hand, pulling me behind him. I don't know where we are going, but I would follow him anywhere. Stepping off the dance floor, he begins walking towards the side door, which leads to an outdoor area. Once outside, he continues a bit until we are away from the crowd.

I'm terrified about what will happen next. Is he mad? Did he want it too? I can't think of anything in between.

He places his beer bottle down and leans against a railing, watching me, still holding my hand, his thumb rubbing circles on the top. I hold his gaze wondering, *Is this like a game of chicken, waiting to see who breaks and speaks first?*

Not yet secure in the words I want to say, I take the step forward and lean on him, tucking myself into his strong chest. His arms envelope me, holding me close. I wish we could stay like this and skip over any talk that doesn't lead us to where I am right now.

"What just happened?" His voice is low and deep, for only me to hear.

I don't move, not wanting to see his expression if it's not a receptive one. "I kissed you."

I feel the laugh huff before he says, "Yeah, I caught that part." He pushes me back. "But I want to know why."

My cheeks are heating up. "Cause I wanted to."

He stays quiet, so I figure I need to go all in and show my cards. "I wanted to because I'm attracted to you." I may have just played my hand, but I wasn't quite ready for a negative outcome, so I take a step back, placing space between us.

His Adam's apple bounces as he takes a breath and swallows. His silence speaks volumes.

"Uh...so well...that's all, so I guess I'll go back inside now."

But before I can walk away, he begins, "Wait. I'm just digesting information." His hands come up rubbing his face roughly. "Sweetheart, I'm no good for you. You deserve so much better than me. I'm a lucky bastard you like me at all. I can't have you and be proud of myself."

"Why do you keep saying that? You are good enough. I hate that you don't think you deserve anything and everything. Stop being a fucking martyr." Hot, angry tears are beginning to collect.

"Please. Don't cry. I think you're perfect. Your smile lights up a room. I hate pushing you away, but you know where I'm from. I didn't even have a high school diploma until a couple of months ago."

"I know all this. I know all of it and still. I. Want. You. It says more about you that you went back. You weren't too prideful to try. You take care of those you love. You give of yourself to ensure those around you are safe and happy. How could you not think you are good enough?"

"You have your whole life ahead of you. You can have any guy you want. They will have a career to take care of you."

"But I don't want any guy. I WANT YOU." I step closer to him. "But the question is, do you want me?"

He shakes his head, and my stomach falls. Is that his answer?

"Of course I want you. But—"

As soon as I hear he wants me too, I lean right into him, saying, "Nope, no buts..."

"But—" I place my finger in front of his lips shaking my head.

"Kiss me." I initiated our first kiss. This time he has to. He has to believe we can do this.

He holds my face in his hands, my eyes search his for an answer. He comes in close, brushing our noses together before softly kissing me. He keeps it short and sweet, so different from what his rough look would suggest.

"You realize you just kissed me, sealing the deal that we are now together, right?" I tease, hoping it's true.

"I just sealed the deal?"

"Yup." *Please let this be it.*

His lips come back to mine again, needier than before, and I happily oblige. He pulls away again before it becomes too much and says, "Just making sure it was sealed properly." The smile that spreads across his face is a rarity, and my heart thumps loudly knowing I'm the one who was able to put it there.

"I'll stay out here while you go let Toni know what just happened because I know she will have loads to say." He stands to his full height, grabbing his beer and taking a drink.

Rolling my eyes, I respond, "Chickenshit."

"I was already in the doghouse for being an asshole to you. Now I'm kissing you. She's going to let me have it."

"Ugh...fine. That is, if they didn't notice us on the dance floor." He raises his shoulders then crosses his arms in front of him. "I'm just going to let her know we are leaving. I don't want to get into it here."

"Good plan."

Back inside, I make my way to our table to let them know we would be leaving. I see Javie first and wonder how he will get home if Alex leaves. I scan the area for Toni but only see Garrett.

"Quite the display on the dance floor." Her voice comes from behind me.

Turning around to face her, she has one brow cocked, seriousness rolling off of her.

Shit, this isn't going to be good.

"We are going to take off," I blurt out, tucking my tail between my legs and running.

"One question and one statement first." She halts my retreat.

I nod, nervous about what's to come. I shrink in a bit, ready for a possible tongue-lashing.

"Do you really care for him, or is this just some bad-boy fantasy of yours?" That question stung. Would she really think I would do that to her family?

"I care for him. I really do." I glance around, wondering if people are watching us.

"Okay. Fair enough. Now my warning to you." Her face stays stoic, reminding me so much of Alex's. "He has never kept anyone around. He goes through girls. They chase him, he uses them, and he's done with them."

I'm left speechless. What do you say to that? Nothing. I've seen a couple of girls pursue him, but he always seemed to keep them at a distance. He was never grossly inappropriate with anyone that I ever saw. Why is she telling me this?

I nod my head, letting her know I heard her, but refuse to respond.

"We'll take Javie home. See you there?"

I still have no words. Alex didn't say where we were going. For all I know, he's taking me back to my apartment. I nod yet again.

She walks past me towards the table. I refuse to look back for fear of who is watching us.

"Wanna go to my place?" He asks as he veers onto the freeway.

"Yes." I'm nervous about messing this up. About whether or not he will toss me to the side too.

Music from the radio fills the silence hanging over us. Dating has never been hard for me. You hook up, it works or it doesn't, and that's it. This feels so much heavier. More people are involved. I don't want to lose Toni if this all blows up. And Javie. He is like the brother I never had.

I'm lost in my thoughts the entire ride back to their house. He exits the car, and when he realizes I haven't opened my door yet, he walks around, opening it for me.

"If you would rather me take you home, I can." His lips pull down nervously.

"No, we need to talk." I get up, not knowing how to begin this conversation. Dating someone has never been this complicated.

Walking into the house, he goes straight to the kitchen, and I take a seat on the couch.

CHAPTER 8

ALEX

I GRAB A GLASS OUT OF THE CABINET AND FILL IT WITH water. There is so much more to this than saying, "Yes, I'm interested." How much am I willing to reveal? I've never let anyone in. Never shared my feelings. Never had a talk like the one I'm about to walk into. No one has been important enough to care about.

I take a few long gulps, buying myself time to formulate something, anything, to say to her. I need to take control. I grab a second glass and fill both up before facing her.

"I brought you a glass of water."

"Thanks." She looks up at me as her hands fidget on her lap.

I take a seat next to her. "I'll start." The relief I see in her eyes at those two words is instant. "I noticed you a long time ago. First, because you're gorgeous, but then for being you. I tried my best to keep you away from here. For my sanity, because it was getting harder and harder to stay away from you, and because you deserve more than what this place is. And this place is me."

"I—" she tries to interrupt.

"Let me finish." She nods and does a cute zipping of her lips. She can't help being adorable. And when has a guy like me used the word "adorable?" "This place is a shitstorm we have tried taping back together over and over again. I'm not Toni. I don't have an out. She is the one with the brains who morphed into something better. I don't see any place other than here for me. I can't bring you down with me. You told me at the club I sealed the deal with a kiss, but I can't do that to you. You can say you want out right now if you want."

"Done?" The cute smile has been erased.

"I think so."

"Now it's my turn." She scoots a little closer to me. "You don't see you the way I do. Even when I told you before, you don't seem to get it. You are the strongest person I know. You have carried this family through everything. You are probably the one who has tried hardest to tape it together. You don't see the determination you already possess. You are lost about what your next step is. So what? So many college students are too. They change majors, drop out, go back… They don't just give up."

She takes a deep breath then continues, "I want you. I want you because I see that determination. I see the pride you have in taking care of those you love. I see how you protect and care for your family. And I'm not gonna lie, you are easy on the eyes too." A flirty smirk spreads on her beautiful face. "I want you. I've wanted you. I've fallen for you."

I can't stay away from her any longer. I'm just going to have to do my best to be the man she needs. "*Amor*, you stole my heart a long time ago."

Her eyes widen in surprise before she climbs onto my lap, straddling me, taking my face in a passion-filled kiss. The excitement of this moment has awakened my cock, and it's straining against my jeans. I know she can feel it because she rubs herself a few times against me before slowing down. I'm not going to take her in a frenzied hurry, and I'm sure as hell not taking her tonight. All we need is the fools coming back from the club to walk in and try to interrupt. That needs to be settled before we move further. I pull back, hating that I'm slowing us down yet again.

She places her head on my shoulder, "Have you said that before?"

"Said what before?" I'm lost at her question.

"*Amor*," she says in a gringo accent.

"Why?" My mind is reeling. Why would she ask now?

"It's dumb. I thought I had a dream of you saying it the last time I spent the night here."

She was passed out. How could she remember? "I may have said it that night." No point in trying to hide that now.

"You did." She lifts her head to look at me.

"Yes. You asked or, more accurately mumbled, about why I didn't like you. When I placed you in bed, I told you, '*Ya tienes mi corazon, amor.*'"

"Which means?"

"You already have my heart, love." I stroke the side of her face. The girl I have been dreaming about is sitting on my lap. I could never have predicted this change of events.

And just as our lips meet again, the front door opens to the family I knew would be close behind. She scrambles off my lap and sits back on the couch, looking at them file in.

"That didn't take long." I catch the irritation in Toni's voice.

"Say what you have to say, Toni. I know you want to, so might as well do it."

She takes a seat in the chair closest to me and Javie takes

the other while Garrett makes his way into the kitchen. Toni stares at me, still holding her tongue.

"Well?" I encourage her to start. "But know this...we will talk about this one time only. Tonight and we're done. This is not, and will not become, a fucking family meeting."

She rolls her eyes, sitting back stiffly. We're locked in a stare-down, and neither one of us will give in.

"Fine, then I'll start." Javie barks out, startling Lola.

I turn to face him, ignoring the daggers Toni is sending my way.

Javie looks to Toni. "We both knew something was up. I don't know why you're being a bitch about it now. You asked me if I knew what Alex was up to. This is not that big of a shock."

"Fuck you!" Toni tells him. "I might have thought he had some sort of feelings, but him acting on them is different." She points her glare in my direction, "Why Lola? You have every hood rat here willing to worship the ground you walk on, and you want to start something with the only friend I have made outside of this place? And when you toss her like you do every other girl, I'll lose her."

"I'm not going to toss her, Toni. I know that's all you've seen from me, but I can promise Lola is not like the others. And you are right, I didn't want to start anything with her. She's too good for me. I believe that now and will always believe it. But I can't tell her no. Not when she wants me too."

Garrett comes out of the kitchen and leans on the door-frame, staying out of the line of fire. I have to admire him, he knows when to fight Toni and when to pull back. This is one of those times.

"She's not one of your hit-it-and-quit-it girls?" The evil smirk that spreads across her face as she says it has me seeing red.

"Enough!" I bark out, standing to hover over her. "You have said your piece, and I have said mine. END OF DISCUSSION!"

"Fine." She smiles. "That's all I needed to know."

She was testing me. She wanted to see how I would react to her poking and whether I would defend Lola. Shaking my head, I remind her, "You're a bitch."

"I know." Her smile spreads wider as she looks at Lola. "Sorry, I was testing him. He passed."

Lola's dumbstruck by the conversation, Garrett looks bored, and Javie, as always, was ready to intervene if we got out of hand.

Toni stands up, announcing she is heading to bed, walking to her bedroom with Garrett close behind.

"You'll get used to them after a while," Javie reassures her. "Just ignore them the way Garrett does. It's safer for everybody." Javie's happy-go-lucky smile seems to calm her. "Good night."

I turn to face her as soon as we are alone again. "You okay?" This is the shitstorm I was trying to warn her away from.

"Yeah..." But it doesn't sound convincing.

"Talk to me." I grab her hand, wanting some connection to her again.

"That's the second time she mentioned you with girls and..." She pulls her hand back wrapping her arms around her legs, which she has pulled into her chest protectively.

"Second?" I want clarification.

"When I told her we were leaving, she mentioned it. She saw us on the dance floor."

"Ah...okay. She's not lying about that. I can't change that either. But you are different. If you are choosing to stay with me, I'm not letting you go."

She stays huddled in a ball, saying nothing.

"Look, if you have changed your mind or want to think about what you want, do that. I told you I was no good for you. It's probably better if you walk now. Nothing has happened and everything can go back to the way it was before. Go ahead and take my room. I'll sleep on the couch." I feel sucker-punched. This is the reason guys like me should not expect more.

"Go on. It's fine." I can't look at her anymore.

"Are you sure?" she whispers.

"Yes, go on, take my room." My head drops back, the ceiling becoming the most interesting thing in the room.

"No. I meant about not tossing me?" I look back at her as she bites her bottom lip.

"I'm absolutely sure."

"Okay." She tucks herself in my side, "I'm trusting you."

I have so much to prove to this beautiful girl. I can't let her down.

LOLA

"I'M TIRED." I begin to stand, nervous about sharing a bed with Alex but wanting and needing to be close to him at the same time.

"Go on, *amor*. I'll stay on the couch." He stays seated.

I extend my hand to him. "No, sleep with me."

"Are you sure?"

As soon as I nod yes, he grabs my hand, following me to his room.

"Here you go." Alex hands me a T-shirt.

I watch as he strips down to his boxer-briefs. Everything I have been fantasizing about is right in front of me, but the fear of being used is overruling my desire. I pull his shirt over my head and push down my shorts, maneuvering in Houdini-like moves to undress modestly.

I crawl into bed, nervous about his intentions.

"Come here." He extends his arm for me to cuddle in his side. I move in close, placing my head on his chest and my hand on his stomach as his arm curls up around me. He places a soft kiss on the top of my head. "Good night."

And here it is, the safety I longed to feel with him. Apprehension about what's next keeps me up until I hear his long, deep breaths. Listening to his breath and soft snores has a calming effect, and sleep soon finds me too.

I wake in an empty bed to the familiar sounds of Toni's family home. Unsure how things will look in the light of day after all the words that were spoken last night, I turn over, not ready to face anyone. I need to hash it out with Toni on our own but am not yet in the mood or the right headspace. How can I fight for Alex when doubts are screaming loudly?

A few minutes pass, and the house quiets down. I'm confused where everyone could have gone on a Sunday morning. Sneaking out and calling him later is looking pretty appealing right now, especially if he just left without telling me anything.

"Wakey, wakey..." Toni's voice comes through as she opens the bedroom door, "princess."

My stomach knots, not wanting to discuss things right now. I watch her walk in with two cups of coffee; she sits on the foot of the bed. She extends a cup to me. "Just the way you like it. A little coffee with your cream and sugar."

I take it, grateful for her version of an olive branch. She takes a sip then pulls her legs up and crosses them comfortably.

"I asked the boys to leave and get breakfast. I figured you and I needed a bit of alone time."

I nod and take my first sip, not knowing how to start or even what to ask.

She begins, "First, you know Alex and I go head-to-head on everything. You've seen it before."

Words still jammed in my throat, I nod again.

"I was caught off-guard last night. This was something I didn't expect. And as much shit as I like to give you about," she air-quotes with her fingers on one hand, "'being besties,' you are my best friend. All I could see was this blowing up, and then I would lose my best friend. The only friend I've made who doesn't live in this shithole." She takes another sip.

I'm beginning to understand, but it doesn't make the hurt or fear go away.

"Talk to me," she pleads.

Holding the mug in both hands, I let the warmth spread. Taking a slow drink, I gather my thoughts.

"Look, last night was surreal. I never thought it would happen. I was ready to live with my unrequited love. And then somehow our worlds came together, and everything I wanted was right there. And it was the happiest and most afraid I've been. We talked, and the pieces were slowly being put together, and you came, flipped the table, scattering them all."

"What in the hell are you talking about?" she quips back, almost angrily.

"You and all your talk about Alex using girls. That's all I can think about now. I can't. I can't be used by—"

"I wa—" she tries to interrupt me, but I put a hand up to stop her and continue.

"Don't. Don't try and explain it away. You opened the can, and it's out now. As much as I want to be with him, having him use me and walk away is something I'm not equipped to deal with right now."

"I'm sorry. That's not what I wanted to do. I was

surprised. I had to ask that in front of both of you to see his reaction."

"Like he would say, 'Oh, yeah she's a'—how did you put it —'hit-it-and-quit-it girl.' He was saving face, and I have to save me." My chest begins to tighten.

"He was not saving face. He's an asshole and would toss them. Maybe not like that, but he definitely wouldn't have stood up to me." She tries to grab my hand, but I pull it away. "He told me off. He was mad at me for pushing. He's in this with you."

Not convinced, I pull the covers away to get dressed. I need to get home. Self-isolation to drown in my thoughts is what I want right now.

I place my mug down and grab my phone from the table by his bed and pull up my Uber app to find a ride. Frustrated with the time it would take them to get here, I feel the tears begin to fall. I can't think straight. The need to run away is in contrast to the pull I feel for him.

"Talk to me," Toni pleads.

I shake my head, "I'm not ready. You and Alex may work like that, but I don't. I got caught in your crossfire, and I'm the only one who got hurt. Please go."

"No."

Voices come through the closed door, and I know the guys are back from picking up food.

"Let's go eat," she tries to persuade me.

"I'm not hungry." Which is a lie. I'm starving, but I will not go out there.

A soft tap on the door before it opens to Javie sticking his head in. "Food is here."

Toni gets off the bed, opening the door and walking past Javie. He looks between the two of us before asking, "Coming?"

Words still refusing to come out, I shake my head.

He walks into the room, closing the door behind him. At the side of the bed he asks, "May I?" while pointing to the bed.

"Yes."

He sits on the bed, his back against the wall. He extends an arm to me, and I quickly curl myself into his side, letting the tears fall. The fear of hurt is overruling any good sense I thought I had. Admitting my feelings last night has left me susceptible to more hurt than I'm ready to endure. He lets me stay here in the quiet, not forcing me to talk. Not explaining away their behavior. Just letting me wallow in the unknown.

I awaken with a start, not realizing I had fallen asleep. I'm still curled into Javie, his soft breath revealing he dozed with me.

"Hey." I shake his chest trying to wake him.

"Hey," he responds, opening his eyes and rolling his neck out.

"I'm sorry," I admit to him. I'm not sure what I'm apologizing for, but it seems appropriate.

"For what?"

The shoulder shrug, which seems to be the only way I know how to answer questions now, is all I can give him.

"What do you want?" He begins to sit up from where we had slid down. I pull myself up, allowing him to get comfortable. I sit facing him.

"Define 'want.'" I buy myself some time to wrap my head around all that has transpired.

"You and Alex surprised everyone last night. Me included. I gotta admit, I thought he may have had a thing for you, but I didn't see the reverse happening. But it did." He takes a breath. Is he buying himself some time? "But now you are hiding out. Did you change your mind?"

Javie is not asking to make waves. He won't pick sides. He

doesn't want to be the one in the know with the latest gossip. He is truly worried about what is happening. Alex may be the head of the house, but Javie cares for all that live within its walls. He makes sure the inhabitants are emotionally happy and comfortable.

"No. I have not changed my mind, but I got scared. Toni was unhappy, Alex uses girls, and my heart is on the line. I don't know if I can do this." I can admit all this to Javie. He will keep my words safe.

"We are a family of dysfunction, little one. You kind of knew this, but you were only an outsider looking in," he begins his story, his gaze staying with me. "You have seen those two go at it, but you have never had to survive it. They have been like this for as long as I can remember. Toni loves to push. Alex does not like to be questioned. Garrett got caught in the crossfire in the beginning. I don't know how he figured it out, but he stayed back and let them do their thing, and all was well in the end."

"I don't know, Javie. It's the part about Alex and the girls he tosses away that has me. I'm freezing. I don't want to be tossed." I admit my fear out loud.

"He won't. He wants you. Badly, now that I am seeing clearly."

"And if you're wrong?" I'm still hesitating.

"I'm not. But if I am you can punch me." The carefree smirk he gives eases me some.

I crawl up to him wrapping my arms around his neck, hugging him.

"Thank you."

CHAPTER 9

ALEX

I LEFT LOLA IN BED AT TONI'S REQUEST SO SHE COULD TALK with her. We get back, and Lola is still hiding in the room. I send Javie to check on them, and instead of seeing her beautiful face, I come face-to-face with Toni, the reason I am in this fucking mess.

"Well?" I ask angrily.

"She's mad at both of us." I watch her as she sits at the table, dropping her head into her arms.

Our dysfunctional life is one of the reasons I wanted to keep Lola away. And literally, day one, we go at it, and she is scared to come out. How can I subject her to any more of what our life is like? There is no use in going after Toni again. No good will come of it. The need to leave is heavy, but I have to ensure she is okay when she does decide to step out of my bedroom.

I sit on the couch waiting. She will need to come out eventually, and when she does, I will let her walk away if that's what she chooses to do. All my previous fears of allowing myself to have her are front and center. She was not built to survive the world I live in.

Not watching the clock, I'm unsure how long I've been sitting here, but I finally hear a door open and footsteps coming my way. My heart stops beating, wondering what is coming. Javie comes around the corner first, giving me the head nod. It eases some of the tension that has built in the last couple of seconds. Lola follows him looking straight at me as she comes around the corner. She pauses briefly, I can't read what she is about to do by the look on her face. My ass is stuck on this couch, fearing whatever I do will make matters worse.

One foot, and then the next, moves in my direction. She stands right in front of me before a small smile emerges. She sits on my lap, curling herself into me. I wrap her in my arms, not wanting anything bad to ever touch her again.

"It's all good now," she whispers into my chest.

I bring my head down close to hers, "Are you sure?" Wanting so desperately to keep her but knowing I need to let her go if that's best for her.

"You're stuck with me." I can hear the smile in that statement. Her sunshine personality making its appearance again.

"Still mad at me?" Toni asks, leaning against the doorframe leading to the kitchen.

Lola sits up, her back straightens giving her a small power-play edge before answering. "No. I'm not. But before you get too happy with that answer, I have something to say." She pauses. "I'm not going to be your punching bag when you're mad at Alex. Whatever happens between us," she waves her hand between the two of us, "is between us. End of story."

Lola taking on this authoritarian attitude is sexy as hell. She is usually the go-with-the-flow, happy-go-lucky one. Putting her foot down and telling Toni as it is has me getting hard.

"Okay, fine." I know those two words were hard for Toni. She likes to push, but she is learning when to back down. "Hungry?"

"I'll get something in a bit." Lola responds to Toni, then turns around to face me. "You. In your room now." Her command is my pleasure.

She stands up heading to my room, and I am right behind her. I would follow this girl anywhere. She walks into my room, waiting for me to enter behind her, and she closes the door. Immediately she comes up to me, tiptoeing and wrapping her arms around my neck, pulling me down until her lips meet mine in a heated, hungry kiss. My arms come around her, picking her up as she wraps her legs around my waist. My body wants me to get in bed with her, but my mind, still in overdrive, does not want to scare her off. I slow us down to make sure we are on the same page.

I pull away slightly, still showering her with small kisses. "We're good?" Being on uncharted ground, I need to make sure I'm on solid footing.

She drops her legs, so I place her back down. "Yes, we're good. Just one thing." She takes a breath before continuing. "I don't want to hear about your past girls again. I know you have a past, as do I, but the way it was thrown at me last night...I don't know... I just wasn't ready for it, and the visual of you being a jerk goes against how I think of you."

She thinks I'm more than I am. I can't let her be fooled. She only knows what she sees here at the house. She has no idea what my life has been or everything I have done. I'm way past being redeemed.

"Sweetheart, I'm an asshole. I need you to know this. I don't want you coming into this with rose-colored glasses. I don't think I'm the guy you've made up in your mind." This is not going the way I hoped, but more like what I'd originally imagined.

"No," she shakes her head. "Like I said last night, I don't think you see yourself correctly. You don't see what I do. I told you last night I saw a guy who is protective and caring. Look at how you are trying to protect me right now." She grabs for my hand and wraps it with both of hers. "I know you can be a jerk. I've seen that too. What you fail to realize is everyone has both sides. I just don't want to be reminded that you have been that way with every girl you have dated. Because I will be the girl you are dating. I don't want to put myself in that category."

"First, I don't date. Or I should say I didn't date. Second, you would never be in that category. You're special. You deserve more than me, but if you want me, I'm yours. Only yours."

The smile that reaches her eyes lights up my heart. I rub her cheek and slide my hand around to the back of her neck, pulling her closer to me until she is leaning against me. He arms come around my waist, her small hands rubbing my back until her stomach growls with hunger.

"Come on, there's tacos waiting for us. But they are cold by now."

LOLA

AFTER A LONG NIGHT and morning of drama, I'm enjoying a quiet night back at my place with Alex. While I don't mind being over there, I wanted this time, right now, to be ours. It is new. We are both nervous. For completely different reasons, but it's there. He's still battling demons of thinking he's lacking. And if I'm honest, I'm scared he's not ready and will run. I'll push too hard or expect too much, and this deli-cate beginning will crumble.

"What time do you have to leave to make it to the ranch

on time?" I ask, knowing spending the night at my place is adding another thirty minutes or more to his commute time.

"I can't leave any later than five. Hopefully traffic won't be bad that early in the morning."

I glance at my phone and realize it's already after ten. We have been mindlessly watching shows, letting the next one begin automatically when the previous one ends. Words have been scarce; we are allowing ourselves the magic of touch to soothe. Hands grazing, slowly, softly, but not quite seductively. It is more calming, reminding each other we are here. I'm nervous about whether I can live up to the fantasies being played on a continuous loop in my head for too long now.

"Come on, let's go to bed. You have to be up early." I press the power button on the TV, turning it off and getting up from where I have burrowed myself into Alex's side.

It is odd going about my usual night routine with Alex laying in bed with nothing on but his boxer briefs. I tell myself this will become normal; it's just the first night. Walking out of the bathroom, I still; he's propped up on pillows, one arm behind his head, with his delicious chest, abs, and tattoos on full display. I feel like I just walked into a *GQ* photo shoot. A heat washes over me as I look at him.

"Come here." His voice is deep, filled with a seductive rasp.

I make my way to him slowly, my chest pounding with nervous anticipation. I lift the covers and crawl in next to him laying on my side, my head propped on my hand to look at him.

"As much as I want to take you right now, I'm not." One sentence obliterates the idea I had of tonight.

Not wanting to sound whiney, but curious about why he would wait, I search my brain for a way to ask *why*.

"I'm not going to because I don't want to rush things. I

want to take my time. I want to cover every part of your body with kisses. I want you to feel me worshipping the body I have been dreaming about. That, *amor*, will not be a quick. And I do have to get up very early and do who-knows-what outside in this heat all day tomorrow."

Thinking of his lips all over me has my body clenching already. A need I have never felt before hits hard and fast. My lips are on his wanting him to soothe the ache building. I let my hand follow the ridges of his chest and stomach until I reach his *V*. I slow down, inching my way closer to feel him.

All of a sudden, I'm on my back, and Alex is above me. Arching my back, I lift my hips with a desperate want. His lips leave mine as he slowly begins kissing down my neck. He palms one breast as his lips come closer to the other. A small nip of my nipple sends a spark south as I buck up needing friction. His hand slides down over my panties. I'm sure he can feel my arousal. He slides my panties to the side and lets his fingers play.

I have never come so fast. I'm spinning from the heady feeling. A few deep breaths and my senses return, I try and slide my hand between us to continue.

"I told you I wasn't taking you tonight. I just wanted to make sure you were taken care of." He places a soft kiss on the tip of my nose before rolling off me onto his back. He extends his arm in invitation for me to come closer.

I take him at his word, not wanting to push, but I am secretly excited for next time. How will I survive all he says he has in store for me?

CHAPTER 10

ALEX

THE SUN IS POUNDING DOWN ON US ALREADY, AND IT'S NOT even noon yet. I take a rag out of my back pocket to rub my face. This is not the future for me. As the summer heat begins to rage, it becomes clearer that I need to find my path. I can't continue on with Lola and have no direction. How would she ever be proud of me or proud to be with me? Until I get my shit together, this will have to be it.

My phone vibrates in my pocket. I pull it out to find a picture of Lola giving me a wink, her blue eyes sparkling. I'll make it my life's mission to ensure she is safe and happy. She deserves nothing less. Not a fan of taking selfies, much less sending them, I reply with a quick *See you Friday night*. She replies with a winky emoji.

I slide my phone back in my pocket, wanting to knock this out and get into a cold shower and the air-conditioned house.

. . .

Back in my room after dinner, I send Lola a text. *What are you doing?*

Lola: *watching TV. You?*

Laying in bed

Lola: *Already?*

Yup. So tired

Waiting for a reply, my phone rings instead with her gorgeous face on the screen.

"Hey," I say answering her video call.

"I just wanted to say good night if you were already in bed," she says with a smile.

"What did you do today?" I ask, wanting to keep her on the phone so I can stare at her just a bit longer.

"Not much. Bummed and did some work for my class tomorrow." I watch her lips pull down a bit before she adds, "I guess that sounds dumb when you've been hard at work, huh?"

"It does not sound dumb. It sounds like you did what you needed. You earned it."

Her lips pull out in an awkward, embarrassed way.

"*Amor*, I put myself in this situation. I'm working hard to find a way out. Never apologize to me because you have it good. Those were your cards and never be ashamed of them. Especially around me."

Her eyes twinkle just a smidgeon.

"Do you ever talk about your past?" Her question is quiet, like she was scared to ask.

"Not really. It's a sad, fucked-up story no one wants to hear."

"I would, if you ever wanted to share anything," her voice still hesitant.

"Why?" That is the real question. Who would want to

know the crap I have gone through? It's a messed-up story with lots of fucked-up mistakes along the way. The only thing is, most of those fucked-up mistakes kept us afloat.

"To know you better. I know things weren't easy. But maybe if I knew some things, I could better understand why you react the way you do or why you do the things you do now." A sliver of a smile appears.

"What do you want to hear?" I want to give her something.

"Whatever you are willing to share. I don't want to ask about something you are uncomfortable talking about."

"I'll share one thing with you tonight. I'll let you choose." I give her the power because I would hate to divulge something she's not ready to hear. My past is best ignored or taken in small doses.

"Why did you drop out of high school?" she asks an easy question.

"To work. I had to help pay the bills." The frank answer comes out easily.

She frowns, and I am confused about why she doesn't seem happy with my answer.

"I've heard that before. But why?" She pauses, and when I stay silent, she continues, "People work and go to school all the time. Why did you really drop out?"

"I don't know. That's what I thought I needed to do." I'm unsure what she's asking. But it hits a small nerve when she says other people work and go to school, because that's the truth.

She is seeing through the easy answer I have always been able to give people. Truth is there was so much more going on at that time.

. . .

I HAVE MADE enough connections for them to seek me out. Now all I need to do is lay low and I will be able to roll in it; these were the thoughts of a poor sixteen-year-old kid from the hood once they had a few hundred dollars stashed away. Everyone in school knows me. I'm every teacher's nightmare, not because I'm a true discipline problem, but because I refuse to work or even listen to their lectures. Sleeping in class after staying out all night smoking and drinking or turning in blank assignments or just refusing to show up to class—all the teachers are at their wits' end with me.

I've found myself surrounded by The SEV (San Eduardo Vatos). I've been able to make my way into their circle, running errands and spreading the word. I have been able to increase their business with my high-school crowd connections. Thanks to dear ol' dad and his former friends, I've been able to make a few easy bucks.

"I THOUGHT it was easy money until I saw someone get caught with it in school. They went right to juvie. It wasn't a place I could be. I couldn't leave Javie and Toni to watch out for Güela on their own. My dad was still a fucked-up drunk. It was easier to stop going to school and have everyone come to me."

"So you dropped out to sell weed?" Lola asks, sounding confused.

"Yes. In my teen mind, I thought I was going to build an empire. It wasn't until I saw the bigger picture that I realized I would always stay a small fish. I may have done some questionable shit, but I wasn't going to jump into what I saw the Vatos doing."

"What were they doing?" Her question is innocent.

"That, *amor*, I will never repeat." I may have earned their respect and been able to make some of my own calls, but I know it's a relationship that can quickly sour. No one needs to know what I have seen while in their company.

This has been the most I have ever shared with anyone about this part of me. My family "knows" my prior business, Javie even helped me.

"Okay." Her smile seems pained.

"I didn't tell you this to make you feel sad. If this is what's going to happen when you ask about my past, that's where it will stay. I will not have you feeling sorry or sad for me because of it."

"I don't feel sorry for you. Not at all. I was just thinking how different our lives are. If it weren't for you, I would think that world only exists in movies."

"I hate that I am ruining your picture-perfect view of the world." She does not need to be a part of this life, yet she still pursues it.

"Don't. Please don't do that. Is your world foreign to me? Yes. But I want to know it. I *need* to know it. That's the only way we are going to work. I don't want to be just some girl who's with you for the now but gets tossed because she doesn't know something or doesn't understand something. You have to be honest with me. I don't want to be blindsided by your past someday."

Her feistiness is one of the things that attracted me to her in the beginning. No matter what I would say, she would do what she was going to do. She is so much like Toni, but without the bitter chip on her shoulder. Strong women. I need to keep remembering that she can handle herself, even if I feel like I need to do it for her.

"You're right. I'm sorry."

"Don't be sorry. Just let me in. That's all I ask." Her voice sounds softer now. Why she wants me will always be a mystery to me. "I'm going to let you sleep now. Thank you for sharing with me. Good night." She blows a kiss through the phone.

"Good Night, *amor*."

LOLA

I LAY in bed thinking of Alex. Sleeping in his arms the previous two nights was not enough. I'm craving him again. The strength and power he exudes without ever trying is soothing. And sexy. Did I mention sexy? I just want to wrap myself in him. Feel his warmth against my body.

Weekdays are going to be the worst. With him gone all week at the ranch, I am stuck with Facetime.

FACETIME throughout the week turned out to be fun. As each day passed, he got more comfortable, and the conversations flowed. He has shared a bit more with me. It came up naturally when I spoke about missing my mom.

He doesn't remember much about his, and she never came back into their lives once she left. But to hear him talk about how abusive his father could be was hard. I know he didn't want pity or for me to feel sad, but how could I not? They were children. When he told me how he would hide Javie to protect him, taking all the beatings himself, I just wanted to hold him. But I couldn't. I could only offer an ear and keep all the sadness locked away.

Maybe it's not such a bad thing to be separated. If I had him here, I don't think we would have done much talking. That is something I hadn't considered. When the week began, all I wanted was his hands all over me. The separation has forced us to talk.

Now I don't have to wait much longer. He is on his way back into town. He said he was going to stop at his place to shower and change and then come to my apartment.

I've cleaned my apartment with nervous energy fueling

me all day, knowing I would be able to see him tonight. I have tried everything to keep myself occupied, but it's not working. I'm sitting on the couch, mindlessly scrolling through channels, but not listening or paying attention. The thought of being able to kiss and hold him has my body tingling. These are only thoughts, and I feel like I might combust. I can only imagine how I will feel when he shows up.

ALEX

I KNOCK on her door and wait. It has been a long five days, but my prize is on the other side. The door swings open, and before I can even take my first step in, she has her arms around my neck pulling me down to meet her lips.

Damn, I was going to try and contain myself, but with this type of welcome, I don't think I'll be able to. I reach down and pull her legs up, and she wraps them around my waist. I step in carrying her and kick the door closed behind me.

Our kiss is frenzied and rushed, building from the days apart.

"Please, I need you," she mumbles through our kisses.

That is my undoing. I take the few steps to the couch, sitting down with her straddling me. I grab the hem of her shirt and pull it off exposing her perfect breasts. The frenzied foreplay continues until she has her release.

I carry her into the bedroom to make good on my promise of kissing every inch of her body before I claim her as mine. Laying her on the bed, I pull down the boxers and panties she is wearing. She lays back, fully exposed, watching me. I grab one foot and kiss from her ankle up her leg until her breath hitches the closer I get to her warm center. I avoid the area purposely, wanting to build anticipation. I move to her stomach kissing my way up slowly while letting my hands roam over her soft, silky skin.

Fantasies can be wicked. Sometimes the real thing can never measure up to it, but I could not dream up this kind of perfection. I have yet to undress myself, and I'm not bothered. All I want to do is continue worshipping her body.

"You're killing me," Lola moans out as she begins squirming underneath me. Her hands grab my shorts, trying to unbutton.

My hand rubs her center softly, causing a bit of friction to pacify her slightly as I continue trailing kisses up and down her body. I brush my tongue over one hardened nipple, and she arches, pushing it further into my mouth. I suck slightly, enjoying the moans of pleasure leaving her mouth.

Not able to take it anymore and wanting this orgasm to be with me buried deep inside her, I stand to undress, grabbing a condom from my pocket. I crawl back into bed, and she takes the condom from me, tearing it open and sheathing me. Her taking control excites me, and I feel like I may explode.

Our lips meet as I slide into her. Her body pulses and tightens around me, extremely responsive. I begin sliding in and out, encouraging her next release. She grips my shoulders tucking herself closer when it hits. I follow her lead, not wanting to torture myself any longer by waiting.

I roll to the side, pulling her with me as we catch our breath. I don't need a fantasy anymore because I somehow managed to get the real thing.

BACK IN THE LIVING ROOM, we are lying on the couch with a half-eaten pizza on the coffee table and a movie we aren't paying much attention to on in the background. My focus is on her. It has been her for too long, and now I have her. She has given herself to me completely. My hand is lazily running up and down her thigh.

"Did you need to do anything this weekend?" She turns around, facing me.

"No. Do you?" I ask, wondering if that's her polite way of asking me to leave.

"Just a study group at one tomorrow." She brings her hand up and places it on my scruffy cheek.

"I should go then. Let you get some sleep." I begin to get up and make the agonizing trip to collect my things and go.

She moves her hand to my side holding me down. "Where do you think you are going?" Her eyes widen at my movement.

"I was going to go home." I answer her honestly.

"You don't want to stay here with me?" Her voice has dropped to almost a whisper.

"Of course I do, but you have things going on. I don't want to get in your way." Relationships are new for me. I have never been in one, much less with someone who has their shit together. How the hell am I supposed to know the rules here?

"Then stay. I want you here." She curls herself closer to me, tucking her head in my chest.

I hold her against me, not wanting to let her go. My mind is overloaded with feelings I have never before experienced. I have fallen so far down into this, I don't know what the hell I will do if it goes astray.

A phone vibrating on the coffee table gets our attention.

"Yours or mine?"

I peek up over her and see my screen lit up.

"Mine."

She turns and reaches her arm to pick up my phone, handing it to me.

Javie sent a message, *Warning I have people over.*

"Javie warning me about his party," I tell Lola.

"Did you want to go?" The hesitation in her voice is apparent, and her body tenses fractionally.

"Hell no. Now that you gave me the green light to stay here, you're stuck with me." I use her words, tossing them back at her. With my statement her body relaxes.

Her fingers begin tracing one of my tattoos lightly.

"How old were you when you got your first tattoo?" Her eyes leave the tattoo and meet mine.

"Seventeen," I answer, not knowing where this conversation is going to lead.

"Which one?"

This is not something I ever thought I would be discussing.

"READY TO BE A MAN?" Hector asks. He's only a few years older than me, but his father is the SEV's leader, which gives him power. We are sitting at his kitchen table with some dude who works on the side for them. Not of age to get a tattoo? That's fine, because we're not in a in shop.

"Just start the fucking thing," I answer, tired of his damn dramatics about a fuckin' tattoo. I refused to be branded as part of the SEV, but to prove myself, I had to get some sort of tattoo. It took some smooth-talking on my part, but I was able to avoid being jumped in. Lucky for me, I had already started proving my loyalty the past couple of years as I was bringing in the younger clients.

The buzz of the tattoo gun begins, and I tried to relax, not wanting to flinch and show weakness. It hits the skin on my upper arm, and I stay as stoic as possible as the feeling of someone scraping me slowly begins. I chose a design similar to the SEV sign, but one that would not tag me as one.

That's another thing in this neighborhood. As soon as one person is busted for something, all the rest begin to get knocks on their doors too.

I don't need anyone knocking on Güela's door or Javie being attached to this shit.

I have one foot in but will not walk fully through door. It is not an easy thing to balance, but since I have become helpful, I have been able to keep a safe distance.

"MY RIGHT FOREARM, THE CIRCLE," I answer her.

Javie and Toni know all my dealings but stay in the background. I didn't want it to affect their lives going forward. Lola sure as hell should not be in the know, but how will I ever have a forever with her if she doesn't know what I've done? It wouldn't be fair to her if she found these things out some other way or if my past decides to haunt me.

Her fingers begin circling my first tattoo, then slowing make their way down to the others. My arm is covered in a sleeve.

"And the rest? Why did you continue?"

"Do they bother you?" Her questions are making me wonder whether she would be happier if I didn't have them.

"No. Just wondering. I feel like I know you, but I don't really."

Cupping her face, I kiss her lips softly, enjoying being able to do it whenever my heart desires.

"The rest were to mask the circle, which is very close to the SEV mark. I was still worried it would bring attention to me, so I thought I could mask it. Let it get lost in the sea of other tattoos surrounding it."

I had let a local guy come up with a few designs, which I told him would embellish the original ink. The neighborhood knows who's who and where your loyalties lie. I couldn't risk them finding out I was trying to camouflage it. All SEV wear theirs boldly, mostly on their forearms, to bare if anyone questions their power.

A smirk appears before she says, "And the camo just continued right down your whole arm?" There is laughter in her voice.

"They say you get addicted to them. I guess they were right."

"I've got my own bad boy." Her voice lowers seductively as her hand makes its way down between us before grabbing my length. "Ready for bed?"

CHAPTER 11

LOLA

LONG-DISTANCE RELATIONSHIPS SUCK. SUNDAY NIGHT always comes too fast, and Monday morning, he's gone before the sun rises. We have been jumping between my apartment and his house the past several weeks.

But last night when Javie called people over, he got my bag and led us out the door. I can't help but wonder if he is trying to hide me from his neighborhood or the girls he has been with. The fear that he could toss me creeps up occasionally, even though I ignore it most of the time. But last night, when people started arriving and he had us leaving quickly, my insecurities rose.

He explained he would never be able to sleep with people there, but it was still early when they started showing. I hate the nagging feeling. And now another five days of separation.

ALEX

FAVOR. We need to meet.

That's the text I have been dreading. I thought I was able to make my exit from the SEV when my dad was busted and sent to prison. The heat so close to me was too much, and I was able to make a clean break. But now Hector texts again.

Not in town until Friday night, I respond.

Hector: *Where r u*

Working on a ranch south of town

Hector: *ranch?*

Yes. what do you want

Hector: *we need to meet*

Fine. Bar highway. Tomorrow 8

I send him a map pin to the place.

I'm not looking forward to this meeting. Nothing good can come of it.

I ARRIVE A FEW MINUTES EARLY, making sure no one from the ranch is here. It's not usual for the guys to be out here early in the week, but I had to make sure no one would be coming up to us. I sit at the bar and order a beer while I wait.

"Hey, *guey.*" Hector takes the stool next to me.

I turn to him, giving him a small nod, not knowing what type of visit this is. I lift my beer to the bartender while raising a finger ordering another one.

I pass him the beer she brings over, and I get up, walking towards a table in the back corner. Even in this place, with only a couple of other people around, I don't need anyone overhearing what Hector has to say.

Taking a seat, my vision line to the door, I wait for him to join.

"What the hell are you doing working at a ranch?" he starts, then takes a long drink.

"Keeping clean with the mess my old man left us with." I

answer as vaguely as possible. No one needs to know who Toni's boyfriend truly is.

"I think it's been long enough," he begins, too frankly.

"Sure... if I don't mind them sniffing around me." I try and divert, knowing where this conversation is going.

"I need you to step up again." His facials meaning nothing but business.

"*No puedo*," (I can't.) I tell him. "You know I promised Toni I would stay clean after my dad's bust. I can't risk Javie either." I try to sound as casual as I can, but deep down I know, there is only one way this conversation is going to go.

"*Si puedes y vas hacer lo*." (You can and you are going to.) His brows pull in as he studies me.

"And where am I going to tell them I'm getting my money from? My job is out here in BFE. I can't be in business and spend all week out here." I use the ranch as my way out.

"I'll get you a job in town. You should probably be at the bars or clubs anyway. I'll make some calls."

"Why now?" I inquire, knowing I shouldn't. You never question.

"A couple guys were pinched. *Pendejos* that started thinking they were going to be big shit. I can't have those fools around for a while. Jefe sent them away."

I don't want to know where Jefe sent them because, either way, it won't be good. If they were new, he needed to make sure they wouldn't talk.

"They were pinched, and you aren't holding back a bit?" The words fall out of my mouth before I have time to think them through. Lola is first and foremost on my mind, and I can't be in this shit while dating her.

"*Que onda*?" (What's up?) he asks. "You were never one to hesitate." I'm not handling this meeting well. I need to get my shit together, or I'll be the next one they send away.

"*No mas*. Trying to keep my promise to Toni." Everyone knows how stubborn she can be, so it's not a stretch.

"Then don't tell her."

"Javie stays out of this too." I need to get in and get out as quickly as I can.

"Fine. But I'm calling in the favor you owe. We let you skirt the SEV. Now you pay for that generosity." The conversation is over, and there is nothing I can do to avoid this.

"Not long? I can't hide it forever from Toni." I know I'm pushing, but I don't know what else to do. I can't live that life anymore.

"*A ver*." (We'll see.) His tone tells me the discussion is over.

The only response now is a head nod, letting him know I understand.

"I'll be in touch. Let you know which club and when." He finishes off his beer before standing and walking out the door.

FUCK! FUCK! FUCK! I can't escape this one. I head to the bar and ask for a couple of tequila shots. I need something to take the edge off tonight. Tomorrow I will be planning how the hell I'm going to lead a double life.

MY MEETING with Mr. Anders went well. I thanked him for the opportunity but told him it wasn't going to be my long-term. I mentioned I was looking at places and would work up until I found something else if he was agreeable with it. My being related to Toni was probably the reason why he was generous about anything less than a two-week notice.

Now to figure out how I was going to manage in town. I needed to make my plans. I would not be keeping product at the house anymore. I can't risk it with Toni, Lola, and Garrett in and out constantly. The money and the books are another bitch to figure out, along with purchasing another burner phone. This is even harder to coordinate than before.

Each evening, after getting off the phone with Lola, I stay up, trying to come up with a way out. Each night, I come up empty-handed. You don't tell these guys no. I was the dumbass who wanted this life, and now it's time to pay up. So much for being the big dog. I'm getting my ass handed to me now.

BACK IN TOWN, I stop at the store, purchasing the phone before I head home and dig out my list. I haven't been out for too long, and everyone knows my product. It shouldn't be too hard to start back up.

At my house, I make my way to the backyard. The rickety shed has nothing but old tools that haven't seen the light of day since Güela passed. The only thing we have managed to do is to keep the grass cut. All of Güela's plants are either dying or overgrown.

Everything I used before is just like I left it. All the hidden money is gone. I pull out the notebook in plastic bags hidden under empty pots.

Here we go. Let the game begin and pray I can keep it a secret until I figure my way out.

LOLA

I THOUGHT I would surprise Alex with our plans for tonight. We have only spent time just us or with his family. As much as I love Toni and Javie, I want to go out. We have established ourselves as a couple, but no one but his family and Garrett know about us. I planned for us to meet friends at a sports bar. It's a laid-back place with pool tables and dart boards. I figured this would be the best way to introduce him to my world.

I thought I would surprise him so he wouldn't have too much time to think about it or find an excuse to say no. He doesn't take long to shower and change so he can do that as soon as he gets here.

Which is weird because he is usually here by now.

Are you coming over? Text sent.

I scroll through our past texts to see if I missed a message where he told me he wouldn't be coming over.

Came to the house for a bit. Taking off in 5.

Would he rather be home than come over here on Friday nights? Should I have offered to meet him at home?

I pour myself a glass of wine, hoping it calms the nerves I still get around him. His intense, brooding personality is a turn-on from afar, but up close, it can be intimidating. While he's been sharing his past, there is still so much more behind what he shares. Behind a second curtain, there is a whole other life he doesn't speak of, and I don't think he ever will.

Curling up on the couch, I dream of what could be, eventually, once he lets go of the past that has a hold on him. Once he steps into believing he can have more than he thinks. I need my bad boy to believe he's more than just that. His past may have shaped who he is, but it does not dictate who he will be.

Keys in the door draw me out of my thoughts. Alex walks in, looking a bit frazzled. He places his bag on the floor before taking a seat on the couch and pulling me on top of him. His kiss feels desperate. Our lips separate, but he clutches me to his chest, holding tightly.

"What's wrong?" I ask, worried something has happened.

He clears his throat, "Nothing. I just don't like the time away from you. I started looking for something in town. The ranch is not my going to be my long-term." He pushes me back, looking in my eyes before giving me a chaste kiss. "I was so desperate for you, I sat on your couch before showering. I'm sorry."

He helps me up, and once I'm standing, he notices I'm dressed to go out, not in my usual boxers and tees I've been wearing to stay in.

"Going out?" His brow cocks up in question.

"We are going out. We can get something to eat then meet some friends at a bar. Play pool and darts." I smile brightly so he won't even question saying yes.

"Anything you want." He kisses my forehead, heading to the shower.

I'VE ONLY BEEN to this bar a couple of times, as I am not a pool player, but I thought it would be the best place to break the ice with Alex and some of my other friends. I know he is self-conscious about where he comes from and not fitting into my life. It's weird to think of him doubting his place anywhere with his cocky, almost arrogant, attitude.

At the bar, I watch how he leans in slightly, placing his arms on the counter. His sleeve on full display in the snug black T-shirt he is wearing. The female bartender notices him right away. She gives him a sexy smirk before slinking her way towards us.

"What can I get you?" Her eyes take him in as her gaze travels from his eyes down his strong chest. She would probably spread herself right here if he told her to.

"What do you want, *amor*?" Alex turns to me, giving me a cocky smirk.

"I'll take an Ultra." I answer sweetly, looking at Miss Bartender, smiling. Her eyes narrow in question before making their way back to Alex.

"Budweiser," he announces for himself.

She turns to the coolers behind her, and Alex turns his body towards me, grabbing my waist and pulling me in closer. Bottles are placed loudly in front of us as she pops the tops off of them.

Alex pulls out his wallet and places a card on the bar in front of him.

"Keep it open. And she can order on it," he informs her.

He comes in close to my ear and whispers, "Thought I would make sure she knew I was here with you."

This small gesture, soothing the jealous beast that began to roar, is greatly appreciated. When he pulls back, his lips are so close to mine, I feel his breath, but not close enough for me to taste.

His smoldering eyes boring into me now make me wish we were in the privacy of my bedroom, but we can't solely live in there.

"Lola!" Hearing my name said with such excitement draws my attention away from Alex to the person calling me.

"Hey, Jasmine!" I greet her as she leans on the bar trying to get the bartender's attention. "Jasmine, this is Alex, my... uh...friend."

Shit. I stumbled over my words because we haven't had *The Talk* yet.

"Hi." She smiles at Alex as the bartender comes up to her. She turns to place her order and faces us again.

"Nice to meet you," he responds to her.

"We have a table toward the back if y'all want to head on over."

I grab Alex's hand wanting to get away from my faux pas, pulling him, making my way to the others. I am tugged as he stops walking. I turn to look at him, and he pulls me to the side.

He leans on the wall bringing me between his legs, his lips pulling out, holding a smile he can't keep from his eyes.

"What?" I ask, not knowing what is so funny. The embarrassment is creeping up my neck heating up my face.

"Do you want to call me your boyfriend?" His eyes dance with amusement.

I drop my head on his chest not knowing if this is a pity ask.

His hand comes to my chin, pulling me to look up at him. "Because I want to call you my girlfriend." His lips meet mine in a gentle kiss before pulling back. "So do I have a girlfriend?"

I nod my head as a huge smile engulfs my face.

"Now you can introduce me to your friends. Lead the way."

I grab his hand again, this time more secure in who we are.

My friends found a great spot at a pool table right next to a dart machine. There are already games in progress as I go around introducing him to everyone.

"We're playing doubles next game now that we have another guy around." Charlie yells to the table before turning to Alex asking him, "You do play, right?"

"Sure." Alex answers while tipping his head back a bit. His domineering nature making its appearance. His at-home, relaxed, gentle side is in contrast to this serious, in-control attitude he shows the world. I've seen him do this before when he and Javie had people over.

He takes a seat on one of the stools by the table, watching the guys as the girls playing darts pull me toward them. I see Charlie trying to chat Alex up, and I hope Alex will come around.

"Where did you pick up sexy bad boy?" Jasmine comes close to me while glancing in Alex's direction. Jasmine is one of my sorority sisters; one of the few I continue to hang out with.

"Yes! That is the question." Steph jumps into the conversation.

"It just happened." I shrug nonchalantly, not wanting to explain. Why does everyone care all of a sudden who I'm dating?

"He's Toni's cousin." Ariel's voice is flat, trying to down-play it. I forgot Ariel was at the country bar the weekend of our first kiss.

"He is?" Jasmine's eyes widen.

I nod my head, hoping this is the end of the conversation.

"So you not going out at all the past few weekends has been because you have locked yourself in your apartment with him?" I can see desire in her eyes.

Tonight is the first time I am seeing Alex through the eyes of another. Before I just saw him as Toni's sexy, domi-neering cousin, but now, watching Jasmine and Steph drool, I am seeing him as they do. He looks like every girl's bad-boy dream come to life. I always knew he was sexy, but having it thrown in my face that others do too is something else entirely. Jealousy spikes again thinking about the bartender eye-fucking him and now my friends not hiding their side-glances well.

Just as I turn to look in his direction, he is up and walking toward me.

"Do you need another beer?" he asks me.

"Yes, please." I try and smile.

He pulls me in close, coming to my ear and whispering, "What's wrong?"

His nearness eases some of those pangs away. "It's nothing."

He pulls back, looking me in the eyes, "Tell me what 'nothing' is."

Not wanting to talk about it here or probably anywhere, I tell him, "I'm fine. Can we talk about it later?"

"Yes, and I'm holding you to it." He cups my chin, bringing my face up to meet our lips in a short, but sensual, kiss. Pulling away he asks, "Do you want me to get the beers from the bartender or do you?" The cocky bastard has the audacity to smirk, knowing the power he has with the women around him.

Not amused, I roll my eyes at him, "You go. See if she slips you her number." The green-eyed monster is on full display.

"I don't want her number. I have everything I want right here." He comes in close, his breath tickling my ear as he goes in for a quick kiss on my neck.

The trepidation dissolves with his attention on me. With my lips pursed, I shake my head at him teasingly. I need to regain my footing with him.

"I'll go get them," I tell him.

Alex is so unlike any guy I have ever dated. Cute, preppy, boy-next-door types have been my usual type. A couple did turn out to be wolves in sheep's clothing, thinking their privilege excused anything they did. But for the most part, they were nice guys who ended up being boring.

He is so opposite from me. His dark, wavy hair, brown eyes, and tanned skin are in contrast to my blonde, blue-eyed, fair complexion. Polar opposites. What does he see in me when he could literally have anyone in this bar if he wanted?

I lean against the bar, waving at Miss Bartender to come my way.

"A Budweiser and Ultra, please."

She grabs them, placing them on the bar, and while popping the tops she says, "Eight."

"Put them on Alex Martinez's tab."

"You're Alex Martinez?" The bitchiness in her voice is not lost on me, which pisses me off. Who the hell does she think she is, and what does she think she can accomplish by playing this game?

"No. I. Am. Not." I stress each word to make it easier for her to understand. "But my boyfriend is, and he told you when we got here that I was able to place things on his tab." I cock my head to the side patronizing her with a fake smile.

"Sorry, but—" she begins before she is interrupted by Cocky himself coming up behind me, wrapping his arms around my middle, and tucking his head in my neck.

"What's taking so long?"

"I'm not able to place things on your tab according to..." I wave my hand dismissively in Miss Bartenders direction.

"Huh?" He looks up at her, and she looks anything but amused. "Put them on the tab now, then close me out." Her eyes widen at his request. His take-control demeanor showing.

"Sorry, this place is busy, and I forgot you asked to have her order on your tab," she stumbles.

"Close me out." His voice lacks any humor or patience.

I wasn't sure what he was doing. Were we were leaving? I stay quiet, letting him handle the situation the way he feels he needs to.

She turns to the register. I turn in his arms, asking quietly, "Are we going to leave?" Which I didn't want to do.

"No. Cash until the next bartender shows up."

I squint my eyes at him, not understanding. "She won't be the lone bartender here long. There should be another one here already, or up soon. This place will get too busy for only one to be behind the bar."

She places the tab for him on the counter, then grabs it and walks away after he signs.

"How do you know so much?" I ask him, surprised by his answer.

"I've had several odd jobs in bars since I dropped out of

high school. I was never able to run a place since I didn't have a diploma, though. I do make a mean cocktail." The seriousness in which he began his explanation disappears with his playful, flirty wink.

"But you finished high school now. You could do more now if you wanted," I offer to him. I know he doesn't see the ranch in his forever.

He nods his head as he considers the idea.

"Come on, let's get back to your friends." We grab our beers from the bar top to join the group again.

The remainder of the evening goes well. Alex's posture never weakens, but he participates in the conversations and at least smiles on occasion.

Chapter 12

ALEX

THE WEEKEND PASSES QUICKLY. NOT HAVING A REAL excuse to leave anywhere on my own, all I was able to do was text out a few feelers to old customers and wait for Hector's direction. Not having a job or place to go in town makes what I'm doing more difficult. No one can know what I'm involved in again. This could damage them permanently.

You start at el mundo this weekend. A text from Hector comes through. This is the premier nightclub for the elite Mexican internationals or those with enough money.

Doing? I ask, not wanting a shit bouncer job or barback again. There is no future and no money there. How can I explain leaving a real paying job for that?

Door. Fuck. I knew it. This won't work.

I can't leave a good paying job to work the door. Fuck that! I respond angrily, frustrated I'm finding myself in this predicament again.

What else can I get a hs dropout? And there it is. I'm no longer a dropout, and he doesn't know it.

I got my diploma now. I want something better. I demand, knowing it may not be the best move.

Since when?

Toni helped me. Let me know when you have a better offer. I stand my ground. If I'm going to stand a chance of escaping this, I need my edge back.

No response, which hopefully means he knows I'm not messing around. I may respect them out of fear, but I know the easiest way to fuck this up is by playing it easy and not pushing back. The key is to find the balance between pushing and offending. And that is the finest of fine lines. One you will not walk away from.

COUNTING down the minutes until the end of the workday, my phone begins ringing.

"Hey, baby." I answer Lola's call. "Is everything okay?"

It's strange she would be calling me during the day while I'm still working.

"Hey, sexy!" I can hear the smile in her voice. "It's nothing. I didn't think you were going to answer. I was just going to leave a message about plans for this weekend. I was thinking we could get away. Maybe head to the coast for a couple of nights?"

While going away with Lola is at the top of things I want to do, I can't leave town right now. Not while I have Hector on my ass and trying to start this shit again. I only have a couple of days to get things in motion before coming back here.

"*Amor*, I would like nothing better than to get away with you, but I can't right now. Not while I'm trying to find something in town. It's just not a good time." I hate disappointing her.

"It's okay. I just thought I would try." I can hear the defeat in her voice.

"I promise, we will. Just not this weekend. Okay?" I hate being the one who placed the sadness in her voice.

"Okay. I better let you go."

"I'll call you tonight." I reassure her about our nightly Facetime call.

This is fucking crazy. I have never felt bad about letting a girl down. But Lola, I would do anything to not make her sad or disappointed.

REPORT TO EL mundo on wed. Trey likes you and will try you out as a bar manager. Hector's text comes in Thursday night. He's probably sitting with Trey right now.

My time here at the ranch is coming to an end. As much as I didn't want to be here, now knowing I'm not coming back feels wrong. Probably because of what I will be involved with soon. Or maybe I did like it and never allowed myself to feel it. Whichever it is, I'm now dreading leaving the stability this place provided.

"What's with the face, city boy?" Juan asks, not missing a beat, as I come into the kitchen.

I didn't think I was that transparent. "Looks like tomorrow is my last day," I answer honestly. The guys here accepted me from the start.

"What are you going to be doing?" he asks.

"Bar manager at a nightclub." This will be the only part of my life going forward I will be able to share honestly.

"Nice." He laughs. "And how is Lola going to like you being around drunk women every weekend?"

Fuck. I hadn't considered that. And after last weekend, I should have thought more carefully about it.

"I don't know, but I got a shot. It won't be forever though.

It's just a foot in the door after all the time I spent fucking up." I try and place a positive spin on it for my sake more than his.

I decide I'll tell Lola in person this weekend. This is not something I want to break to her over the phone. Even if it is Facetime.

I HAVE a few errands to run. Be at your place about 8. I send the quick text to Lola so she does not worry about me not showing up at her place at my usual time like last weekend. No need for her to start being curious about my whereabouts.

I stop at Hector's, or more accurately, Jefe's home to settle some last-minute business we have yet to discuss.

Walking up to his house, the familiar people hanging around, a sense of deja vu creeps up. I walked these steps so many times up until a little under a year ago. But it feels like a lifetime ago. I know this game well, but this time it is so much different. I have more to lose if I'm caught.

I raise my head to the men I walk past going into the house, my presence expected. These men only respond to confidence. You either have it or you'd better fake it because they will eat you alive. They are many years older than me. Been playing much longer. Most have been in and out of jail, always keeping their lips sealed and earning a higher status for taking the fall and not bringing anyone down with them.

I have been able to last. One because I have never been caught, and it pleases El Jefe, The Boss. And two, for my age, I have hung with the big dogs; I know my place but also assert myself. The guys my age are hungry to make names for themselves. They want to do it quick and ruffle the older generation's feathers. Those guys fell from grace hard and fast.

Thinking I'm meeting with Hector, I'm surprised to be escorted into his dad's office.

"I'm pleased to have you back." He extends his hand out to me.

Shocked by this meeting, I smile and take his hand. I have nothing to say since this was forced upon me.

"Sit." He moves around his desk, and I wait for him to sit before I take my seat. "Hector tells me we were able to get you in at El Mundo."

I nod my head; again, no need for words. It will only be when he asks a specific question that I will be expected to talk.

"He also said you were hesitant to come back. Is that right?"

Now it is my turn. I nod again. "I am. Not much time has passed since my father's bust and court date. I don't want anyone coming around sniffing."

"Yes, yes. I know about your dad. *Pero no vale para nada.*" (But he's worthless.) Jefe shakes his head back and forth, looking at his desk, disappointed. He may have been friends with my dad in the past, but now, my dad has somehow placed himself on Jefe's shit list.

"*No eres to papa. Tu piensas.*" (You are not your dad. You think.) He taps his finger on his temple. I'm getting the feeling he is buttering me up for something. Before he does, I need to lay out my requests.

"I would like to think so." I begin, jumping in. "So to begin, I mentioned to Hector I was not getting Javie involved this time. He now has a clean job, making money, and I would like to see him continue."

His eyes widen just a fraction at my courage in making demands. Other than that quick slip, his features stay the same.

"Fine. Your business. You run it the way you see fit."

"Thank you for respecting that." I want to stay respectful, especially with what is coming next.

"I need a place to store. I can't keep it at the house anymore. Too risky. With Javie there, he will suspect, and Toni is visiting more since my Güela's passing."

"Anything else?" I can see my request is not going over well.

"Not right now." I answer with confidence. That will do for now. I know when to stop.

"Fine." He taps his fingers on the desk. "We just closed up the tire shop on First Street. You can use that as your base." He opens his desk and passes me a set of keys. "If you don't want anyone sniffing, you better keep that place quiet." He warns me about doing business in an abandoned business like I don't realize the risk he just placed me in. This was deliberate, because I won't work out of my house.

Working out of my house gives me sole responsibility for the bust if ever caught. If I'm working out of the closed shop, I can hold others accountable if I choose to. It's easier to raise suspicion, too, if I'm seen coming in and out for no reason. Not the best outcome, but it will have to work for now.

I want to mention how temporary this assignment is, but he says, "You better be going. Business waits for no one." Dismissed, I know better than to say anything else. I stand, nod, and walk out.

Back in my car I receive a text from Hector. *Meet Trey at 2 on Wed at the club. Your tire will be ready on Monday.*

His dad has already relayed the message, and my supply is set. Fuck. This just became real, and my shoulders start to tense. Game on.

LOLA

DISAPPOINTMENT that we couldn't get away this weekend weighs on me, but I understand his desire to stay in. Traveling back and forth every weekend and looking for a job in town probably has him exhausted. He does not need a "get-away," which is fancy for "more driving and work before you can relax." Not wanting to lay around the apartment yet again, I think of what else we can do here in town.

"Hey, baby," Alex says as he walks through the door, seeing me laying on the couch.

Seeing him always brings a smile to my face. The days spent apart are lonely. I get up to meet him before he showers.

"I missed you." He kisses me then pulls away. "I have something to tell you, but I need a shower first."

He lets me go before I can get my question out—"What is it?"

"Patience. I'll be right back," he says, retreating to the bathroom.

I watch him walk away and hear the door close behind him. It couldn't be anything bad if he is taking his time to tell me, right? Or he's buying time because it is bad? Is this the reason he was late getting here today? The suspense getting the better of me, I strip down and decide to persuade him to tell me what is going on.

I open the bathroom door and pull the shower curtain back to a glorious sight. I don't think I thought this through all the way because all I can see is him. Water cascading down his tattoo-covered body.

"Just gonna watch or are you getting in?" he taunts, reaching out to me.

I step into the shower, placing my hands on his well-defined ab muscles letting them slide up his chest. The ridges of his body silently announce his strength. He takes my mouth, kissing me with such force. Entwined so tight, I don't know where I end and he begins. The need for him is instant.

He turns me around, my back against his chest and lets his hands roam over the peaks of my breasts and down between my legs. His fingers enter me as his thumb rubs over my clit. His other hand comes back up, kneading my breast, and his lips softly suck my neck. The warm water rushing down part of my body while cool air hits where the water does not reach has my senses in overdrive, and I come quickly, my knees weak. His arm comes around my middle keeping me steady.

"What was this about, *amor*?" he whispers into my neck.

I turn around to face him, "I thought I was going to ask you what news you had, but I got distracted." I press myself to him, wanting to feel him in me. Or truthfully, needing to feel him in me.

He turns off the water and grabs a couple of towels from the rack, wrapping them around us before stepping out and walking us to my bed. He pushes me lightly, sitting me down before kissing me and unwrapping the towel.

"Lay down." I do as he says as he crawls on top of me.

He's holding himself, weight on his arms accentuating his shoulder muscles. This part of a man, when you're laying under him, shows strength and is sexy at the same time. My hand slides over his shoulder down his arm as I feel him enter me. The delicious fullness and connection we have when making love is what I needed.

His kiss is greedy as he slides in and out. I watch his shoulders, move, tense, and relax with each movement as my center begins tightening. The sheer strength he displays in all facets of life awakens my body. I free fall into an orgasm, wanting to pull him closer. He lets go, allowing himself to fall on top off me. I clutch him tightly as the delicious full feeling dissipates and we catch our breath.

He rolls off me, pulling me to him. My head on his chest, he kisses my hair. After a few quiet minutes enjoying the afterglow, I can't take the suspense any longer.

"What was your news?"

"Today was my last day at the ranch. I found another job." He answers, but his voice sounds off.

"Really? Wow!" I'm proud of him but curious where he will be working. "Where did you get a job?"

"El Mundo. I'm going to be a bar manager." His voice is level, giving me nothing.

"A bar manager? Cool." My brain is spinning in overtime with what this means. Working every weekend. All night. In a club filled with exotic, rich women. When would I have time with him anymore? I don't want to take anything away from him, but disappointment is instant.

"Yes, which means things will change for me yet again, but at least I'm in town all week."

I wish I could ask more, but fear if I do, my voice will betray me, so instead I stay quiet holding on to him tightly, not wanting this to end.

After a few quiet moments he asks, "You have nothing to say?"

"No." I'm keeping my concerns locked away.

"Really?" he pushes. He rolls me onto my back and rolls to his side resting his head on his hand.

Keeping my mouth shut is much harder when his questioning eyes are boring into me.

"I don't know." I close my eyes and roll over, tucking myself into his chest so I don't have to look at him anymore.

He pushes my shoulder so that I am lying flat again before he begins, "Look at me, *amor*." He waits until I open my eyes again before continuing, "Tell me what's wrong."

"It's stupid, so I would rather not." I try to weasel my way out of admitting my jealousy.

"It's not stupid. Please tell me." He's calm as he waits.

I'm not getting out of this, so I might as well come clean, at least partially. "If you work in a club, you will be working every weekend, which means no weekends for us." I shrug my shoulders in disappointment.

"Is that all?" How does he know there's more?

"Nothing. It's stupid." I try and deflect.

"If it is bothering you, it's not stupid. Now spill." His tone is more demanding.

"You. Around all those beautiful, exotic, scantily clad women every weekend." I turn away from him, embarrassed I voiced my insecurity.

"I don't want those women. I want you and only you." He creeps up closer to me, placing soft kisses on my shoulder. His hand comes around my middle and gently pulls me back against him. The warmth of his chest is soothing, but not enough for the nerves prickling.

"I did this so that I could be in town with you all week. I don't have many skills. You know this. I just got my diploma. I'm a dumbass that doesn't deserve you, but for whatever reason, you have chosen me. I have bar experience. I have done every odd job there that did not require a degree. I can finally do something more. Maybe I won't like it, but it gives me some experience to move on if I want." His hand is splayed on my stomach. I feel his permanent five o'clock shadow brushing along my shoulder as he continues his kissing assault.

"But I've seen the way women respond to you." I exhale loudly. "You and I both know they will be throwing themselves at you. Last weekend the whore bartender was ready for you to take her right there."

A soft chuckle vibrates against my back which raises my anger at what I feel is a dismissal of my feelings. I try and pull away but he holds me still.

"*Amor*. You know what that words means, yes?" He pauses, waiting for me to answer.

"Yes." I whisper, not really wanting to participate in this conversation anymore.

"Tell me what it means then," he probes.

Not wanting to play whatever game this is, I stay quiet.

"Well if you aren't going to answer, then I'm going to tell you. It means 'love.'" He pauses for a moment before continuing. "I call you, only you, "love." I call you "*amor*" because you are the only woman who has brought me to my knees. You are the only one I have ever wanted to spend time with. I told you before, but I will remind you in case you forgot. *Tu ya tienes mi corazon*. You already have my heart."

I turn around, looking into his dark eyes, searching. Is he really in this as deep as I am? I place my hand on his scruffy cheek then let it slip down slowly to his chin, brushing my fingertips lightly along his lips. Nerves of uncertainty and fear fill me.

He puckers his lips, kissing the tips of my fingers. "*Te amo*."

A lone tear escapes and travels down the side of my face. "I love you too." I bury myself in his chest as his arms tighten, holding me close.

Things have gone so fast. Or did we just torture ourselves unnecessarily by denying our feelings the past several months? I've known I was in love with him long before we even had our first kiss. Any guy who came up to me during that time I immediately compared to Alex. No one ever came close.

CHAPTER 13

ALEX

MY MEETING WITH TREY WENT WELL. HE GAVE ME A TOUR of the club even though I was already acquainted with it. He went over my responsibilities and the dress code. I will need to get a few things because you have to dress for the clientele the nightclub attracts. The hard part of this job is inventory with the amount of alcohol and bottle service that flow constantly. They have plenty of procedures to ensure all is accounted for. I will be going in early for the next three days to meet all the bar staff, from the lead bartenders to the barbacks. I have much respect for the barbacks, as I was once one, because they do all the grunt work. Washing, cleaning, refilling the ice, restocking glasses, showing patience with customers who are angry because the barbacks cannot serve them drinks, and being respectful toward the wealthy, who just hate to wait—just a few of the things they do behind the scenes to make a bar run efficiently. Without them, the bartenders would be in over their heads.

How's it going? A text from Hector comes through as I'm walking out of the club. It's only been a couple of days since I've been in town, and they are expecting progress already. Unfortunately for me, I can't move that fast anymore. I don't have the freedom to do I as I wish without people wondering what I'm doing.

Fine. Met with Trey and I start tomorrow. Will pick up then.

I visited the tire shop once this week while Lola was in class. Checked out the layout and traffic. I don't want to be caught visiting there too often, so planning everything in advance is going to be key. The supply they left makes me nervous. I wasn't planning on moving that amount. I didn't even move that amount when I had Javie helping me. The only positive, I won't be having to weigh and package as they have already done that for me.

Strolling the aisles of a resale men's clothing store is not my idea of a good time.

"Why don't we just go to the mall and look?" Lola quips behind me as I drag each sport coat and suit jacket across the metal bar in frustration. She means well but forgets our differences.

"Because I don't really want to pay full price for these things, especially if this job is not going to be forever," I answer diplomatically without admitting I don't have the cash for such extravagances. At least not yet. If I'm going to keep a girl like Lola, I will need to figure my shit out.

"Oh." Her quiet response is an indication she caught my meaning.

She moves to the next aisle, looking through dress shirts. A black suit jacket catches my eye, and I take it off the hanger and slide it on.

"That looks good," Lola says, coming around again with a few shirts in her hand. "Turn around," she directs me, as she hangs the shirts on the rack.

Her hands are running along my shoulders down my back to my waist. She comes around and tugs on the sleeves.

"This one won't need any alterations, and it looks good." Her eyes are wide and happy. "And changing the color and print of your shirt will keep it from looking the same." She is inspecting each shirt she picked out in front of me. I, of course, let her since she seems to enjoy it. "You said you have another jacket at home?"

I nod in the affirmative.

"Okay. And slacks?" It now seems she is on a mission.

"I have a couple pairs."

"Keep looking for one more jacket, preferably a dark grey if you can find one. If not, we'll look again another time. I'll get you a couple more pants." Her attitude quickly went from hesitant to take-charge.

"Hungry?" I ask her as we walk to the car.

"I am. Tacos by your place?" I can't believe how much this white girl loves spicy Mexican food. And now that she knows the small restaurants on my side of town, that is where she insists on going when the craving hits.

I shake my head at her as she smiles in victory. Little does she realize, I would walk through fire for her. I don't think I have it in me to tell this girl no for anything. She is my weakness, and in this business, I can't have one. The only good thing about this is she is only known by few and they may know of her, but nothing about her.

We take a seat at her favorite taco shack for a late lunch. I'm feeling guilty I have to leave her tonight for my first real shift. I guess it's not about working at the club, but all the other stuff that comes with it. I'm not sure what arrangement

Trey and Hector have, but I need to find out quick. I need to know if product will be going into the club.

"What's wrong?" Lola pulls me from my thoughts.

"Nothing." I shake my head, not wanting her to begin suspecting anything. She can never know what I'm doing. I will get the wrath of Toni if she finds out, but I know she can handle it. Javie will be disappointed but understand my predicament. Lola. Lola doesn't understand this side of town and what I need to do to stay alive.

"I was thinking, maybe I'm doing too good of a job dressing you, and I may regret it," she teases.

"And why will you regret it?" I lean in a bit, raising an eyebrow in question. I suspect jealousy is behind this statement.

She rolls her eyes, knowingly. "You know why. And stop acting so damn innocent because we both know you are anything but." She moves back in her seat until her back is flush against the booth, arms crossed.

I open my hand, palm up on the table, "*No seas asi, amor.*" I wiggle my fingers wanting her to take my hand.

"You know I don't speak Spanish." Her lips pull down automatically.

I know this, but quick sayings in Spanish come out first out of habit. This is just how I learned to communicate. I have never had to learn to be anything but who I am. Now I'm beginning to understand how hard Toni must have had it in college trying to "fit in" with people so unlike the ones we grew up with.

"Don't be like this. I love you." I tap my fingers on the table, hoping she places her hand in mine.

"*Que onda guey?*" (What's up, man?) Hector's voice pulls my attention away from Lola.

Panic strikes having Lola here with me. Him seeing me

with her and knowing about her... FUCK! Did he just hear me tell Lola I loved her?

Stone faced and refusing to look at Lola, I answer, "*Nada, y tu?*" (Nothing, and you?)

A smirk appears as he cocks his head towards Lola, "*Estas jugando con gueras?*" (You're playing around with white girls?)

I shrug nonchalantly, hoping he leaves, "*Por ahora.*" (For now.) I'm relieved right now that Lola doesn't speak Spanish, and Hector does not need to know she is my kryptonite.

"Hi. I'm Hector." He extends his hand to her.

"Lola." She places her hand in his, and he gently shakes it.

"If you ever get tired of playing with the help, you should find me." He gives her a sleazy wink. She smiles politely, but I can tell she is uncomfortable.

A waitress comes by and drops off our food, interrupting Hector.

"I'll let y'all eat." He turns and walks toward the counter.

She waits until he is out of earshot before asking, "Who was that?"

"No one you want to know," I whisper, putting my finger to my lips, letting her know to stay quiet.

Eating on this side of town will not be so easy anymore. I won't ever know who will come up to me asking for things while I'm with her. I can't risk being with her here.

She begins eating, but her eyes follow Hector until he exits the restaurant. As soon as he does, she begins again, "Now do you want to tell me what that was about?" She lowers her head, whispering softly.

I knew she wouldn't let it go. "His dad runs this side of town. Those things I refuse to talk about...they all revolve around him and his father. That's all you need to know about him."

"Oh." Her eyes go down to her food as she begins breaking a tortilla chip nervously in her hands.

"Hey." I place my hand on top of hers, halting the mess she's making.

She looks up at me, fear written all over her face.

"It's the past, baby. Let's just leave it there." Now I have told a bold-faced lie.

She nods, her face attempting a smile, and picks up her taco, taking another bite.

"I love you, and I will never let anything hurt you." I work at trying to comfort her. She has never seen the ugliness of this side of town. She was sheltered in our home and the few people we chose to let in. People I knew were somewhat trustworthy and who I could control. But I'll be damned if any of the ugliness the hood holds touches her.

LOLA

FLIPPING through the channels while I wait for Alex to finish getting dressed for work is killing me. While I don't want to be the jealous girlfriend, I can't seem to squash the feelings each time they come up. The strength with which I feel them takes me by surprise each time. It's an awful feeling.

I hadn't decided if I was going to stay home tonight, but I'm leaning towards going out. At least it will help me keep my mind occupied and off of Alex. I hope.

He walks into the living room, and my jaw hits the floor. I know my boyfriend is *hot*, but damn. He walks out with the perfect dressed-up bad-boy look. The only guy I have ever seen pull this off is David Beckham, and he's a celebrity. My stomach instantly knots with thoughts of all the women who will also think exactly what I am.

"I'm off. Wish me luck," he says, reaching his hand out to me.

I get up to see him out. "Good luck." I run my hands down the lapels of his jacket.

"Do you want me to head home after work?" he asks, placing his hands on my waist.

I shake my head nervously, not knowing why he would ask that. "No. Why would you want to go home?"

"I don't want to go home. I just didn't want to wake you when I get in." He comes in closer, kissing me softly.

"Come here. I want to wake up with you." I may have answered too honestly.

"Good." His sexy smirk appears as he brushes his nose past mine and kisses me deeply before walking out.

I flop myself on the couch, alone with my thoughts. Not wanting to second guess us, I pick up my phone.

Doing anything tonight? I send Toni a text.

Garrett went out to the ranch. What did you have in mind? Her response comes quickly.

WE FIND a table at a swanky bar. Not usually our scene, but I needed an excuse to get dressed up. I was hoping I could stay up until Alex got home and I would be looking just as good as the girls in the club.

"What brought you out tonight?" Toni asks taking a sip from her martini.

"Alex started at the club tonight." I shrug, taking a sip of the fruity concoction I ordered. "I didn't feel like sitting home alone."

She gives me a knowing smile. "I'm sorry for that day at the house. You both shocked us. I have to admit, I didn't see that coming. Javie said he suspected it, but I really thought Alex didn't like you and was being nice because you were my friend."

"To be honest, I didn't think he liked me either." Thoughts of that time swirl. "I really thought he was going to be my unrequited love."

"Unrequited love?" Her brows raise in surprise.

"Probably." I try to evade the conversation. Toni may be my best friend, but she is also his cousin and I have learned quickly watching their dynamics; nothing comes between them. For them, blood is always thicker than water.

I look around, watching people laugh, mingle, and meet. It seems so easy, but we all know there is a game and finesse to it. The way we dress to attract, the smiles, the eye contact...all tell-tale signs of the art of seduction. One that I learned and mastered quickly but realized did not make me happy. And now I am in love and unsure of my footing. The confidence in my game is gone.

"Where did you go?" Toni's voice breaks through my thoughts.

"Sorry. Never mind." I place my well-rehearsed bright smile on to continue. "Why did Garrett go to the ranch this weekend?"

"You're changing the subject." She cocks a brow at me.

"How?"

"You know how. Now why are we really here, and what is going on with you and Alex?" she pushes, bluntly.

I take a deep breath in, letting it out slowly, and take a slow sip, buying time to figure out how to say something without saying anything.

"Alex and I are fine. He's working, and I didn't want to sit home alone. I told you." I pull my lips into a forced smile like I have learned to do to make others comfortable.

"First...you have on the fake sorority smile. Wipe it off. It's not real, and that's not you. Second...you are never at a loss for words. You are a-mile-a-minute if we let you, and now you seem to be tripping over yourself. So I know something is up."

"I can't." I shake my head at her. My smile disappears.

"Can't what?"

"Can't talk to you about it. I was about to, then remembered who you are." I take her hand squeezing it, missing my best friend.

"Who am I?" she asks, confused.

"Alex's cousin. Or more like his sister." I pause, letting that soak in for a bit. "I've watched y'all together. Y'all are tight. Nothing is coming between you. I can't talk to you about Alex. What if he does something to make me mad? Not saying bad but you know how guys can irritate us. I can't vent to you. That's your family. That's just weird."

"You—" she begins, but I interrupt her.

"I didn't think it through when I fell for him. The exact reasons I fell for him are the exact reasons I can't speak to you about him. He's so freakin' loyal, as you all are. If you had to pick sides, you would pick him, and I wouldn't expect it any other way."

"Are you done yet?" There's irritation in her voice.

"Uh...I guess so." Crap. I really don't know where to step.

"You can talk to me about Alex because even though I will always be by my cousin's side, I know he is far from perfect. I know he will probably fuck up because that's what guys do. You forced me to be your BFF, and now you are taking it away? I'm not letting you. You need to vent? You can always come to me." She turns her hand over where I am still clutching her and tightens her fingers around my hand in return. "I just don't really need to know about him intimately, if you know what I mean." She smirks with a twinkle in her eye.

"Fine. You win." I surrender to her.

"So why are we here?"

"Because I'm jealous." The truth falls right out.

"Jealous of who?"

"Of all the girls who I figure are throwing themselves at him right now. It's freaking exhausting watching girls overtly flirt with him in front of me. And if I'm not around, I can only imagine how brazen some will be. Especially if they are drunk." My fear is out in the open, so I grab my drink and chug the remaining fruity liquid.

"And what does he do when they flirt with him?" she inquires.

"Nothing." My shoulders slump in defeat.

"Nothing?"

"Well he doesn't flirt back, if that's what you're asking. And he usually flirts with me to ease the jealously he has seen a couple of times. He makes sure the girls know he is with me."

"I'm going to let you in on a little secret." The mischievous twinkle in her eye sparkling. "He doesn't flirt. With anyone. Not that I have ever seen. I'm telling you this so you can see what I didn't. At least not right away. He used girls. Every time I would ask why he would go through girls, his answer was if they let him, he would."

"See? They make it easy. Ugh..." My head falls back in defeat.

"No. You didn't let me finish. He wants you. He finally found the person who got him to stop. That night at the house when I pushed, I was doing it because I was not going to lose you because he couldn't keep it in his pants. I needed to make sure he was thinking. He fought for you. He has never done that. I could push any of his girls, and he would just shrug and drop them. Not you. With you, he fought me back. That's how I knew he was in. You said it yourself. He flirts with you. That is not something he did. He didn't care about making girls feel comfortable or loved or cared for. But he does that with you. You. You are what he wants, and he won't purposefully hurt you with another girl."

"Thanks." Hearing it from someone else and not the broken record of self-doubt is eye-opening.

"Look. How about we head to the club next weekend. You can see him in action."

"Okay," I agree quickly. I wasn't sure if it would hurt or help, but I have been dying to go to the club everyone has been talking about lately.

KISSES in my hair and an arm coming around my side wake me. "What time is it?"

"Almost three-thirty. Go back to sleep. I didn't mean to wake you." I feel his stubble brush over my shoulder as he brings his body tightly against mine.

"It's okay. I tried to stay up and wait for you, but the martinis I had made me sleepy." I turn to face him.

"Martinis, huh? Where did you go?" He smiles at me, cupping my cheek softly.

"I met Toni at the new martini bar downtown." I kiss him softly.

"Did you have a good time?" His fingers are softly gliding up and down my arm.

"I did. I haven't been out with her in too long. We needed it." Spending time with Toni tonight after breaking the ice with the new dynamics was necessary. I felt much stronger after.

"Good. Because I never intended to get in the middle of your friendship. She needed you back then, even if she didn't want to admit it. She needed to see there was a whole other world for her. She refused believe. You forced her. And for that, I will always be grateful."

"I didn't do anything except make her be my friend." I didn't understand what he meant.

"That may have been all you did, but to her...it gave her a way to stop leaning on the shithole part of town she was scared of leaving. And for me...you are pushing me to be a better man. The one you see me as." He brushes his lips past mine gently. "Go back to sleep, *amor*."

CHAPTER 14

ALEX

I'M USING THE TIME WHILE LOLA IS IN CLASS TO RUN MY errands. As much as I didn't want to go into the tire shop more than once a week, I've found that that is an impossibility. I will need to go daily since I can't store anything. I need to figure out a way to consolidate trips. I fear this way will set me up to get busted.

Need new tires? A text from Hector wanting to resupply the shop. I haven't even managed half of what they left, and he already wants to make a new delivery.

Mine are still good. I respond, knowing it's not the best answer, but it will have to do right now.

I learned that EJ, a bartender at the club, was friends with Hector. I will be supplying EJ, and he will take care of business in the club. This is good news—I am not dealing in public. All I have to do is watch his dealing to ensure he is playing it safe. The club is not a place to get sloppy. Too many prying eyes.

I park in front of a house I know too well. Toni hooked me up with one of my best buyers. I started small on her campus, doing all the leg work until I met Chad. He was able to move so much more than I did since he was where the students were.

I knock on the door and wait. As nervous as I may be on the inside, I can't let it show.

"Hey! It's been a long time," Chad greets me after opening the door. "Come in."

"It has." I pat him on the shoulder, walking in.

He closes the door and gestures for us to sit.

"Are you back?" he asks me directly.

I can't show weakness, but I don't want to answer this question either. Because I'm not back. I am in this for the short-term.

Coded discussion takes place, neither of us fully trusting the other. A handshake and a swap of goods has us back in business.

I meet with several of my old buyers. All found new suppliers, which is no surprise, but I'm able to get most back with me. A couple of the smaller ones didn't like how I dropped off the grid.

It hasn't been easy trying to maneuver a "night" job with trying to build business during the day. I don't want Lola curious about my comings and goings while she is in class.

LOLA

THE NERVES STIRRING in my belly about tonight are on fire. There are no flutters or cute jitters. It is a full-on cramp, moving up and tightening my chest. The talk with Toni calmed me all week, but all of a sudden, tonight feels different. Alex has already left for work, and I am in his room getting dressed. He didn't want me riding home alone, so I will be going with Javie and meeting everyone else there. He added our names to the list, so we will not have to wait in line.

"Almost ready?" Javie yells through the door, tapping it a couple of times.

"Give me five." I respond. I've been dressed ready to go, I just need to center myself for what I may see.

Knowing there is nothing I can do but go and experience the club Alex works at, I walk into the living room asking, "Have you ordered the Uber?"

My eyes widen at Javie polished up. I've never seen him like this. He looks like he could grace the pages of *GQ*. While Alex has the bad-boy, intimidating, sexy look, Javie is boy-next-door with an edge. I had never seen him this way as we quickly fell into a comfortable platonic relationship.

"My, my. Look who cleans up well!" I wink at him.

"Shut up. And yes. The Uber is about five minutes away." His usual jovial smile brightens his eyes.

"I'm serious, Javie. You look very handsome." I stand in front of him. "You are going to make some girl very happy." And I truly mean it. He is kind and affectionate.

He shakes his head in embarrassment, not responding.

We are on our way. Toni's text comes through.

"Toni and Garrett are already on their way," I inform Javie.

"We'll meet them inside."

See you there. I respond to Toni.

Stepping out of the car, I'm surprised by the amount of people in line. I've only seen this type of club hype on TV in LA or New York. I didn't even think this type of thing happened here. We are in freakin' Texas. Scanning the line, I see people dressed to the nines. I wonder if everyone will eventually get in. If not, what's the point?

"Come on." Javie's hand is guiding me on my lower back.

"Will people get mad if we skip the line?" I whisper up to Javie.

"No. They are used to people going up. But you better have your name on the list or enough cash to buy your way in, or you will look like a jackass."

At the door, Javie casually shakes the bouncer's hand as they do that slight chin raise greeting to each other. His mannerisms are so much like Alex's right now. I'm seeing Javie in a completely different light. Alex has always had this intense take-charge presence, but Javie was always so laid-back. Seeing he also has this side is a bit mind-blowing.

He grabs my hand and pulls me in front of him. He guides me as we walk in through a dimly lit hallway that opens to a full club. Now I understand the line outside. The club already looks to be at capacity.

"Come on. Let's get a drink?" Javie says in my ear.

"How will we find Toni and Garrett?" I ask Javie as we wait for our drinks.

"Walk around." He shrugs, unaffected by the crowd.

"Have you worked here before?" My curiosity gets the best of me. His transformation into a mini Alex is strange.

"Yes. The door was my only job, unlike Alex who moved around the club."

"Did you like it?" I wonder why his demeanor is still stiff.

"It was a job."

The bartender drops our drinks off, and I quickly go to pull a card out of my clutch to pay. Again, Javie does that chin raise, and he grabs the drinks from the bar, handing me mine.

"Did you start a tab?" I ask.

"Nah. I've worked with her before. On the house. Come on. Let's find Toni." I let him lead me again.

The dance floor is packed with people, and I am in awe watching them dance to the Spanish pop music playing. Their movements smooth and fluid, hips swinging to the beat of the song. It's a little intimidating.

"Hey," I greet Toni and Garrett, who are sitting at a table.

I take a seat on one of the chairs facing the dance floor. There are a couple of empty tables, which I think is odd considering the amount of people here.

"Why aren't people sitting at these empty tables?" I ponder out loud.

"You have to pay for these," Toni answers. "Garrett refused to be out there all night, so he reserved and paid for a table." She rolls her eyes in his direction, smirking.

"You are more than welcome to head on out there if you want," he teases her back. I know she has had to make some adjustments because he is stinking wealthy. Her pride fought him so much in the beginning, but she is slowly coming to terms with their discrepancy.

"Shut up." Her smile is relaxed.

Hands on my bare shoulders and a kiss on my neck startle me.

"You look beautiful tonight." Alex's voice soothes me.

I turn to face him. His powerful demeanor is on full display. His fingers gently stroking my shoulder is the only soft thing about him right now.

"I've got to get to work. Enjoy yourself." He places another quick kiss on my neck. He stands announcing to the table, "I set up a tab for you with Jen. End of the bar." He waves his hand in her direction. "Javie," he waits until he has Javie's full attention, "you take care of her."

Javie only responds with a quick nod of his head. I watch as Alex makes his way through the crowd. With the amount of people here, I don't know if I will get to see him again.

"Why do you need to take care of me?" I ask Javie.

"Because I brought you here."

Toni snort-laughs holding the liquid she just sipped in her mouth. She swallows and coughs before saying, "Shut the fuck up. You are doing it out of some machismo duty, thinking us girls can't take care of ourselves."

"What-the-fuck-ever. Alex tells me to watch her. I'm watching her," Javie counters.

"And Alex has you watching her because as much as he hates to admit it, he still holds a machismo card," she comes back.

"Okay. Stop," I interject. "Machismo or not. Why do you need to watch me? Why don't you need to watch Toni?"

"Toni is now Garrett's responsibility." Garrett remains quiet, as usual, when they begin the familial arguments. "Besides, we trained her well. She didn't have it easy, so she knows the game."

"I lived in Europe by myself for almost a year. I think I know how to take care of myself," I announce proudly.

"Maybe so. But this is a whole new world, *guera*. Until Alex tells me to let up, sorry." He shrugs and a hint of the Javie I know appears.

"You agree with this Garrett?" I want another male point of view.

"Sort of." He pauses. "It's a fine line. I was raised to look after and respect women. It's the cowboy way. Not because they can't do it themselves, but it's part of being a gentleman. I want to be able to shield when I can. I want to save the day when I can. It's a touchy subject. But know, most of it comes from a good place of wanting to protect. Not always, but then again, nothing is ever an always or never."

With Garrett's answer, I decide this is a debate that could go on for eternity and one that I wasn't truly invested in. If Alex wants to keep me safe, why fight it?

"You remind me so much of your brother tonight. I've never seen you so..." I couldn't find the right word.

"I haven't needed to be this person in a while. Not since leaving..." He leaves his sentence hanging.

"Leaving?" I ask.

"Yes. They can both be hard asses. Only it doesn't come naturally to this one." Toni gives Javie a genuine smile. "Now your guy. Sorry to tell you, Lola; you are stuck with the true hard ass. He doesn't know how to drop it."

A waitress comes by and drops us off a round of drinks and shots. I look around and see Alex behind the bar. He nods, and a slight smile appears for a second before disappearing.

After a couple of drinks, the beat of the music is calling. I watch as Toni and Garrett hit the floor. Garrett is not as smooth as many of the men, but he is holding his own with Toni.

"Let's go dance." I turn to Javie.

He extends his hand standing up. "Come on."

On the dance floor, I see his dominant presence again. He has transformed into someone larger than life. He has gone from laid-back and fun-loving to hard and intimidating. His moves are fluid as he takes the lead, holding me close to him, but not in a sexual way. He's strong and in charge.

After a couple of songs, we make our way back to the table. I fan myself with my hand sitting down. I look around for a waitress to get a couple more drinks but don't see anyone around. Garrett and Toni come back and announce their departure.

"You're really leaving?" I ask Toni.

"Yup. I know this place can go to the wee hours of the morning."

"Okay. I'll see you later. Bye." I watch as they walk away.

"One more drink, and then we'll head out too?" I ask Javie.

"Sure. I'll go get them." He makes his way to Jen.

I look around for Alex so I can at least say a quick goodbye.

"Hello, gorgeous." A good-looking guy sits next to me.

"Hello," I respond politely. "I'm waiting for someone."

"Not anymore you're not." He grabs my hand on the table.

I pull it back placing my hands on my lap, away from him.

"I think you're at the wrong table." Javie's voice has an edge I've never heard before.

"Nah. I found the perfect table," Stranger responds arrogantly.

"Lola, go to the bar." Javie instructs me.

"Wait. What?" He seems angry, and I'm confused why I'm being dismissed.

"Now." His eyes are hard.

Hesitantly, I stand. Javie takes a seat in an empty chair. He is cold and calculating.

"You have not done what Javie told you." Alex's voice comes from behind me. "Now, *amor*."

Startled by their behavior, I follow their directions and head to the bar. Alex stands confidently next to the table. The guy looks up at Alex, then back at Javie. A few words are spoken, and strange guy gets up, the arrogance gone. Alex and Javie exchange more words before walking to me.

"I'll see you at home." Alex cups my cheeks kissing me firmly.

He turns to Javie. "Thanks."

"What was that about?" I ask Javie once we are in the Uber on our way home.

"What?" His posture is more relaxed than I've seen all night.

"With that guy? He was going to hit on me. Big deal. I told him I was with someone."

"You can never show weakness. That guy knew you were with someone. We were at the same table all night. He wanted to spread his damn feathers is all. You dominate or get dominated." He's saying the words, but they sound odd coming from him.

"How would a random person dominate you?"

"Most people at the club know us. Regulars know us. That guy is a dickwad with too much money. He thinks his money excuses his behavior. We just reminded him otherwise."

"Oh." I'm surprised by this.

"Lola, you need to understand this world is different. Without saying too much, we have a reputation to uphold. Or at least Alex does. And I will do my part."

"Okay." The alcohol flowing through my system makes his explanation hazy, so I decide to drop it for now.

Alex was expressionless and professional all night. His facial expressions hard and determined with everyone he spoke with. I watched him when he was close to the table. Many people called him, and the radio he wore in his ear seeming to go off often. I could tell when he was trying to listen as he would bring his hand up to his ear. When women would stop him, he seemed polite, but never gave them a smile or any hint of interest.

Remembering him with the guys at the ranch, he seemed to turn into someone else at the club. The friendly banter he had with those guys did not exist with anyone I saw him interact with tonight.

"Lola." Javie breaks me from my thoughts as I was about to head into Alex's room.

I turn to face him.

"He won't be there forever. I don't know what he's trying to prove, but as soon as he gets it out of his system, he'll find something else. Just don't tell him I told you that. Let him figure his shit out. He fought what he felt for you for so long. Doesn't think he can live up to what he thinks you need."

"But I just want him. Nothing else."

"Maybe. But he's a man and wants to prove himself worthy. Let him." His soft thoughtful nature returns.

I nod even though I don't truly understand or agree.

CHAPTER 15

ALEX

Walking up for a meeting with Jefe is not what I expected today. Falling back into a groove, I have done everything to build myself back up, all while hiding this part of me from Lola and ensuring I don't raise Javie's or Toni's suspicions. The same usual strong-arms are out front, acting casual for anyone not in the know passing by. They are Jefe's most trusted *camaradas*, proving their loyalty many times over.

"Hey, Toro," Bruto says to me as I pass. I inwardly cringe at my old name. I haven't been gone from it that long, but I also didn't think I would hear it again when I walked away.

I give him the head nod. We were never on friendly terms. It was always only business. I may have been able to avoid getting jumped into the SEV, but it didn't mean I didn't have to pay certain dues. And since I wasn't officially one of them, I was always kept on the outside.

I'm let into the house and am escorted back into Jefe's office. Stepping in, I see Hector and a younger guy, who doesn't look familiar, scrolling on his phone. Jefe is at his desk reading something on his tablet. Everyone ignores my entrance for several seconds until Jefe decides to set his tablet on the desk, looking up in my direction.

"You finally decide to join us?" Jefe begins, annoyed.

"I'm sorry. I had to wait to get away." I know it's still inexcusable, but I tried to warn them in the beginning that I wasn't dealing like I did in the past, and I don't have Javie's help.

"Wait for?" His displeasure shows.

"I mentioned I am not bringing Javie back in, and I don't want Toni to know what I'm doing. I promised her I would stay away. She doesn't want me to end up like my fucking father," I explain and instantly regret it. They don't care. They just want results. I'm sounding weak. This will not go unnoticed.

"Well, then maybe you need to find your cock. Looks to me like you lost it." And there it is. They saw my weakness.

No words are needed. I keep my mouth shut and wait to find out why I have been summoned.

"Alejandro, meet David." Hector begins, so I turn to face him. "He is learning the ropes. I wanted you to meet him so when he's around, you know he's safe. He will be helping me check the different venues we are working in." Hector gives him a signal, and my phone vibrates in my pocket.

"He just texted you his number. If I am unavailable, you can contact him." This is a strange turn of events. I know better than to ask who this kid is and how in the hell he got to be Hector's right-hand man. Either he's family or they are getting too cocky, which is making them sloppy. Either way, this is not good business.

I nod in understanding.

"The tire shop is doing well. I had my doubts the first couple of weeks. Too much product still sitting there. But I'm glad you were able to get it moving again."

"Yes, sir. And thank you for the shop to work out of." I turn to Hector, knowing he's in charge of my comings and goings in there. "And the system for payment is working?"

I have been leaving a coded receipt with payment in a lock box.

"Yes. It keeps everything in the shop." He wasn't going to give me credit for thinking of it, but that it's working is all I need to know. I don't have to come here at all unless I'm forced.

"Anything else?" I don't want to spend more time here than I need to.

"Why the rush?" Jefe questions.

"No rush." I cross my arms, waiting, careful not to offend.

Jefe picks up his tablet again, and I watch as he begins tapping it. Out of the corner of my eye, I see David on his phone, and Hector is watching me. I will stand unmoving however long it takes.

A few minutes pass in silence, Hector going back and forth from watching me to tapping on his phone each time it vibrates. Jefe acting like I'm not even there.

Finally, Hector speaks, "I have to head out. Want Toro to stay, or is he dismissed?"

Jefe does not look away from his tablet, just lifts his hand and dismisses me with a flick of his wrist.

I spare a glance at Hector and David before I turn to face the door and walk out. A couple of months in the game again, and I am in the hot seat.

Relief settles in as soon as I am in my car. Driving away, I head to the house. I need to drop off some money in the shed. I check the gas cans Javie transformed into a place we could hide things. He was able to weld a compartment in the bottom, which turns it into a perfect place to hide money. In the shed, I take the false bottom off and tuck in most of the money I've made.

. . .

I WALK into Lola's apartment, knowing she is already home from class. Luckily, I have the club to use to cover my tracks with business. Being at the club during the day to check inventory and place orders has been a great excuse to cover my comings and goings.

"Hey, babe!" Lola calls out from the kitchen as I walk in the door.

I go straight to her, needing the feel of her to help erase the crap of today. She is wearing a cute, short little dress. Taking her mouth in a passionate kiss, I pick her up and sit her down on the small island. She wraps her arms around my neck, holding me. My lips start trailing down her neck.

"Dinner will burn if you keep distracting me" She giggles as I tickle her neck.

"Let it." My mind wants to forget the shit I'm caught up in. The more I think about my way out, the less I believe it's a possibility, and I can't keep Lola with me if I'm in.

I hold her to me, hoping the feeling of drowning dissipates.

"Hey, baby, what's wrong?" She pushes me back, looking deep into my eyes.

I need to man-up, or she will get suspicious. "Nothing. Just a crap day." I place my lips on hers again and let my hand lazily trail up her leg, leaving a trail of goosebumps in its wake.

"I like when you wear dresses." My fingers trail the edge of her panties as her breath hitches.

"Turn off the stove. I need you." She does not need to tell me twice. I reach over and turn the knob.

I let my fingers glide over her panties, feeling the warmth and her slight squirm forward. Her fingers tangle in my hair holding me close to her. The jeans are constricting my growing bulge. I push the thin fabric to the side gliding my fingers back and forth a couple of times, teasing her a little more. The sexiest moan leaves her lips, slightly muffled by my kiss. She drops her head back giving me full access to her body.

I pick her up as she wraps her legs around me, and I walk us into the bedroom. I need more space than just this small island to satisfy the need we have.

Getting lost in everything Lola, her touch, her skin, her scent, *her*...is necessary to wash away the stink of what I am involved in.

She consumes every part of me when we are making love, but once it's over, my mind begins racing again, and my body tenses.

"Are you okay, baby?" I continue to hold her tightly, wishing the orgasmic afterglow would hold off all thoughts of doom that came crashing in right after.

"Yes. I told you, just a crap day." I answer her, not knowing why she would ask again. I thought I was able to distract her from her questions.

"Are you telling me everything?" She persists.

Not understanding where her line of questioning is coming from, I have no other way to go but to tell another lie. "Of course, I am. Why would you ask that?"

Her shoulders shrug as she tries to turn over.

"Nuh-uh." I hold her to me. "What's going on?"

She drops her face down and stays quiet.

"*Amor*, you need to talk to me. What's going on?" I press, worried she knows.

"I don't know."

I move to sit up, pulling her with me. She grabs the sheet, covering herself. Her eyes searching mine for all my hidden secrets.

"Tell me." I need to shut this down without scaring her.

She takes a deep breath, her eyes never leaving mine.

"You've been changing. Ever since you started at the club." Her gaze drops, and I stay quiet. "You are...I don't know, *hard*...for lack of a better word...most of the time now. I mean, I knew you were a badass," a small smile appears, "but now it's different. This badass persona you wear is always with you. You're closed off again. Like when I first met you. You were a vault that no one could penetrate. But as time went by, I saw *you*. Your determination, your loyalty, your love, the way you protect...That's why I fell. I fell for the person you are trying so hard to hide again."

"*Amor*, you have me. All of me. No one has ever penetrated so deep." I stop trying to find words to soothe her. "I have some things to take care of. Things I don't want to do, but I have to. Things I can't speak about. Nothing, and I mean nothing, will ever touch you. I will never let anything ever happen to you. Not while I'm alive."

Alive. That is the word that has been worrying me after my meeting today.

"Why can't you tell me? I will support you no matter what. You just have to be honest with me." She's pleading with me now.

"I am being honest. As soon as I can tell you everything, I will. I promise. I just can't risk it right now. Please understand. I'm trying to finish this shit up and move on. I'm moving on to be the man you need me to be." I take her face into my hands. "Please do not say anything. I will be fine. I just need a bit more time, baby. You don't need to worry about me."

She lets go of the sheet and crawls on my lap straddling me, holding tightly.

"Then just stop. Stay with me. I can support us until you find what makes you happy." A muffled whisper escapes.

"I can't let you do that. What kind of man would that

make me? I need to be able to take care of you. This will all come to an end and be forgotten history."

A nod of her head as she continues clutching me is my answer.

"I need you to keep this between us. You can't share what I just said with Toni and Javie. They will try to get involved, and I don't need to be worrying about them too." I push her shoulders back, separating us. "Promise me?"

"I promise." She comes back in, holding on to me tightly.

CHAPTER 16

LOLA

I know whatever he's doing isn't good. May not be legal. And I don't fully understand why he's doing it. As much as he's scaring me, I don't want to let him go. I can't let him go.

Finding the strength, I search his face for any clues.

"I promise not to say anything to Javie or Toni, but then you have to promise me something." I wait for him to agree before I continue.

"It depends," he answers.

"No. Not 'depends.' Promise me or don't." As fearful as I am of a tragic ending, I need this.

His eyes bore into me. I begin to move off of him, showing I can be just as much of a hard-ass if I want to. His hand grips into my hip, holding me in place.

"Okay. I promise," he concedes.

"If you find yourself in trouble, in between a rock and hard place or in over your head...anything of that sort, you let me know. You tell me what is going on. You are honest with me about everything."

"I don't need to. I will figure it out." He tries to take back his promise.

"Too bad. You already promised. Are you telling me that you are already breaking your promise to me?" I won't let him weasel out of this.

"I won't let anything I'm doing touch you. You will know everything once I'm away from it. Only then. That I will promise you." Pain is written across his face. I have never seen him look vulnerable. Even when his grandmother died, he was the rock, holding the family together. His bad-ass façade has fallen, exposing feelings.

"I love you." These are the only words I have left to say, and I hope they can hold us together.

SUMMER HAS COME TO AN END, and Greek rush life is back. A sorority-fraternity party is not Alex's idea of fun, but I was able to talk him into going since Garrett and Toni would be attending. And he couldn't fight a good cause. My sorority and Garrett's fraternity have come together to raise money for the food bank. We have rented out a club, and all the money raised at the door, and a portion of bar sales, will be donated.

"Thank you for getting tonight off." I say to Alex as we are getting dressed.

"I would be a dumbass if I let my girl go to this without me." He is pulling on his jeans as I am going through my dresses, trying to decide which I want to wear.

It's being held at a club, but attire is everything to this crowd. These people are not my idea of fun, but I did spend the past few weeks helping plan and organize. I need to participate in something to keep my active status.

Throwing a few options on the bed, I begin to panic I don't have the right dress. I look up at Alex, and he is dressed ready to go.

"How is it you look like you just stepped out of a high-fashion magazine?" His intense bad-boy appearance contrasts with his dark jeans, button-down, and jacket.

"You can wear your pajamas and still be the most gorgeous girl there." He steps up to me, wrapping me in his arms.

"Not true." I pout as the nerves about being surrounded by vapid sorority girls all night hit. I have chosen to distance myself from them the past couple of years. The materialistic, plastic attitude is everything I have come to despise. My time away in Italy showed me what was important and what I was missing in my life. But I still come back to it, for my mom. It is her legacy I want to live up to.

"To me, you are the most beautiful woman." He places a quick kiss on my forehead. "Are you going to pick one?" He points at the dresses I laid out on the bed.

"No. You are. Choice one." I slide the first dress on and give him a nice turn for the full view. I continue modeling each dress.

"The white one," he says automatically after I slip on the last one.

"I haven't even shown you this one."

"Don't need to. I was just waiting for you to finish, so I could tell you to go with the first one."

He chose a dress with a white, fitted top and a slightly flared skirt. The top was cut deep in the front and low in the back. He seems so sure, so I slip out of the last dress and place the first one back on. I find some nude heeled sandals, and I'm ready to go.

. . .

As we walk up, I watch as Alex transforms from the relaxed guy at the apartment to his dominant persona. At the door, he nods in recognition to the guy I hand the tickets to. I hid the amount I paid for the tickets from Alex. I didn't want him to feel obligated to pay.

Once inside, I ask, "Did you know the door guy?"

He nods giving me no other information about him. I decide now is not the right time to be talking about this.

"Let's get a drink." He places his hand on the small of my back, leading me through the small crowd.

At the bar, we order our drinks, and I begin to look around for Garrett and Toni. Not seeing them, I find Jasmine and Ariel with a couple of the guys Alex met over the summer. We exchange pleasantries for a few minutes before they excuse themselves to mingle with others. It was easy to ignore the difference between Alex and I all summer. But here, it is a stark reminder we don't have much in common except our love. As we move around and others come to say hello, Alex is not a part of it. He stands proud, exchanging greetings, but otherwise not participating in any of the conversation. Talk about classes, majors, internships are all things he has never been a part of. But through it all, he never faltered, his mask of intimidation firmly in place.

"So how long do we have to stay?" Toni startles me from behind.

"It's still early. What are you complaining about?" I turn to her, smiling.

"I know, but no matter how many of these Garrett forces me to go to, they are not my thing."

"What? Was I supposed to attend minus my girlfriend? You know that would have caused more drama than making you come," Garrett teases her in return.

Some people did not make it easy on Toni when she and Garrett became official. His wealth and her lack of it was a sore spot for many girls who thought they would be able to be the next Mrs. Anders. Watching the struggle Garrett had with people trying to use him for his money, power, and connections, I am glad mine is hidden. It is all tied up in a trust I ignore. My mother was the one with the true wealth, not that my dad is hurting for money. After her passing, my father refused any of her estate, instead placing it all in my name with a manager in charge. While my mother's name is prominent old money, I have my dad's last name. Only a few people have put together the connection, and since I don't flaunt it, I've been able to fly under the radar.

"These are exactly the places and connections I wanted you to make. This is the world you belong in," Alex directs at Toni quietly.

He is Toni's loudest cheerleader and will sacrifice himself in the process.

"I know, and I'm here, aren't I?" she replies, rolling her eyes at him.

"While I don't particularly care for this world either, you" I hit his chest with my index finger, "are more than you think."

He stays quiet, not showing any emotion, yet I know he is absorbing what I said.

"Come on. Dance with me." I grab his hand, dragging him behind me. I have wanted to dance with him since I was at El Mundo dancing with Javie. I want to get lost in the music with him.

I weave through people, finding a spot on the dance floor. I turn to face him and see his mask drop ever so slightly, showing a sexual longing. No one but me would notice that miniscule change in him.

His hand comes to my waist, and as soon as he begins moving to the music, I'm lost in him. I come in close, needing to feel him. His strength and masculinity are instant turn-ons. I'm lost in the feel of him, the bass thumping, and the lights. I don't know where we are headed, but I do know I don't want to go without him.

"Hey, Lola!" a sorority sister yells over the music, interrupting.

I turn to face her.

"Hey," I answer as I take a step away from Alex.

"The student newspaper is here and wants pictures of everyone who helped organize for an article."

"Oh. Okay." I turn back to Alex, grabbing his hand leading him off the dance floor. "Give me a few minutes. Let me go take this picture."

He tips his head slightly. I squeeze his hand before letting it go.

Rebecca, sorority president, is talking to a couple of my sisters as I approach.

"Ugh...where have you been? We've been waiting on you for this damn picture." Her frustration is clear.

"I was on the dance floor," I answer honestly.

"Whatever." She takes a deep breath, rolling her eyes.

She has never been the nicest person, but this is attitude is surprising.

"Let's get together." She swings her arms for the few girls gathered.

"What about the guys?" one girl asks.

"Since Lola decided to get lost, they took their picture already. We will have separate pics in the paper." Her exasperation exaggerated.

The underclassman looks at me sadly before moving to the couch in the corner. We all take our seats and smile on cue.

After he takes a few pictures, the photographer thanks us, walking away.

I begin to follow his lead, not wanting to spend any more time around them, but Rebecca stops me.

"Who the hell did you bring as your date? I have never seen him around," she lays in on me.

"His name is Alex, and he's my boyfriend." I answer her casually. Never has she shown any interest in anything I have done in all the time we have known each other.

"And he is?" she probes.

"What do you mean?" I don't know exactly where she's going with this line of questioning, but I have an idea, and it's not good.

"Does he go to school with us?" Her lips spread with a saccharine-sweet smile.

"I don't see how Alex is any of your business. Excuse me." I choose not to play her game.

I enter the ladies' room to take a few cleansing breaths, away from the shallow people I try so hard to avoid. I don't know why she would start in on me. We have spoken to each other on maybe a handful of occasions in all the years we have been sisters.

"Lola." As I walk out of the ladies' room, I hear my name called. I turn to see Jared, one of the fraternity brothers, taking the last couple of steps to reach me.

"Great job on this fundraiser. Some of the guys told me you were the driving force behind it." I smile at the unexpected praise.

"Thanks! I was hoping if we went big, we would have a greater donation to offer. I'm just glad it worked out," I reply proudly.

"Let me get you a drink." He takes my hand.

I pull away. "No need. I'm going to go find my boyfriend."

"I insist." He steps in closer to me.

"Not necessary." I move back a step, and I hit the wall.

He comes in close again, placing his hands on either side

of me; his lips are so close to my ear, I can feel his breath. "Drop the guy. He's a nobody. You took a ride on the wild side over the summer, and now you can check that off your bucket list."

I place my hands on his chest to push him back, repulsed by his sentiment. He's strong, and my shove doesn't do much.

"You know we make a much better match, right?" He kisses my neck. I try and push him back again unsuccessfully; his arrogance sickening.

Just as I was going to try and duck under his arms, he is pulled back. I look up to see Alex tugging him away from me.

"Your lips on my girl are not welcome." Alex's voice is even, but the rage in his eyes can't be missed. Alex steps in his personal space.

"She wanted it." Jared squares up.

I grab Alex's hand, "Come on, let's go." I try pulling him, but he stays firm shaking his hand until I release it.

"If she wanted it, why was she trying to push you back?" Alex's jaw is ticking. His intimidating stature is one thing, but this anger is something else entirely.

"She was just being a little shy and playing hard-to-get. You know how they are. She'll be riding me later." Jared taunts him by winking at me.

"Let's go, Alex." I try and get his attention, getting angry he won't let this go. All we need to do is walk away.

"Fuck with my girlfriend, you fuck with me." I watch Alex's hands begin to clench and unclench repeatedly.

"Look, dude. You were her summer fling. She needed to date a bad-boy low-life, and now she has. You're not her future. I am."

"Let's go!" I yell again. I look around and notice they have drawn a crowd.

"I'm going to say this only once. Touch my girl again and you will regret it."

"I don't think you want to start anything with me. Remember, I can buy my way out of anything." Jared answers coolly.

"That's right. The pussy way to go about things. You should probably learn to man-up and take care of business on your own without daddy's money. Be a real man. That's what Lola needs. A *real* man." Alex shoulders roll back just a fraction, and he has an evil glint in his eye.

"Fuck you!" Jared spits out, taking a swing at Alex.

Alex does not move, taking the full impact of Jared's punch without flinching. His lip busts, and blood starts running down his chin, but he is unmoving.

"Like I said, *pretty boy*," Alex taunts him, "Grow a pair of balls, then come back and we can talk."

Jared takes another swing, but this time Alex ducks, avoiding the hit, and comes back up, punching Jared in the gut. It knocks the wind out of him. Jared collapses on his knees, trying to catch his breath.

Just then, a couple of bouncers show up, grabbing Alex and Jared escorting them out. I watch, frozen in my spot.

"Time to go." Toni grabs my arm, pushing me in front of her, following in the wake the bouncers create as they pass through the crowd.

"...press charges!" As soon as I walk outside, I hear those two words leaving Jared's mouth.

"On who? You threw the first punch. We can call them, but they will take both of you in for disorderly conduct." One of the bouncers informs him, smiling. "We can do that if you like." He reaches into his pocket.

"Never mind. You are worthless." Jared takes a few steps towards the door, but another bouncer moves in front of him.

"Where do you think you are going?" The other bouncer chimes in.

"This is my fraternity party. You have to let me back in," Jared demands.

"We don't have to do anything. An organization rented it. Not you. You have no voice here. You can't go back in." He stands firm, unmoving. This is the same guy who Alex nodded to on our way in.

"Fuck this shit." Jared exclaims loudly continuing to complain as he walks towards the parking lot.

"Hey, Toni. Been a long time." The first bouncer greets her kindly.

"It has." She smiles brightly rolling her eyes. "Thanks, Mark." She winks at him, then turns to the bouncer at the door, "See you, Jay."

"Come on, princess, before your carriage turns into a pumpkin." Toni teases me, but I am far from being in a joking mood.

"Thanks, man." Alex claps hands with the first guy and lifts his chin to the guy at the door, who responds in kind.

"What the fuck, Alex? What the hell was that for? Just to put on a show?" I exclaim.

He comes up to me, reaching his arms around me, "Come on, babe, I'm tired. We'll talk when we get home."

I step back out of his reach. "Go home, Alex. I need to think."

"What?" His eyes narrow. "You need to think? Think about what exactly?"

"Tonight. I don't know why you thought you needed to go all effing caveman. I could have handled my own crap." My voice increases with each word. "But instead of letting me deal with my people, you go and make a scene and embarrass me in front of everyone. Like I wasn't already the center of talk. Now I'm going to have to listen to this to."

"*Es mi vieja o no?*" (Are you my woman or not?) Alex's eyes fill with an anger directed at me.

"What? You know I don't know Spanish!" I exclaim frustrated, mortified, and furious.

"Never mind. You go ahead and deal with *your*," he air quotes with his fingers as he emphasizes the word sarcastically, "people. I don't know why I believed you would be different."

Toni steps in between us. "Hold up, guys. Tensions are high and adrenaline is still flowing. Maybe you both need to stop talking."

"Uber is here," Garrett calls out.

"Can I have it?" I turn, walking away from Alex.

CHAPTER 17

ALEX

GARRETT OPENS THE DOOR FOR HER AND WAITS AS SHE GETS in, closing it behind her. I watch as he opens the passenger door, talking with the driver.

Fuck my life! Everything happened so fast. If this is how she wants to handle things, then let her. It probably wasn't going to work out anyway. I'm not surprised. This is the story of my life. Managing all the crap the universe likes to throw my way. She's just another girl.

"Come on." Garrett claps my shoulder, getting my attention. Toni is climbing into a car. "We'll go to y'alls place tonight."

THE FREEZER IS the first place I head once we get home. An ice-cold bottle of tequila greets me. I grab a glass in one hand and the bottle in the other, walking out into the living room. I place both in front of me on the coffee table, sit on the couch, and fill the glass.

The cool liquid leaves a nice burn as I take a large swig. Leaning back, my head hits the wall. Another swig. As much as I don't want to care about her walking away, I do. My chest physically hurts knowing she doesn't want me. Knowing that, in trying to protect her, I somehow fucked up. Shouldn't surprise me. I've fucked up more times than I can count. Leaving destruction everywhere I go. I don't know if I'm more pissed at her or myself right now. I know the game. I know better than to get attached to anyone. I know everything crashes and burns around me. I know good things don't happen to me. I know this, and yet I let myself foolishly believe they could.

And I'm pissed at her for pushing things. Why the hell did she push so hard for us if she was just going to walk away so easily?

Another swig.

"Mind if I pour myself one?" Garrett enters the room.

"Help yourself."

He grabs a glass from the kitchen; he comes back and sits on the chair, pouring himself a drink.

"So what happened?" he asks.

"I handled business, and Lola got pissed."

It's quiet for a couple of minutes, neither of us talking.

"Can I give you a few words?" he starts cautiously.

"Yeah..."

"I don't know what started it, but Lola hates attention from that crowd. She can be the most persistent, happy, and caring person, but she doesn't want to be in the spotlight for it. Especially if she could be judged for it."

What is he talking about? How could she not be the center of attention?

"I'm confused." I take another swig, hoping numbness comes quickly. Home is the only place I can do this. I will never lose control of myself where I can't control my surroundings.

"I don't know exactly what happened her freshman year, but whatever it was it stayed with her. Toni's told me some things. And last year, she invited people to her place and almost had a panic attack. She really doesn't like her sorority. She is only in because it was her mother's sorority. She only did it for her mom."

"Then why did she go out of her way to be a part of this thing tonight?"

"She had to in order to stay active. In order to keep your status, you have to participate. I don't know how much she has done to stay active."

"Oh..." I'm beginning to feel like a jackass.

"Just thought you should know." He finishes what he has in his glass and stands up. "Good night."

Pulling out my phone I type out *I'm sorry. I love you*

I press send. Then wait. And wait. Three dots appear, announcing I may get a response.

I love you

Hope. The only problem with hope is, I don't know if I should have it. What if it causes the fall to be even more painful when it comes?

Sleep is what I need now. I polish off the tequila in my glass and head to my room.

KISSES on my back and soft hands on my shoulders wake me.

"Good morning, *amor*." Seeing her here in my room, with no makeup and puffy eyes, breaks my heart all over again. "I'm sorry for last night."

"I'm sorry too. I shouldn't have left you like that. I panicked." A couple of tears escape her eyes.

I bring her down, clutching her tightly against me. The

wetness from her tears now flowing freely down my chest as her body trembles slightly with the soft sobs. How could I have gotten it so wrong? In jealousy, I hurt her.

Jealousy. That is a foreign word for me. Never having those feelings for anyone. Never giving a shit about anyone. All the girls before Lola could come and go. There was never an emotional attachment. I could care less if they left because I was sure to find another to satisfy me.

"Shhhh," I whisper trying to help calm her. "I've got you." And in saying these words, I know I don't want to let her go again.

Her arm comes out from between us to wrap around my side. Her deep long breaths an indication she is slowly calming down. After a few minutes she begins to wiggle out of my embrace, sitting up. She crosses her legs in front of her, facing me, and I sit up, leaning against the wall.

"I'm sorry." she begins.

"Babe, I'm the one who should be sorry," I interrupt her before she can go any further.

"Maybe, but I *do* need to apologize." She wipes her eyes as a couple more tears fall. "I should not have left without you. I handled everything wrong last night. I freaked out and ran."

"Why did you freak out?" Is this what Garrett mentioned last night?

"I'm sure you have noticed that I don't hang with many people from the sorority. I have a couple of friends there, and even then, I don't trust them fully. I don't know if their loyalty would lie with me or the '*sisters*,'" she air quotes. She takes a deep, calming breath then continues.

"I was them. I was as shallow as they come. If you had met me in high school, you would have hated me. I was a superficial bitch. But life kicked me, and I re-evaluated. When my mom died, I was broken. I was lost my freshman year. I tried to keep up appearances for my sisters, but when

I would break down, they weren't there for me. Times when I was grieving, weekends I needed a shoulder to lean on, they were more interested in getting wasted and partying and who they could pick up. My pain was an inconvenience."

She squirms a bit. "After a while, I was at a low. I couldn't find a reason for joy. I plastered on a smile and went on. A mask to hide the parts that others found to be a bother. Then came the critiques and judgements. Anything I did was wrong. Not superficial enough. So I left. That's when I decided on a year abroad. I ran."

Listening to her story is painful. I can't believe this perfect beauty could be judged for anything except being the warm, generous person she is.

"I'm—" I begin to apologize again, but she stops me.

"Don't. You didn't know. I couldn't sleep last night. All I kept thinking is, "Why am I still letting these fools dictate my life?" Why did I care what they thought of me? I have stayed in the sorority for my mom. She always wanted me to be a part of what she said was the place she found some of her best friends. But if she were here and I wasn't happy with these people, she wouldn't want me to stay just because. I'm sorry because I gave them the power last night. I let their opinions of me take me away from you. I left you. I ran again."

She scrambles into my lap, wrapping her arms around my neck, holding me tightly. One hand comes up to cradle her head, and I let the other run up and down her back gently.

"I don't want to run away from you again," she mumbles, her face tucked in my neck.

I let her stay like this for a bit. Holding her, wanting to protect her from anyone who could hurt her.

"Is it my turn yet?"

Her head nods while still laying on my shoulder.

"I was jealous last night. And I didn't handle it well." She pulls back, looking at me.

"Wait, what? You were jealous?"

"Yes. I saw him try to kiss you, and I saw red. I wanted to kill him right there, but I do know better than to lose complete control. I didn't realize it was jealousy last night. I just reacted. The thing is, I have never reacted that way because of a girl. Not once. Girls could come and go, and I didn't care one way or the other. There would always be another. But when I saw you with him...my heart dropped, and it was instant rage."

"I don't want anyone but you." She grabs my face with both her hands kissing me passionately as she rocks against me. "Make love to me."

"I love you." I tell her before rolling her over covering her body with mine. "You are beautiful and strong. Never doubt that."

Just then Lola's phone chimes. We ignore it, our lips coming together in a need-filled kiss. Another chime...then a few more.

"What is going on?" I pull away from her reaching over to the side table to get her phone and hand it to her.

I roll onto my back, giving her a moment to check her messages.

"Oh my gawd, Alex." I hear fear in her voice.

"What?"

"They might arrest you for assault." She rolls to her side, giving me her phone.

I swipe through the messages from Ariel and Jasmine, giving her a heads up; then some guy sent her a video of me punching the asshole and him dropping like a pansy.

"What are we going to do?" Her eyes fill with fear.

"Nothing yet." Sitting up I crack my neck to the side, hoping Toni hasn't lost her edge. "Come on."

I pull on a pair of shorts before walking out into the kitchen, hoping they are up already. Garrett is in the kitchen putting the coffee on.

His lips pull slightly when he sees Lola behind me, "Good morning."

"Is Toni up?" I ask him.

"Nope, still in bed." He continues with the coffee.

I turn back to Lola. "Babe, go wake her up and tell her to come here."

She looks at me, perplexed, but turns away, walking back to the bedrooms.

I take a seat at the table to wait for her. Garrett takes an empty chair, "Do I want to ask what is going on?"

"You can, but let's wait and see if Toni is still walking both lives."

"Not even gonna ask what that means." He shakes his head.

"Everyone is here today?" Javie walks in. "Just as I was getting used to the peace and quiet alone here." Toni is living with Garrett, and I have spent so many nights at Lola's, I hadn't thought much about Javie being alone here at the house so much.

"Sorry," I apologize to him, even though technically it is my home too.

"What the fuck for? It's our house. Y'all can come and go as you please. You know that." He goes to the counter and stands in front of the coffeemaker. "But I do get the first cup." He yawns, rolling his neck.

It's quiet for a moment before Javie asks, "Should I be worried?" His brow cocks in question.

"Don't know yet. Waiting for Toni," I answer, knowing never to show fear.

He tips his head once then turns to the counter to begin fixing his mug.

"I swear y'all have your own way of things. One day I will know exactly how things go." Garrett smiles, truly curious about our life.

"If you stay with Toni, you'll probably learn more than you want. But you can also help us live both lives. I don't think we will ever forget the life lessons engrained growing up here, but we do need to be able to assimilate into a world away." The more I think about a life with Lola, the more I know I can't stay planted in the hood. I forced Toni to stay away, and I will need to do this also. I will need to be able to handle a normal life. I will need to be the chameleon I told her to become. And if I leave, Javie will do the same.

"What is so important you had to wake me up?" Toni comes into the kitchen plopping herself in a chair, crossing her arms on the table and placing her head down.

"Did you take any video last night?" I ask her.

"Really? That's what you woke me for? What do you think I am? An amateur?" She hasn't lifted her head, speaking with her eyes closed. "Lola, get my phone."

Lola walks back out and returns with the phone, placing it on the table next to Toni.

"Check for yourself." Toni remains unmoving.

I open her phone to the pics, and sure enough, there is a longer video of the frat guy hitting me, throwing the first punch. The relief is instant. This is all I need to contain the assault charge, but I may still get charged with disorderly conduct. Doubt he will want to have to go through that, though.

"I taught you well."

"Are you going to fill in the others who are still confused?" Garrett asks.

Lola comes closer to me, and I pull her onto my lap.

"People just sent Lola texts warning her that they are going to press charges on me for the incident last night. Sent her an edited video of me punching that asshole. Nothing before. Toni has the full video of him punching me." I explain.

"Good thing you haven't lost your edge, Toni." Javie pipes in. "So why are you punching people at a frat party?"

"For trying to kiss Lola." My blood pressure rises thinking of it again.

"Good reason. Now show me the video." Javie holds his hand out for the phone.

"Hold up." I send the video to myself and Lola, then hand him the phone.

"And you take video because?" Garrett questions.

"You never know. Here in the hood, it could be to calm families and friends from trying to get involved. Kick someone's ass and then they want revenge, so they get their families involved. Video can prove that you didn't go looking. Many times people wanted to come after us. We needed a way to avoid shit when possible. Sometimes it was to send a message." I shrug because most times it wasn't needed, but when you do need it, it can be a lifesaver.

"Damn! Why did you take the hit?" Javie asks.

"To see what I was up against. If he dropped me, I knew I would get back up. If he didn't, I knew I didn't need to put in much effort."

"What?" Lola exclaims looking at me.

"That's one way of doing it." Garrett nods, impressed.

"Contain the testosterone, please." Toni says, bored with the conversation.

"Lola, send this video to whatever guy texted you and your friends. It needs to get out there." I'm taking a risk by spreading it to others. It could embarrass him into staying quiet and letting things go or embarrass him into wanting to take things further. "Wait. Hold up." I place my hand on Lola's phone, halting her typing.

"Garrett, do you know this guy?" I ask the only person who may know how things will go.

He nods his head.

"If it goes around, will he try and retaliate because of embarrassment or let things go?" I need to play this smart with Lola involved. I don't want her to unnecessarily take heat because of me.

"He will retaliate. He's big, new money who thinks the world owes him." He answers honestly.

"New money" means nothing to me, but I'm sure it is something I will need to learn soon.

"Just send it to the guy that sent the video, then. No one else. I'm sure he will get it back to his friend. To your friends, just tell them I'm handling it. Nothing else. Let him back off quietly. I'll let him save face."

"You sure?" she asks me.

"Yes."

She picks up her phone, and I watch her do exactly as I said.

"If there is nothing else, I'm going back to bed." Toni gets up yawning and walking away.

"She is no rancher." I laugh at Garrett. He may be an early riser, being trained his whole life to wake early for work, but Toni loves her sleep.

He shakes his head in resignation.

CHAPTER 18

LOLA

NOT WANTING TO BE ALONE TONIGHT AFTER ALL THE chaos of the day and with Alex going in to work, I decide to stay at his house. Javie agreed to stay in with me for a movie night. Once Alex knew I wouldn't be home alone, I saw the visible relief in his shoulders. I'm not sure why he insists on carrying everyone's burden. Pizza and popcorn fill the coffee table in front of us.

"So what did you want to watch? And please don't torture me with some girly movie," Javie asks me, laughing.

"I'll let you pick since you are giving up a Saturday night for me."

"Why was that guy trying to kiss you if you are with Alex?" Javie asks without looking at me. He is scrolling through shows and movies.

"Guys like that think they can have whatever they want. They think their money makes them more attractive than what they are." This is the best explanation I can give.

"Every guy thinks they are more attractive than what they

really are." His laugh booms. "Except me of course. I know exactly how good I am." He winks at me teasingly.

I roll my eyes at him. "Yes, you and your brother know exactly how cute y'all are and use it."

"Correction. I use it. Alex does nothing, and they still come sniffing around."

I shove him playfully. "Don't remind me. They even like to sniff around while I'm with him."

"Sorry."

"Don't be. Not your fault."

"I know. But I also know he does nothing for it or to encourage it. Does he?" His eyes narrow, waiting for me to answer.

"No. He never encourages and always makes me feel like the only girl in the room." Pride fills me, knowing he loves me.

He nods knowingly. "Found one."

Javie clicks play to an action movie.

LIGHT through the blinds wakes me. I creep out of bed quietly so I don't wake Alex. I'm not sure what time he got in last night, because I didn't hear him. I slept so soundly in his bed. I didn't experience the uneasy feeling I usually have sleeping at the apartment when he is working. I don't know if it was because I was in his space, because his brother was next door, or just because of all the drama we endured the night before.

We had our first fight, and I'm not proud of the way I handled myself. The thing he wants the most, to protect me, I didn't let him do. I punished him for doing what comes naturally to him. He is a protector, and I took that from him. It hadn't dawned on me before.

I grab my backpack and head into the kitchen for coffee

and to take advantage of the quiet to get some homework done. It's my last year, and I can't wait to be done and away from so many people.

"Hey, gorgeous, how long have you been up?" Alex comes up to me a couple of hours later, giving me a kiss then taking a seat.

"For a bit. Got lots of work done. Javie took off about an hour ago."

"So we are finally alone?" A suggestive smirk appears.

"We are." I close my laptop placing my elbows on the table leaning into my hand.

"You know I've heard make-up sex is the best kind of sex." He winks at me.

"Is that so?" I tease.

"Well, I couldn't tell you for sure because I've never had a fight, but I'm willing to give it a try to test it. You in?" He stands, extending his hand to me.

I place mine in his, letting him lead us back into his room to see what all the talk is about.

ALEX'S HEARTBEAT is thumping softly as I lay my head on his chest. I'm lazily dragging my fingers around his stomach, watching him tense slightly when I hit a ticklish spot. While I agree that make-up sex is pretty dang good, for me, it was reconnecting with him. Realistically, I knew a fight would come up, but I didn't think it would be caused by my actions. Being close to him again was necessary for me.

"Have you heard anything more from the texts you sent yesterday?" Alex asks, breaking the silence.

"No. But I was going to see if Garrett heard anything. He may hear things before I do. Not everyone will speak to him because most of them have probably figured out you are Toni's cousin." I really wished we didn't need to talk about this. I wish it would all just go away. He does not need another burden to carry.

"Yeah. I was going to ask him myself. I just wanted to make sure no one was giving you any trouble."

"No one has said anything to me." I tell a little white lie.

While they haven't brought up the fight, many have been critical of who my boyfriend is. I have ignored many texts today from sisters wondering why I'm dating "beneath" me. They begin by celebrating his good looks, but then switch it up, letting me know I should only "bag the help," then move on.

And Jared did text me. He didn't mention the fight, though. He wanted to remind me who he was and how suited we are to each other. He knows who I am by the tone of his text. He wants me for my name, not for who I am. Before now he has never paid much attention to me except pleasantries. If he is pushing this hard without even actually asking me out on a date to get to know me, he just wants my name to boost his.

"Good." His hand is softly stroking lines up and down my back.

"What are you going to do if he decides to press charges?" I don't want to think what could happen, but I can't live in ignorance.

"I will handle it. Just like I've handled everything else that comes up. I'm a survivor. But that is not something that you need to think about. I'll take care of it."

I lift my head to look up at him. "But I do worry about it. I know you like being in charge. I get it. That is one of the first things I noticed about you. But you are in a relationship now. You will need to trust me to help. However I can."

He begins his shaking his head. I nod in response.

"I know I didn't handle things well."

"Stop. I will take care of things if and when I need to. End of story." His is voice somber.

"I don't want to fight with you again, so I'm backing off. But I will not be some princess who can't take care of things. I will be an equal in this relationship. I know you will have a hard time with it. I know you are a control freak. But I will wear you down with time. Because that's what we got. All the time together."

"Maybe." His lips spread in a small smile. "Come here."

I crawl up, meeting my lips to his.

I pull back, running my finger over his lip where it is split from the hit he took. He grabs my finger wrapping it in his hand, kissing the tip then bringing me back to him.

"Anyone home?" Toni's voice breaks through as she shouts.

"No!" Alex yells out.

"Okay. I guess you don't want to know what I know." Her voice is on the other side of the door now.

Alex quietly groans. "We're coming out."

We dress grudgingly before exiting his room.

"What news?" Alex inquires as soon as he enters the living room, where Toni is sitting on the couch.

"You don't need to worry about anything." She scrunches her nose, smirking. "He wasn't happy when the video was spread by his friend. The guys seemed to be more impressed with Alex not going down on the first punch. Ass would rather let it die down and forget about it than have to continue living through it if he took it to another level."

I've watched the video several times. At the time, I was scared by the situation but seeing it again after the fact, Alex taking the hit without flinching was a complete turn-on. He was in charge and never gave an inch. That powerful and intimidating man is mine. He loves me. And I am hopelessly in love with him.

"Good." Alex responds.

"That's it?" Toni asks.

"Yes. It's over, and we don't have to think about it anymore. I don't want it to affect Garrett at his frat house. Those are his people, and you are with him. I can't let our relation set about another round of crap for y'all."

"We're good. Lola on the other hand..."

"I don't know if I'm going to stay in."

"What?" Alex turns to me.

"I don't like those people anyway. What am I doing there?" My lips turn down as my shoulders shrug in defeat.

"I won't have you giving up anything for me."

"It's not for you. It's for me. It doesn't make me happy."

"Good for you." Toni smiles at me. "You do you."

CHAPTER 19

ALEX

I HADN'T HEARD FROM DAVID, HECTOR'S LACKEY, UNTIL I received this cryptic text to deliver to a new location. I was hesitant to do it, not wanting to take orders from a new kid. I considered telling him no, but I obliged, not knowing how he fits into all this. The first time he contacts me is to make a delivery I'm sure he can handle. The amount is strange, not enough to be for a true supplier, but too much for a single toker.

Parked in front of the house, the only thought floating through my mind is *trap*. I'm in a nice, family-friendly neighborhood. Nothing about this feels right. I look around, trying to get a feel for it. The burner chimes.

Forget the drop.

I don't think twice. I put the car in drive and speed away. Hector's text confuses me, but I'm not questioning it right now. A few minutes pass then another chime.

House now.

Something is off if I'm getting conflicting direction. I

haven't needed to go to the house since meeting David, and now two different orders and I'm being dragged back.

I walk up, ignoring Jefe's guys stationed outside. I want to know what happened today before this little inexperienced shit gets me busted for something I don't even want to do.

Hector is waiting at the open door.

"You got here fast."

"When I feel like I'm being set up to get busted, you better believe I'm going to get my ass here fast." I may be overstepping, but I refuse to go down because some asshole is trying to make it big too fast and not learning the game.

He lowers his voice. "*Calma.*" (Calm down.)

I stay quiet, waiting to see what Jefe says about this. I follow Hector into the office, and David is sitting in a chair opposite Jefe. I stay standing against the wall behind David.

"Alejandro," Jefe leans back in his seat as he greets me, tilting his head to me. "Want to tell us what the fuck happened today?"

"You tell me. I get one order from David and then another from Hector." I'm reining in my temper right now.

"David?" Jefe directs at him.

"I got a lead. I thought it would be a clean, profitable, long-term relationship." The shit is trying to justify his stupidity. I got to give it to him, he is holding his own.

"And you did what with this information?" Jefe presses.

"I texted Alex to get the product to them." I study David, trying to learn more about him. I need the upper hand on this one.

"And this lead came from? *Dime todo ahora porque,*" (*Tell me everything because*) Jefe growls, "I'm getting fucking tired of asking questions." It seems Jefe is getting close to losing it.

"I met this guy at Frankie's Billiards. He was drunk and bragging about his product. I offered him a better deal if he upped his purchase amount. He showed me pictures of his product and cash to prove he was legit."

This fuckwad thinks pictures are enough to jump into a new deal with the amount he wanted me to deliver. *Fuck*.

"That's it? No recon. No questioning. No letting Hector check up on things. You just sent in my guy? Do I have that correct?" Jefe bangs his fists on the desk.

David's color drains from his face. He stays silent.

"And you *pendejo*?" (*dumb ass*) Jefe turns to Hector. "You let this happen?"

"I will watch him better."

"*Que´ te dije?*" (What did I tell you?) Jefe's face is turning red; he's not bothering to hide his anger any longer. "After the mess with the other two, I thought you learned!"

Hector, knowing better, stays silent; no explanations or excuses will be tolerated.

"*No aguantare´ esta estupidez.*" (*I will not tolerate this stupidity*.)
"Yes, sir."

"*Vete. Los dos.*" Jefe dismiss them from the room. He has not looked in my direction. I'm unsure whether I should stay or go.

"Alejandro." I stay unmoving. "*Siéntate.*"

I sit on the chair Davis vacated at Jefe's command.

"Why did you go?"

"I got an order. When you introduced him before, he was below Hector. I was questioning it, but what did you expect me to do?" I hate to admit I was following blindly, but that is the game we play.

"But you knew it was a bad idea."

"Hell yeah. First, he gave me no info on the buyer except name, address, and amount. Nothing." If I'm going to get out, I need to make my stand now. "What kind of shit is that? I don't work that way. You know that. I play smart or not at all. The address he gave me was in some nice cookie-cutter neighborhood. Pill poppers there, probably, but weed? C'mon. This isn't my first day on the job. I'm doing this for now, but it won't be my forever. I want normal. If I'm going to get normal, I need to make sure to keep my nose clean."

"How far did you get?"

"I was in the car, contemplating whether to get down and how I was going to do it. I never met the person he sent me to."

"Good. David is new, and Hector should have known better than to leave him to his own devices. You do not take any more orders from David. You do your business, and all other orders will come directly from me. I'm doing David's dad a favor right now. He has been in lock-up for the past twelve years. Now that David's of age, I'm taking him under my wing."

I stay silent, knowing there is nothing to say to it.

"You want out?" He caught that.

"The only reason I came back was to repay the debt. You have been good to me. You have let me call my shots. Gave me the freedom to do this without going all in. You didn't need to do that, but you did."

He stares at me, and I am worried about how it's being received.

"Do you know why I did that?"

I shake my head, wondering if he will change his mind and demand I'm jumped into the SEV now.

"Because you have been loyal since the beginning. You are not like your dad at all, except in the loyalty department. He would die three times over for me. This last time he was busted, he took the fall and took no one down with him. He is a loose cannon and flies off the handle too much, but when he goes down, he goes down alone.

"You have kept your head down. Worked hard. Didn't play into all the crap that goes on. And you stay quiet. That is why.

That is the only reason why. What are you planning for later?"

"To be honest, I don't know. Toni is making something of herself. So is Javie now. So I figured maybe I should give normal a try."

Silence consumes us. The fear of breathing too loudly is causing me to hold it a bit.

"You can go. Remember, do your business and nothing else" he finally says after a couple of minutes.

Without another word, I stand exiting the room.

In my car, I can't help but think of everything that just happened. Jefe didn't tell me no. He didn't force El SEV on me. He didn't give his permission or blessing, but it's a start. So much of what I had been dreading about walking away is beginning to fade. I just need a bit more time, and I may be able leave with no hard feelings.

LOLA

WALKING to my car after my last class for the day, I'm excited Alex has his first weekend off. He has been working every weekend, only taking one night off to go to a frat party that caused him more trouble than just going in to work. I didn't plan anything, not sure if Alex wanted to stay in a relax or go out.

A few more months and this journey will be over. A full load this semester and only two more classes next one, and I will be done. I never really decided what I wanted to do, so I settled on a business degree, specializing in marketing. Not that I will stick to it, but at least I have completed something. It feels like I have been floundering with no direction for so long, finishing something makes me proud.

I can bounce around life all I want, and I will still be okay.

I can go to school, take time away, do whatever, and still land on my feet. Alex does not have this freedom. It just occurred to me that I am doing exactly what he is doing, trying to figure out the next step. But I have the comfort of failing and not hitting bottom. If he fails, he may. He does not have the security of family and money to pick him up again.

I don't know how this has never come to mind. We are like souls, looking for our future, but going about it very differently. We have to. Life has dictated the way we search.

"Lola!" Ariel yells my name as she exits the building I'm walking past.

I stop, waiting for her to catch up to me.

"Hey. What's up?" I greet her.

"Not much. I haven't seen you around since the frat party," she begins. "I just wanted to check on you. I was going to text you but thought it was insensitive. You know with everything that happened. I didn't want you thinking that I was trying to gossip or anything."

With other sisters texting their catty comments, I'm glad she didn't. I may not have trusted her intentions. I've avoided the house and all places the sisters like to congregate on campus so I could avoid their comments.

"It's fine. Really. Not much happened. It just died down and went away. That was best for everyone. Why drag out a stupid bar fight?" I shrug nonchalantly. I want to trust her.

"True. I'm glad for you. It was stupid." She smiles brightly then continues, "So we were thinking of hitting up El Mundo this weekend. Jasmine met a guy that could get us on the list. He told us we could get in six people." Her excitement shows.

"I would love to." I answer quickly. I want to be there with Alex. I wonder if he would go as a patron? "I need to ask Alex. He is off this weekend, so I don't want to ditch him. Who all were you going to ask?"

"You, me, and Jasmine. Jasmine was thinking of Jason

since she wants to try and hook up with the guy who works there."

"She's taking her gay boyfriend to have a dance partner and still be able to flirt with the guy." I laugh at her creativity.

"Something like that."

"Okay. I'll ask Alex and let you know. But you don't need to hold the spots for us. Alex can get us in. He knows people."

"You sure?"

"Yeah. If he wants to go, he can get us on the list. Not a problem."

"Okay. Saturday. Text me and let me know."

We hug and depart in our different directions.

THE SMELL of something delicious assaults my senses as soon as I open the front door of Alex's house.

"I'm instantly hungry now," I announce, walking into the kitchen to find Alex in workout shorts and a muscle shirt.

"*Hola hermosa*." He turns his head, giving me his naughty smile before going back to stirring something.

"Whatcha making?" I sit at the table.

"Everything. Carne asada, beans, rice, salsa...Hope you're hungry."

"Wow. All that for me?"

"Yes. Anything for you," he says easily.

I walk up to him, wrapping my arms around his middle, placing my head on his strong back. One of his hands grabs my arm holding me to him. These quiet times when it's just the two of us, no one would know how different we are. We are just two people who are attracted to each other. Two people who enjoy each other's company. Two people who respect each other. Two people who found love.

"What's wrong?" He turns around in my arms to face me.

I lean into his chest relishing the security I feel.

"Nothing. It just has seemed like a lot lately. I needed to feel you."

"What's a lot?" He squeezes me a little tighter.

"Everything. Nothing. I don't know." Remembering he is in the middle of cooking, I pull away. "I better let you get to it, or you will burn my dinner." I look up to him.

He gives me a chaste kiss, letting me go, slapping my butt as I walk away. I sit down appreciating the view: a tattooed, muscled, bad boy cooking.

"Where's Javie?" I wonder out loud.

"Working, I guess. I haven't seen him since this morning."

"Would you consider going to El Mundo as a customer?" I want to go, but I don't want to push him into going if he would rather not. We can find someplace else to have fun if he would rather avoid it.

"Why?" he asks as he pulls plates out of the cabinet.

"No reason. Just wondering if you would go since you work there." I try to play it off as curiosity.

He doesn't answer as I watch him serve each plate. He grabs them both, placing them on the table and returning to the drawer for utensils. He sits and takes his first bite, smiling while watching me.

I roll my eyes at him before giving in, "Fine. Ariel said they were going Saturday. Jasmine met one of the door guys, who was going to put them on the list. I wanted us to go."

"Since you asked me so nicely, yes, I will take you. Now eat."

I take a bite and am in heaven.

"I don't want to make you go if you don't want to. If you would rather avoid the place you work on your night off, I understand." I shove a bite-size piece of tortilla filled with asada into my mouth.

"If you want to go, I will take you."

CHAPTER 20

ALEX

I WOULD GIVE THIS GIRL THE MOON IF I COULD. I'M NOT IN that position yet, but I will work my ass off until I can. I will be the man she deserves. She loves me, and I need to show her I can take care of her in the way she is accustomed.

Do I want to go to the club? Not really. But if she wants to drink and dance in an upscale club, then that is what she will do.

She walks out of the bathroom wearing only a tiny thong and a see-through bra, making her way to the closet. I'm instantly hard watching her.

"Hey," I call to her.

"What?" She asks without turning around.

"I need you to help me with this." I'm tenting my boxers, and I don't want to wait until later tonight to get some relief.

"With what?" She finally turns around, looking at me lying in bed. I glance down at myself giving her a clue.

She takes her bottom lip into her mouth, holding a sexy smirk.

"And what would you like me to do?" She takes a few steps closer to the bed.

"Whatever you like." I stroke myself a couple of times.

She's by the bed, watching me. My fingers trace the thin strings of her thong, making their way down between her legs. She spreads her legs a fraction, and I feel the moisture of her longing.

She hooks her fingers on the strings, sliding them down her legs, then straddling me. She slides my cock into her slick center. She rocks into me, taking charge. She leans down, kissing me, her tongue gliding over my lips then sliding in. She pulls back again, in control and speeding up her pace. I feel her clenching as an orgasm takes over quickly. I grab her hips and guide her for a few more strokes before letting go myself.

She falls into my chest, her heart racing as she takes a few deep breaths.

"Are you trying to distract me from getting dressed?" she asks. I'm still inside her.

"No. I just got a little excited watching you prance around the room wearing nothing."

"I'm wearing panties and a bra," she counters.

"Panties and a bra that hide nothing and make you look hot as hell." She sits up, rocking herself a bit.

"Keep that up and I'll be ready for round two." I grab her breast, pinching her nipple just a bit, teasing her.

"Okay. I'll play fair." She comes in for a quick kiss before getting up. "I'll go clean up."

I CALLED in to check availability for tables earlier. I won't take a table if they could possibly go to paying customers, but since only a couple were reserved, I asked for one. She texted her friends, letting them know to meet us in the reserved area when they arrive. Walking through the club, it is a much different experience being on this side. I can't help but check stations as I pass though. I have never come to this club to hang out. I have actually avoided it.

"What do you want to drink?" I pull a chair out for her.

"Bacardi and diet please." She looks back at me smiling.

"I'll be back." I kiss her cheek.

I head to the bar dedicated to the reserved area, where Jen smiles at me, "That one looks familiar." She nods in Lola's direction.

"Shut up and make me a Barcardi and diet and get me a Budweiser."

She laughs at me, getting busy.

She places Lola's drink on the counter, then pops the top from the beer bottle. "Would you like an iced glass, sir?" She continues her sarcastic assault.

"No, just give me the damn bottle." She laughs as she hands it to me. "But seriously, if I am not with her, keep eyes on her. Please. That's my girlfriend, Lola. Give her whatever she wants."

"You got it, boss." I turn, walking back to the table.

I learned early on Jen is trustworthy, takes the job seriously, plays it straight, and treats everyone in the club with respect. She may tease and have fun, but she is here to make money and leaves drama at the door. That is sometimes hard to find when you work with young people who want to party while working. I've had to fire a couple of bartenders that were shitfaced by the end of their shifts because they did too many shots with customers.

"Are your friends on their way?" I place her drink in front of her.

"She texted they were at the door, but I haven't seen them yet." She is looking around.

"I'll go check on them."

"You sure?"

"Yes. Stay put."

Her brilliant smile is the only thanks I need.

At the door, I find one of the guys has stopped them from entering.

"Hi, Alex," Ariel greets me, smiling.

"Hello," I respond to her. "What's going on?" I ask the guy who has stopped them.

"I don't have her name on the list." He points at Jasmine. "She says Joe was putting their names on it, but he's not here yet."

"They're fine. When Joe arrives let him know his guests are inside and not to add more to the list."

Out of the corner of my eye, I watch as Ariel and Jasmine's eyes widen at my direction. He unhooks the rope, letting the group walk past.

Walking in, I can see some random guy standing and speaking with Lola. I knew the vultures would come in hard and fast with her. She doesn't realize how gorgeous she is and how many guys want her attention. Just then I see Jen step up, speaking to the guy. He smiles at her, tips his head, and walks away. Lola looks up at Jen as they exchange a few words before Jen walks back to the bar.

At the table, everyone grabs a chair, and Ariel begins introductions. Ariel and Jasmine are accompanied by a girl and two guys I have not met.

"You work here?" Ariel directs to me.

"I do. I'm one of the bar managers," I answer.

"Why didn't you say so when we talked?" Ariel asks Lola. "I was worried this whole time that y'all wouldn't be able to get in." She smiles, shaking her head.

Why would she hide that I worked here?

"I told you Alex would get us in." She smiles timidly. "I

just don't want people always asking to get on the list if they know he can do it. It's not fair to him."

"We won't." Jasmine jumps into the conversation. "Alex, what can you tell me about Joe? Good guy or not?"

How do I answer this? He's a guy. I don't know if he likes her or if he just thinks he can get into her pants. I don't think he's part of any of the questionable business running through here, so I guess that is a plus.

"He's okay, I guess," shrugging and keeping my answer vague, "I don't really work with the door guys, so I'm not sure."

"Urgh." She smiles, but I can tell she wants him and probably doesn't want to be used.

One of the guys they came with, Johnny, comes back with several beers.

He picks up one of them, bringing it in towards the middle of the table, "Cheers!"

"This place is incredible," Ariel comments.

"It really is." Lola's eyes sparkle as she looks around. While she may not like the rich people in her sorority, I do know she likes the good life. I'm not blind to her shopping habits and upscale tastes

The conversation continues for a few minutes until the girls decide they are going to walk around. Not wanting Lola to feel left out with her friends, I encourage her to go with them. I can keep an eye out for her from afar.

"Can you get me another?" I call out to Jen at the bar.

She places another beer in front of me.

"Your girl left you?"

"Her friends wanted to walk around. I did get stuck with one of the other boyfriends, though." Whatever date Ariel brought was sitting at the table.

"Mr. Personality does not play well with others." Jen laughs at my expense, but she's not wrong. I can't say I have friends. I have acquaintances I will go out with, but I have never trusted anyone enough to consider a friend. I have Javie and Toni. They are the only ones I have needed thus far. It took a few months, but I trust Garrett too.

I walk back to the table to wait for the girls to return.

Even though the music is bumping, there is an uncomfortable silence between me and Ariel's friend.

"You like working here?" He finally decides to speak.

"It's a job," I answer.

"It must be a bitch to keep track of all the bar inventory and transactions. Keep people from skimming or bottles from disappearing with all the table service. Huh?"

"It can be. I'm surprised you know so much about it." I'm curious about his knowledge.

"My parents own a few restaurants, and the bar is one of their greatest pains. One of the restaurants has a large bar with happy hour specials every day. That is the one that takes the most work."

This one may have the money, but anyone who is in the restaurant business knows the work that goes into running it well.

"I bet."

"Can I speak with you?" EJ, Hector's bartender, is at the table.

"Excuse me." I tell Ariel's friend.

I follow EJ into one of the empty storerooms.

"I'm out. I need more," he begins.

"Can't do it right now. I won't be able to get anything to you until Monday. You know the deal," I answer calmly.

"I'm completely out. Don't you want this business?" He tries to turn this around on me.

"Yes, but I would also like men who can plan accordingly. If you knew you were running low, you should have called yesterday. You didn't, so now it waits until Monday." I straighten up a bit more, rolling my shoulders back. I will not have anyone question my methods.

"I don't think Hector will like this." He tries to push back.

"I don't think Hector will like his guys not being ready for a weekend." I stand firm. "Now if you'll excuse me..."

Back at the table, the girls are chatting excitedly.

"Let's dance." Lola stands as soon as she sees me.

I extend my hand to her to lead her out to the dance floor.

LOLA

HE STOPS and grabs my hips, bringing me in close to him. My hands land on his chest, and I'm lost in him. The music and lights set the scene for the sensual movements overtaking us. He turns me around placing my back to his chest as I close my eyes, letting the beat lead me.

The heat building from the bodies packed on the floor, the feel of his hips slightly grinding when we move past each other, and his hands on me have turned dancing into the best foreplay.

The song melts into a salsa beat, and I pull away from him, smiling.

"I don't know how to dance this one." I grab his hand to pull him off the floor.

"But you will." He doesn't move, instead pulling me back to him.

I glance around to many people walking off the floor and others staying and beginning the complicated salsa steps.

I look back up to him; he's wearing a panty-dropping sexy smirk as he places one hand on my lower back and grabs the other one.

"Just trust me and follow." He begins moving.

After one song he escorts me off the floor. "Not bad for your first time." He places a kiss on my head.

"Thanks for the vote of confidence, but I felt like I had two left feet."

"Not at all. Just like anything, you learn it."

As we wait for our drinks at the bar I hear "Hey, Alex" from a female voice.

I turn around to a familiar face. I recognize her as the girl who threw herself at Alex when we were at his house. She kept trying to make out with him, but he kept pushing her away.

Alex turns to see who called his name. "Cara." He says her name without any greeting. He turns back around to face the bartender.

"Mind getting me a drink?" She shimmies her way to the bar, leaning against it, close to him. I wonder which door guy is a friend of hers.

"Shouldn't whoever you are with be getting you that?" he responds, not looking at her.

"Aww. Don't be like that. Are you jealous?" she taunts him. "You know I can fuck better than that white girl." She winks at him, and I can't help but stare at the train wreck in front of me.

He finally turns to her, and I'm on the edge of my seat, wondering how he will respond. "You will never speak about my girl like that again. Be mad all you want because you were only a fuck. But leave her out of it."

The drinks are placed in front of us, and just as he is picking them up, I hear, "*Vete Cara.*" (Leave, Cara.)

The sleazy guy from the restaurant comes to stand behind Alex. I watch as Alex's posture stiffens ever so slightly.

"Hector." Alex says without looking back.

"*Me llamaron,*" (They called,) Hector says.

"Y." (And.) Alex responds back in Spanish. I wish they would start speaking English so I could understand.

"*Necesitan proiducto. Vas a ir a recoger?*" (They need product. Are you going to go get it?)

"No." Alex stands firm, and I wish I knew what he was saying no to.

"*Necesito llamar a mi papa?*" (Do I need to call my father?) Hector puffs his chest out.

"*Andale.*" (Go ahead.) Alex finally turns and stands to his full height, and I know something is off now. "*Me dijo que solo tomara órdenes de él.*" (He told me to only take orders from him.)

"*A ver.*" (We'll see.) Hector pulls out his phone. His fingers touch the screen before he places the phone to his ear.

Alex is unmoving, and I don't know if he remembers I am right behind him.

Hector starts speaking to someone on the phone in Spanish. They are staring at each other, and I swear one wrong word, and fists will fly.

He places his phone back in his pocket and stares at Alex. I'm not sure what's happening, but his shoulders slump slightly.

"*Tu novia?*" (Your girlfriend?) He nods his head in my direction, eyes narrowed.

"*Nos vemos.*" (See you.) Alex turns around, gripping my waist and slightly pushing me back to the table.

The others are at the table laughing and talking, but I can't concentrate on anything they are saying, still trying to piece together what just happened. Alex takes a long pull from his beer, his eyes never leaving the bar where Hector is standing. He has now taken Cara under his arm and is kissing her dramatically.

I squeeze his knee under the table to get his attention. His gaze doesn't move, and I can't help but get jealous. Does he want Cara? Is he mad because she is with the sleaze? I squeeze again a bit harder.

His eyes meet mine, and all I see is anger. Tears threaten as I wonder if he is going to walk away from me.

"I want to go."

"Fine. Let's go." He stands abruptly, getting the attention of everyone at the table.

"I'm not feeling well all of a sudden. We are gonna go," I announce loudly over the music to everyone.

"Are you sure?" Ariel asks, confused.

"Yeah. I don't know what happened." A fake smile spreads across my face.

"Stay. Enjoy," Alex says as he steps away from the table.

I pull out my phone to order a car. As we walk past Hector, he tips his head to Alex with a creepy smile.

Luckily cars are always close to this place, and there is one ready once we get outside. I open the door, sliding in, wondering if Alex will come with me. The way he has ignored me since that interaction is unnerving.

Alex sits down, closing the door behind him. A breath I hadn't realized I was holding whooshes out. Not knowing what to ask or how to even react to his change tonight, I stay quiet. I glance at him out of the corner of my eye, and he is frozen, eyes staring forward, detached. His usual attempts to hold me or ensure I'm comfortable are missing.

The car pulls up in front of my building, and I exit the car quickly. I want to get into my apartment and hide.

Alex unlocks my door, and I step in, walking directly to the bathroom. I do notice he follows me in and sits on the couch. In my room, I slide my dress off and pull on a shirt and boxers. I wash my face, wanting no evidence of tonight left on me.

What happened? I'm scared to ask. I'm scared to know

the answer. So instead I curl up on the bed hugging my legs in front of me.

Alex walks through the front door, leaving me. One last look back facing me; his eyes empty and cold, holding no emotion. His mask firmly in place. He turns around, closing the door behind him. I'm frozen in place. How could it end so badly? It can't. I won't let it. My feet finally move, and I run to the door to catch him. I open it, and all I see is darkness.

I'm startled awake and realize I had fallen asleep. I sit up and look around, not knowing how long I was asleep. Is he still here?

I creep quietly into the living room to find him in the exact spot I left him when we walked in. He's slouching back, his head against the wall behind him staring at the ceiling. Timidly, I walk towards him, wanting to curl up on his lap but deciding on the corner of the couch furthest from him. I bring my legs in, wrapping my arms around them.

"What happened tonight?" I whisper, not knowing how to begin.

Silence. The silence that pulls your heart out, strangling it to the point you don't know if it will ever beat again. A silent, sad tear escapes. Not wanting to show how much I'm hurting, I bring my legs down to retreat in defeat to the bedroom again.

"I can't tell you." He sounds pained.

"Why can't you tell me?" Four words are giving me a spark of hope I thought was lost.

"I told you before. I have to finish some business. I'm doing things I'm not proud of. Things I thought I left behind me. Things I don't want you to be a part of. Things that would cause you to walk away from me." The despair in his voice doesn't sound like him. He is strong and capable, and this is not a part of him I have ever seen.

I move a little closer. "Tell me. I told you I wasn't going anywhere. I'm not leaving you."

"I can't. You can't know any part of this." He's a bit bolder.

"Why?" I plead, getting closer, placing my hand on his chest. He has yet to look at me, the ceiling getting his full attention.

"You know I can't tell you. You would then be—" He stops abruptly.

"Then don't do it. Whatever you are doing, just quit. I don't know why you're doing it, but if you don't want to then don't." I'm begging him.

"It's not that easy. I do it, and I lose you. I don't do it, and I don't know how long I live." He finally looks at me, his eyes filled with tears. "You were never supposed to be this close to it. I just needed to fulfill a favor. Be in and out quickly. No one the wiser. And it's been dragged out."

I can't stand this. I crawl into his lap, needing him. I wrap my arms around him tightly, and he squeezes me, holding me close. His face is tucked in my neck, and I feel the moisture of tears. My emotionless boyfriend is finally showing his human side. He hurts just like everyone else. He's just better at masking it. After a few quiet moments, I pull back to look him in the eye. I didn't think I could love him any more, but seeing him so full of emotion, I realize he is even more beautiful to me.

"Who was that guy?" I finally ask, needing to know what we are dealing with.

"There's a guy I owe the favor to. That was his son."

"Okay. So do what you need to do. But you are not leaving me." If I need to be the strong one now, I will do it.

"No. I can't have you with me. He now knows I have a weak spot. If anything goes wrong, they will use you against me." Pain fills his eyes.

"We aren't breaking up." I don't know what he's saying, but I hope that's not what he's insinuating.

"We need to. At least for now."

Anger comes quickly. "Why? So you can go fuck Cara? Is she part of this game you are playing?" Words to hurt him fly from my mouth.

"*Amor*, you know I don't want anyone but you." He pulls me to him again, clutching me to his chest.

"Then don't do this," I mumble out. "I love you."

"*Eres mi unica. Te amo para siempre.*" He responds in Spanish. And while I love to hear him speak it, right now I need to know what he's saying.

"English." There is no holding back my tears now.

"You are my only. I will always love you." His arms tighten just a bit more.

"*Eres la única que tendrá mi corazón.* You are the only one who will ever have my heart. I love you." He voice is hoarse, and his chest heaves.

"No. This is not happening." I refuse to accept that this is it. There must be some other way to get through this.

"It is." He is still clutching me, and I can tell he is crying.

"Neither of us wants to let go. Don't do this!" I pull back, staring at him; anger fills me, and I find I'm raising my voice.

"Don't you think I tried to think of a way to avoid this? I have not slept. All I keep thinking is how I can get out. But I can't. Not until they release me. This is not my game." He takes a jagged breath, then continues, "I would not be doing this if no one knew about you. I promised myself this would not touch you. But tonight, it did. If anything happens, it needs to happen to me and *only* me. But Hector saw me with you at the restaurant and now tonight. He knows I don't date. I don't take girls out. If I did, then it means something. And that he has Cara, who also saw me with you at the house. Now that they know about you, it's not safe."

"Why isn't it safe?" Deep down, I know what he's doing again. I know why he fears for me. I know the answer, but I can't give up on us. I refuse to acknowledge it.

"You know I can't say anything more." His hands cup my cheeks as his thumbs stroke my cheeks, wiping the tears that have fallen.

After all our time together, his stone façade has fallen, and all I see is pain piercing his eyes. I knew he cared for me. I trusted it, even though I couldn't always see it. In this moment, I see how much I mean to him because he looks as broken as I feel.

He pulls me close, our lips meeting in a desperate kiss. A goodbye neither of us wants.

"I need to ask one favor, even though I have no right to one."

"Anything." I would do anything for this beautiful man.

"Javie and Toni can't know any of this. They will try to get involved, and I don't want them on the line. This is my problem, and I will handle it. I won't forgive myself if they jump in too. Tell them we broke up because I fucked up. Whatever excuse you want to tell them. Blame me. Place everything on my shoulders." His fingers go into my hair then slowly make their way down to the ends. "I never deserved you. I'm just a fuck-up that could have ruined your life. I'm sorry I wasn't stronger. I should never have given in."

He grabs my waist and moves me off his lap, standing up. I watch him walk to the door then turn back, "You have my heart, and I never want it back." And with that, he opens the door and leaves.

The emptiness I feel is immediate. I curl up on the couch letting the tears fall freely.

Chapter 21

ALEX

I shouldn't be surprised life has knocked me down again. I don't know why I thought it would be any different. My life is here. A window in the walls around this place may have creaked open for a moment, but it has slammed shut and been bolted. There is no escaping. At least not for me. I was able to get Toni out, and now I'm working on getting Javie out. Once I'm successful, my job is done.

"Why are you here?" Javie walks through the front door, finding me on the couch drowning in tequila.

"Cause I live here." I'm not ready to talk, the wound fresh.

"Technically, yes, but you have spent every day and night with Lola. Where is she?" Javie asks as he walks past me to the kitchen.

Maybe it was a rhetorical question on his part, and I can avoid the discussion altogether, at least for a few days. The TV is on, but I have no idea what's showing as my mind has been everywhere except on the picture in front of mc.

Javie returns from the kitchen, a bag of chips in hand. "Where's Lola?" he asks again.

"At home." This is the easiest answer I have.

"And you're polishing off that bottle because?" He's not dropping it.

"No reason." I refuse to look at him. I'm already a mess, and there is no reason for anyone to know how the fuck I'm feeling. It was a bad idea from the start.

"Look at me, asshole," he says with an edge. As soon as I look in his direction, he continues, "What the fuck did you do?"

"Don't worry about it. It's none of your fucking business." I won't have him lecturing me on jack shit.

"Fuck you. You made it our business when you decided to fuck a friend." He drops the bag of chips he was holding, posturing up.

"Who I fuck or don't fuck is none of your business." I'm trying to rein it in, but with the pain and drunkenness coursing through every fucking part of my body right now—and with him trying to provoke me—I don't know how long I can contain it.

"Again, Lola is our business." I'm stuck between admiring him for caring so deeply for the girl I love and wanting to hurt him for making this harder than it has to be for me right now.

"Since you are evading the question, I know things aren't kosher. You fucked her and threw her out, didn't you? You treated her like you treat all the fucking whores around here. That's what you wanted? To treat her like your fucking whore?"

As soon as he compared Lola to a whore, I saw red and wanted to stop every damn word coming out of his mouth. I am up and swinging, not thinking about what I am about to do. I connect with his jaw, but he expected it and comes at me. Fists fly and soon we are on the floor, wrestling like only brothers can. I want someone else to feel the anger, frustration, and hurt in me.

"WHAT THE HELL?" Toni's voice breaks through. "STOP THIS SHIT!"

We both pause long enough for her to kick us both in the ribs.

"Shit, Toni, what in the hell was that for?" Javie asks her angrily.

"For y'all being dumbasses." She sits down and watches us sit up, our anger still brewing, but tamed. "Why were you fighting like ten-year-old boys?" She has a way of emasculating us when needed.

I refuse to look at Javie. This is exactly what I wanted to avoid. A spectacle of my failed relationship and their curiosity about what I did to provoke it.

"Ask Alex if he's still dating Lola." Javie gives her a bone, and I know she will not let it go.

She sits down, her eyes never leaving mine. I know she's processing, and when she comes at me, it will be full force. Javie has nothing on the sword of a tongue Toni has.

"Spill." She crosses her legs under her, getting comfortable.

I'm keeping my mouth shut for as long as possible. We will be fighting the battle of wills, and I don't intend to lose. She's patient and conniving. She continues to stare in my direction, but I will not flinch. Javie gets up from the ground and sits on a chair. I dare not move, not when I have too much to hold back.

Toni yawns, rolls her eyes, then pulls out her phone. Her eyes finally leave mine as she begins touching her screen. I'm curious about what she is doing until I hear the phone ringing. I wonder who the hell is she calling until I hear Lola's voice in her voicemail greeting. Toni hangs up, not leaving a message.

I rub my face roughly, frustrated I've put myself in this predicament. Why did I ever believe I could leave my place in life?

"We broke up. Is that what you need to hear? I'm a fuck-up, and it's over. My relationship is none of your fucking business, and that's all I'm going to say." I stand quickly, retreating to my room to avoid any further words.

"You know..." Toni begins, and I don't know why I stop to listen. Maybe it was her tone, she didn't sound angry, only sad. "You are the only one who can fix it if you fucked up. I know we didn't have any good role models in this department, but if you love her like I think you do, man up and fix it."

If she only knew. Knew I placed Lola in danger. Knew what I was involved with again. Knew I am acting like the low-life everyone expects me to be. Then she would know I don't deserve another chance. No. A crushed heart is my penance.

In my room, I close the door and lie on the bed. I need to get Javie out, sell this fucking house, give Toni and Javie the money, and disappear. I don't know where, but I can't continue bringing heat to them. This house keeps them too close to the life that is in front of me. I need them far away.

LOLA

SHOCK. That is the only word that comes to mind after this past weekend. I don't know how our relationship could disintegrate so quickly. How is he doing? Is he also destroyed? Is it selfish to want him to hurt as badly as I do? I'm on autopilot, going through the motions. Smiling on cue when necessary, even though I'm dead inside. Alex was supposed to be different, be my last, be my forever.

I've picked up my phone to call him too many times to count. Each time, I stare at his number, wanting so badly to hit the button, have him answer, hear his voice. Have him tell me he's sorry and that we can figure it all out. But then I remember his stubbornness and quickly put my phone down, fearing his rejection will cut through the numbness I have found.

My only problem has been avoiding Toni. I refused to answer her call last Sunday. Each text she sends, I respond with a quick response so I can keep her pacified and off my back until I can figure something out. I can only assume she knows already, as I'm sure Javie told her Alex is back at the house. I don't know what he told them. I know he told me to blame him, but what does that even mean?

WHEN ALL I want to do is hide from the world, my dad's house is the only place to go. He's still at work when I arrive, so I head to my room. I close the blinds and crawl into bed, not having the energy for anything else. I wish sleep to take me because that is the only time I'm at peace. No pain or sadness.

"Lola...Lola..." My dad's voice wakes me. I sit up, still groggy. "What are you doing here? If I knew you were coming, I would have come home earlier."

Still confused. "What time is it?"

"It's after eight. I went to have dinner and drinks after work with friends. You didn't tell me you were coming." Worry mars his face.

I shake my head, the tears coming quickly. "We broke up." That's all I could say before the sobs took over.

I was in pain, then angry, then numb, so I hadn't cried

since Sunday. I was keeping the sadness at bay. Seeing my dad, it comes at me like a wrecking ball, knocking me down. He comes in close and holds me as I finally let the sadness of our ending overcome me.

He continues to sit in the dark room, not saying anything, just letting his presence be a balm. When my breathing evens and the tears slow, he finally asks, "Is it time for ice cream?"

A small giggle escapes, and it feels good. I nod my head, making my way out of bed. Ice cream may be the stereotypical break-up food, but it's been our way of coming together through sadness. When my mom passed, there were many nights when I didn't want to do anything, but as soon as he asked if I wanted to go get ice cream, I would relent. That's when we could talk. The cold, sweet treat has been our constant.

He places a bowl of chocolate chip ice cream in front of me, along with chocolate and caramel syrup.

"Ready?" He sits down next to me at the breakfast bar.

I grab the chocolate and caramel syrup, pouring both on top of the ice cream before I take my first bite. "I don't know exactly what happened to be honest. He ended things because he is wrapped up in something. Things he won't tell me about and things he does not want me involved in." Admitting to your dad that your boyfriend may not be on the right side of the law is not really sane, but I don't have anyone else to talk to.

He watches me as we each take another bite. "And that's all your giving me?"

"I know you may not have the best impression of him. Especially after what I'm about to admit to you, but I need to you to understand. I really feel he's my forever. He didn't have it easy growing up. He had to do things he isn't proud of to help support his family. He works so hard at making sure Toni makes it, and now he's after his brother to do the same, but he sacrifices himself in the process. He has been the man in his family because his dad was a 'worthless alcoholic,' his words not mine."

"Keep going," he prompts, and I know he's trying hard to keep an open mind.

"He didn't and still doesn't have the luxury of being able to hit rock bottom and not get hurt on impact. We've never known that type of desperation. The need to do things, even if you don't want to or know they are wrong. I was sad and depressed, so I took off on an extended vacation in Italy. If he needs something, he only knows what that side of town has taught him. He didn't have a role model to guide him." I take a deep breath, hoping I'm explaining it well. I shove the spoon in my mouth, taking time to consider how much I want to divulge.

"I can see that. To be honest, I'm not so comfortable with this conversation, but I'm open to listening and not judging," he says after a few quiet moments.

"All this is an assumption because he won't tell me what he has done. He wanted to keep it buried in the past, but somehow it became his present. He was adamant about becoming a man who would make me proud. A man I deserve. He never thought he was good enough for me. I have made assumptions about what he's done. The most probable is he sold drugs. And he's doing it again."

"I—" My dad begins, but I quickly stop him.

"Wait. He has somehow started again, but against his will. What I can't understand is why. He mentioned he needed to fulfill a favor and there was no getting out of it."

I had been wallowing in self-pity and heartache all week; I'd never stopped to think about all this. Having to explain it to my dad, I'm seeing things differently. He was in as much pain as I was our last night together. He finally let me see the real him, no hiding behind the mask of indifference or power he wears in front of everyone. Last weekend was the only time I have seen him fall apart. He may experience emotions, but he never shows them.

But he did with me. He let me in. It is love.

"And why did he end it? What happened to cause the breakup?" He's going in for another bite, his eyes on his bowl.

"We were at the club he works at Saturday night with friends. Toward the end of the evening, some guy showed up, and they exchanged words. Everything unraveled after that."

"What did that guy say?" Dad actually seems curious now.

"I don't know. They spoke in Spanish, and we left right after. He said the guy was the son of the man he owed the favor to. And now my mind is racing." I take a bite thinking. "He didn't want me to tell Toni or Javie what happened because they would know what he was up to and didn't want anyone involved. See...he continues to do all the shady stuff, to sacrifice himself for others."

"I can't do anything about this. I won't say I'm comfortable with you chasing him, especially if he doesn't want you or his family involved."

"I know. But I have to do something. I don't know what... but something."

The tightness in my chest that had been squeezing the life out of me all week has lessened in the short time we have been speaking. I was drowning, but now I have found a life vest. I just need to figure out how to get out of the currents. A renewed sense of purpose fills me. He is the one who usually saves everyone, but this time, this time I'm going to save him. Now just to figure out how.

"I'm not giving up on him, Dad." I want to make sure he fully understands that Alex is my forever.

"I want to know what you are doing. I don't want you jumping into something you know nothing about. If he is this careful about your safety, sacrificing a relationship, it's not safe for you."

"I know. And I wouldn't want to do anything to jeopardize him. I'm just holding on to the hope that what he's doing isn't forever. He said it wasn't; now I just need to trust him on it."

CHAPTER 22

ALEX

THE PAST COUPLE OF WEEKS HAVE BEEN A BLUR. ALL MY brain wants to think about is Lola. What she's doing? Who's she with? Thinking about guys hitting on her puts me in a rage, so I've had to stop those thoughts from entering. Her social media sites have been quiet, no new posts. All I have left of her are the pictures on my phone. I fear she will call me because I don't know if I'll be strong enough to stay away. It was torture walking away from her. It was the hardest thing I've ever had to do.

I stare at a picture of us, polar opposites in every sense. My dark hair and eyes in stark contrast to her blonde and blue. My dark and brooding personality is calmed by her light and cheery outlook. She is what I never knew I needed. I want her desperately but know she is a bright light, and I will only dull it.

. . .

I HAVEN'T BEEN SUMMONED to Jefe's house since the incident at the club, so I'm guessing I'm in the clear. He hasn't texted me at all either. It's been unusually quiet, which is weird. I walk into the tire shop to pick up product for deliveries but am shocked by what I find. Stock is low and has not been replenished. I check the lockbox and am surprised to find it has not been picked up.

I'm in and out quickly, refusing to set myself up for a bust. This is unlike anything I have seen from Jefe in the past. I know he hasn't been busted because the whole neighborhood would have heard about it already. If I'm released, he would have let me know. He half-asses nothing when it comes to his business. I don't know what is going on, but it can't be good.

After my last delivery, I receive a text from Javie to meet him for a late lunch before I head in to work. Not really in the mood for it but decide I will need to face him sometime. It may as well be now. I have been avoiding them as much as I can.

I WALK into the burger joint looking around for him. Seeing he isn't here yet, I find a secluded table in case our voices do not stay civil. The server comes by, and I order drinks for the both of us and wait. Everything around me is placing me on edge, business, Lola, avoiding Javie and Toni; I need to focus.

A chair scraping startles me out of my thoughts. Javie sits down, his usual smile replaced with furrowed brows.

"Hey," I say first.

He only tips his head at me, his eyes searching.

The server places our drinks down and takes our order. Silence has surrounded us. Who will break first? I take a jagged, deep breath in, hoping it calms me.

"I figured we wouldn't start throwing punches in a public place so that's why I asked you to lunch," Javie begins.

"Why would we throw punches?"

"Because you don't like to be questioned, and that's what I'm going to do." His features are stone, showing no emotion.

"No need. I handle my own shit."

"You're right. You did. Past tense. Now it seems like your shit is handling you."

"*No sabes.*" (You don't know.) I won't show weakness.

"It took me a second, but yes, I do know." He takes a drink. "You came at me last time because I called Lola one of your whores."

He watches me, but I refuse to show him any emotion. He's trying to get a rise out of me again.

"You love her. Still love her. If you didn't, you wouldn't have cared if I called her that. Your jaw wouldn't tick. Remember, I know your tells."

Fuck... I relax my jaw. What is he getting at? He's getting too close to the truth, and I can't have him trying to intervene or help. He needs to stay as far away from this as possible. Silence is all he's going to get from me.

He plays cool, looks around, takes a drink before starting again. "See. You didn't expect me to come after you like this, and you have slid your mask on. You think because I can't see what you're feeling that I don't know what you're feeling. But that's where you are wrong, brother. I have watched you all my life. I have seen the way you approach situations. I don't think you fucked up with Lola. I think you pushed her away. Something happened."

"Nothing happened. I'm a fuck-up, and she deserves better." The words leave my mouth robotically.

"You're not a fuck-up. We've had to do some fucked-up shit to survive, but no we are no fuck-ups."

"Just let it go, Javie. It wasn't meant to be. She has no business slumming it."

"She didn't think she was slumming it. And I would think her opinion is the one that matters." A small smirk appears.

He knows he's pushing. He knows my weaknesses. He is the only one I trust with my life, but right now I'm protecting his, so I can't give him anything. Silence. I won't show my cards.

"I heard you're avoiding Toni too." He starts again after a quiet pause.

"I'm not avoiding her." I shrug nonchalantly.

"She mentioned some unanswered texts." He has learned well. He sounds bored with our conversation. He's turning my ways against me.

"Why the hell do I need to reply to every one of her stupid 'hello' texts? *Para que?*" (For what?)

Silence. He looks around, sits back, and takes a deep breath. He won't stare directly at me. He's just trying to make me uncomfortable. He's pushing me to get frustrated. Stay calm and keep focused. Another half hour and we will be done.

Our food arrives, and he takes a bite of a fry spitting it out and quickly taking a drink. That small incident breaks the tension that was looming over us.

I decide to try another tactic to distract from the conversation.

"Any new welding jobs?"

"Hell yeah!" His eyes light up, and I know I can control the rest of our lunch. "A ritzy auto body shop that restores classic muscle cars contacted me. My two favorite things together. Cars and welding. So far I've only done a few things here and there, as a test. I'm waiting to get a call to come back. If I can get that job full-time..." The bright smile he is known for spreads across his face.

I hated to jade the happy-go-lucky side of him. But he needed to know how to handle himself where we grew up. It wouldn't always work for people to know I was his brother. They also needed to know he could handle himself. Anywhere you are, you need to show dominance. Power and money are what makes the world spin. We may not have had money, but I earned the power for us.

We enjoy a few bites of our burgers without speaking before he begins again.

"So you're really done with Lola? For good? No going back?"

I nod my head. He needs no more than that.

"Okay, then. I guess it's not going to bother you when guys start chasing her again."

Fuck, Fuck, Fuck. He knew that would hurt.

I shake my head, shoving fries in my mouth to keep from grinding my jaw.

He takes out his phone, swiping at the screen then placing it in front of me. When I look down, it's a picture of Lola with some guy with his arm around her at a party. It didn't take her long to start partying again.

Everything I just ate feels like it wants to come right back up. I can't take my eyes off the picture.

"You lied. You're not okay."

My gaze comes up to meet Javie's. Pain I can't hide anymore rushes in.

"Don't worry. It's an old picture. I searched her social and screen shotted one from way back. She's still silent on social media. Which I'm sure you know because you've stalked her." He looks down at his food, giving me a moment with my thoughts. "I can only guess what you're involved in, and I'm not sure why. I will stay out of it. If you've gone through this much trouble to hide it and push everyone away, I know it's no joke. Just know, she won't wait forever."

My gaze travels back down to my food. I knew I wouldn't

be able to keep this buried forever. I just hoped I wouldn't have to explain until I was out.

"I don't expect her to wait. I expect her to get on with her life. I'm no good for her." I refuse to look up.

"I'll say it again. She wants you." His voice is low.

"She doesn't know what she's getting with me. She doesn't know the shit I've done. She absolutely does not need to be pulled down in life with the likes of me."

I take a bite of the burger, not wanting to disclose anything further.

"If I suspected this, you know Toni will be on the scent soon too, if she isn't already. Get out before this shit blows up."

He doesn't know the half of it. No new product coming in means the walls are closing in.

Chapter 23

LOLA

Classes, eat, and sleep. That is my life now. Knowing Alex loves me is what has kept me moving, one foot in front of the other. I still don't know what's going on, but I won't push. Yet. He will shut down and push me away harder. I know it. need to figure out how to approach this without him pushing me away.

Sitting down at the table, trying to focus on the assignments in front of me and when they're due, I'm shocked at the date in front of me. I should have started my period days ago. Is this really happening on top of everything else? My heart drops. I don't need this problem on top of everything else going on.

Fear travels through my body, paralyzing me in my chair. My head starts shaking back and forth. No. Nope. Uh-uh. It's just all the stress. That's what it is. My shoulders tense. How can this happen? I'm on the pill. Trying to complete any schoolwork while my brain is absorbed with this will be impossible.

I get my shoes on and head out to the drug store. I need to know right now if I'm pregnant or if this is another cruel joke life is throwing at me.

The drive there and back was the longest twenty minutes of my life. Pee on a stick. That's all I need to do. Pee on a stick and wait. I ran out the door like a crazy woman on speed and now I'm holding this stick in my hand, unable to complete the next step. What happens if it's positive? Wait, what do I want it to be? Positive? Negative? I place the test on the counter and throw myself on the couch.

My heart feels like it's beating a million times a minute and growing larger by the second. My chest is tightening, making the thumps so loud. *Deep breath. Calm down. Release.* Close my eyes. More deep breaths until my chest begins to decompress. A single tear slides out. I want Alex's baby.

With that thought, I sit up and make my way to the bathroom. A sense of urgency takes over. Pee. Start the timer on my phone. Three minutes. Don't look at it, just wait. One, two, three, four... fifty... This is not helping. Pace the living room. Walk in circles. The timer goes off.

It's positive. My heart drops at the same time joy fills me. I want his baby. It was never anything I thought of until today, but now that it's in front of me, I don't want to let it go. Now I just need to figure out how to get him to come back to me.

Driving to his house is nerve-racking. A doctor confirmed the pregnancy, and I spent the last couple of days trying to figure out how to tell Alex, but everything that came to mind sounded stupid. Fear about how he will receive the news fills me. But I am determined to get us back together and help him out of whatever he is swept up in. I pull up, and there are no cars. Both his and Javie's cars are gone. Alex usually does not go into work until later, so I decide to wait for him.

I use the key I still have and let myself in. The familiar scent of their home assaults my senses. A calm tingles from my head down being here again. The first home where I didn't need to act any way other than being myself. My feet lead me to Alex's room. I pick up a T-shirt thrown on the bed and hold it up to my nose. A knock on the door startles me.

Walking to the living room, I hear more knocks on the door but harder. I stand in the middle of the living room, unsure if I should open the door. Another pounding, then the door handle begins turning. I didn't lock the door behind me. The door opens, and the guy from the club steps in, staring at me.

"Where's your boy?" he asks, irritated.

"I don't know. I just got here." I mumble, frightened.

"When do you expect him?" His eyes narrow.

"I don't know." I'm rooted to the floor.

"Lunch with you, club with you, and you at his house. I would expect you know something." He takes a couple more steps in, closing the door behind him.

"I haven't talked to him in a while." My voice is barely above a whisper.

"Then we'll sit here and wait for him to return." He moves to the couch, sitting down casually. "Sit, sit." He waves his hand to the seat next to him.

"I should probably go." I hate to leave this creep in their house by himself, but I don't feel safe with him.

"No, please don't leave. You were here to see your boy. Stay. I'm sure he will be happy to see you." A sneer for a smile spreads across his face.

I slowly move to the chair furthest from him lowering myself slowly.

"I'm Hector, and you are?"

I'm quiet, not wanting to say anything. I wanted so desperately to know what Alex was up to, and now all I want to do is run as fast as I can from this place.

"Well?" he continues when I don't answer.

"Lola."

"Ah." He draws the sound out. "Now that's a sexy name if I ever heard one. No wonder my boy has kept you around. White girl with a name like that. You must have shown him a good time to hold on to him. He never keeps any of the hoes around." He huffs a laugh.

I'm scared to move, sitting stiffly.

"You know, if he's not taking care of business, I can show you a good time. No reason to stay with the help when you can be with the king." His arrogance sickens me.

Quiet. Just stay quiet. *Alex, where the hell are you?* I think to myself.

"You don't speak?" He continues watching me. He waits, and when I say nothing, he asks, "Why so quiet? ... Scared?"

My eyes widen a bit as he sits forward placing his elbows on his knees.

"Yes. You're scared. And if you're scared, you know there is something to be scared of. I see my boy has been talking. What do you have? A magic pussy? Because that *culero* has always kept his mouth shut. Word on the street is the heat is coming, and the only difference is a white girl slumming it." He stands and comes in front of me.

I push back into the chair as far as I can get.

"Have you been running your mouth, *guera?*"

His arms are crossed in front of him. I shake my head back and forth quickly.

"You know what happens to snitches around here?"

I shake my head again.

"*Pendeja. (Dumb ass.)* You run your mouth and don't even know the consequences? No one said blonds were smart."

I'm frozen. My fight or flight instincts in shock. You may think you would know how you would react to some sketchy situation from watching this crap on TV. But living it? It's completely different.

The front door flies open, slamming against the wall, startling both Hector and I.

"What the fuck are you doing in my house?" Alex's presence is larger than I have ever seen.

"Just getting to know your..." A sinister smile emerges.

"You know better than to enter a man's home without permission. I can shoot you right now and get away with it." Alex takes another step in, one hand behind his back.

"And you know this whole neighborhood would rain down on you if you did." Hector turns to face Alex, squaring his shoulders.

Alex shrugs, "And if it did, maybe I wouldn't give a damn."

Hector eyes him curiously, each waiting for the other.

"We need to talk business." Hector concedes as Alex gives nothing.

"Fine." He slightly tips his head to Hector, then his gaze finally comes down to me. "You weren't invited either, Lola. You need to go."

"Not so fast, *chingon*. She knows something, so she stays." He refuses to move out of my way.

"Es amiga de Toni. No sabe nada. (*She doesn't know anything.*)" Alex begins speaking in Spanish again. I'm assuming he's doing this on purpose.

I'm able to catch "Toni's friend," but that's it.

"*Si no sabe, por que tiene miedo?*" (If she doesn't know anything, why is she scared?)

"*Es guera. Ella no es de aquí. No sabe nada.*" (She's a white girl. She's not from here. She knows nothing.)

"*A ver.*" (Let's see.) Hector turns back to me without leaving me room to get out of the chair.

"My boy says you don't know anything, but I'm not so sure. Let me ask... Why were you here?"

Nothing comes to mind. I'm not about to blurt out that I came to tell Alex I'm pregnant. *Crap. Think.*

"I...uh...was looking for Toni." Alex mentioned her a second ago. "We were supposed to meet up."

"Nice try, but Toni doesn't live here anymore. You think I don't know what goes on in this neighborhood? She has not lived here in a long-ass time."

"I know that. But we were meeting here." If I'm going to save myself and Alex, I need a damn backbone. This thug is not going to push me around.

"I wanted tacos, and the best are around here. So here is where we meet." I stare back at him. I refuse to cower, especially with Alex watching me. Alex needs to know I can take care of myself, and while I love him protecting me, I need to do this on my own too.

"Text Toni and tell her you will meet her at the taqueria, and you can go now," Alex demands.

"Excuse me." I look up at Hector as I stand up, bumping into him.

He grabs me by the arm as I take a couple of steps away.

"*Déjala ir.*" (Let her leave.) Alex's voice is strained.

Hector's grip on my arm loosens, and I walk quickly past Alex and out the door. He's in trouble, and I wonder if I caused it to be worse. I jump in my truck and drive away, unsure what I should do. I know Alex will be pissed at me for telling Javie, but I don't know who else to call.

I drive to a shopping center and park. My nerves and fear make it hard to concentrate. I pull out my phone, tapping Javie's name and listen to the ring.

"Hey, Lola. What's up?" Javie's cheerful voice sounds so different from what I just encountered.

"I...uh... don't know how to explain this, but something just happened at your house." My voice begins to shake.

"Are you okay?" he asks immediately.

"Yeah...uh...but I don't know." Tears collect in my eyes, not wanting to betray Alex and his wishes, but scared for him.

"Lola. Talk to me. Are you still at the house?" I hear Javie's concern through the phone.

"No."

"What happened?" Javie says softly. The crackling sounds of coworkers welding in his shop are gone.

"I went by to see Alex, but he wasn't there. Then some guy, Hector, showed up."

"Did Hector hurt you?" He sounds angry.

"No. But he was mad. Saying something about the heat was coming, and he called me a snitch. Alex got there and convinced him to let me leave."

"Where are you?"

"The shopping center parking lot off Terrace and the freeway." Tears slide down my cheeks.

"Are you okay to drive home?"

"Yes, but what about Alex? Did I get him in more trouble?" Sobs begin as I think of all the things he could be involved in.

"No. Don't worry about Alex. Hector is an asshole, but Alex can handle him. He's been doing it since he was in high school," Javie reassures me.

"But -" I begin, but he cuts me off.

"No buts. When have you ever known my brother not to take care of business? It's fine. I'll check in with him. Now can you get yourself home?" His voice sounds calm and collected.

"Yes. I can drive home."

"Calm down and get home. I'll check on Alex, and I'll call you later."

I hang up, trusting him.

ALEX

WATCHING Lola walk out the door, away from Hector, I can breathe a little easier. What in the hell was she doing here? I can't think of her right now. I need to focus on the problem in front of me.

"Now tell me what the fuck is going on and why you thought you could walk into my home uninvited." I will not give an inch to Hector. I may show respect for Jefe, but Hector needs to earn it again for not watching over the wet-behind-the-ears prick.

"You tell me. There's chatter of the heat being on us." Hector sits on the couch.

I will not let this asshole try and intimidate me, so I take up the chair Lola vacated, making myself comfortable.

"I know nothing about the heat. I do not want to be busted, so therefore, I work clean. I'm not jeopardizing myself. You better start looking elsewhere."

"The only change is that whore who doesn't belong here."

"Or that fuckwad who doesn't check his sources. Sending me to a place he thought was safe because of one fucking meeting at a bar. Fuck you. You have a loose cannon in that one."

"DO NOT QUESTION how I do business." He angers quickly.

"I can question you all I want. It's Jefe who has my loyalty. Always has." I will not bow down to Hector when he's getting sloppy. He is becoming too complacent.

"Since you mention my dad, he wants to speak with you."

Fuck. I knew it would be coming.

Car doors closing outside have me curious until I hear the knock on the door.

I glance out the window to see police. Everything I tried to avoid is crumbling on top of me right now. I look back to Hector, and he knows. I place my gun on the floor by the door and open it with my hands up. No need to be shot for acting stupid.

Guys dressed in SWAT gear throw me to the ground and rush past me to Hector. I watch from the ground as Hector tries to fight them. It takes three of them to get him down and eventually cuffed. An overturned chair and a broken TV and coffee table are the casualties.

Once SWAT has swept the house, a detective crouches down in front of me. "Alejandro Martinez?"

"Yes."

"This is a warrant to search your house." He throws the paper by my face.

I watch as several cops walk in and begin tearing things up. A couple pick me up and begin escorting me outside, reading me my rights. They place me in the back of one car as I watch Hector escorted into another. Fuck me. This came hard and fast, but not because of me.

The detective who showed me the warrant comes out of the house walking towards the car. I watch him as he opens the door.

"Instead of us tearing up the house looking for the drugs, why don't you tell us where to look?"

He will get no words from me. Telling them there are no drugs in the house, unless Javie has been toking, can and will be used against me. I know the drill.

"They're in there making a mess, and you can stop it." He's frustrated.

I turn my head straight away from him and refuse to say anything.

After a couple of minutes, "Fine. Have it your way." He closes the door.

He speaks to someone, and a cop walks to the car and gets in. The car starts, and we pull away. I watch my house disappear. The life I know, gone. Everything I thought I had left behind pulled me under, and there is no coming back.

Chapter 24

LOLA

Minutes feel like hours waiting for my phone to ring. I've been pacing back and forth since getting home, looking at my phone every couple of minutes to check if I missed a call. Pace. Check phone. Pace. Check phone.

Ping. I bring my phone to my face quickly to see who it is.

It's Toni asking me to come to their house. That's it. No mention of Alex or Javie. I grab my keys and am out the door in less than a minute.

Knocking on the door, I wait for someone to answer, not wanting to use my key. Javie opens the door, and as I look past him into the living room, I see it in shambles. I step around him, taking the mess in. A few more steps to the kitchen, where I find Toni throwing things away and Garrett sweeping.

"What happened?" In my confusion, I'm not sure if I said the words or just thought them.

Since Toni and Garrett continue to work not looking in my direction, I'm convinced the words were solely in my head until Javie says, "The cops executed a search warrant, and this is what's left."

My head spins around to look at him. "For what?" The words come out a bit louder than I'd meant.

"Pot."

I'm surprised, even when I shouldn't be. The evidence of Alex's dealings were all around me, and I chose to ignore them. I knew he was into something, but I refused to believe this was it.

"Did they find what they were looking for?"

Javie shakes his head at me and brings his index finger to his lips. He extends his hand to me. I take it, and he pulls me through the kitchen into the backyard. Toni and Garrett follow us out.

Javie sits down in a chair, tilting his head to another for me to do the same. Garrett and Toni pull up an old cooler and sit next to us.

"Did you know what Alex was up to?" Toni is staring at me.

"I guessed something was up. He had changed. The more time we spent together, the more he seemed to relax, and his guard was coming down. But when he started working at the club, it went up again. I asked him about it, and he told me I had nothing to worry about. He just had some things he needed to take care of. Then it all came crashing down the weekend we broke up. We were at El Mundo, and that guy Hector was there. They exchanged words, and we left. He broke up with me after. Said he couldn't be with me and do what he needed to do. That's it."

"What did he and Hector talk about?" Javie asks.

"I don't know. They spoke in Spanish." I shrug.

"Of course they did." Toni rolls her eyes in frustration.

Javie's phone begins ringing. He looks at it, then answers it quickly.

"Yes. I'll accept." He says then, "Alex."

Javie listens, and I want nothing more than to hear what Alex is saying.

"I got you. I'll bail you out," Javie says.

Javie listens yet again.

"No. Seriously. I got you. I still owe you for all the gas you paid for."

Watching Javie, I try and figure out what is going on, but Javie's expression is so much like Alex's right now. He is showing no emotion. I wait, and he continues listening, then ends the call.

"He says to leave him there. He does not want me to use his money to get him out."

"That damn pigheaded bastard." Toni's anger rises. "He would get us out in a second and yet he will sit and rot in that damn jail cell like a fucking martyr."

"What money of his? I told you what I know, now someone needs to tell me what is going on." Frustration that they are keeping me in the dark sets in.

"We're guessing he was selling again. We don't know why, but if Hector was involved, he was pulled in. We just don't understand why. We were able to quit that shit when dad got busted. But if they got him in again, it's the boss that called him," Javie says.

"But how do you know for sure?" I ask, still lost.

"I found his money in our old spot. He wasn't keeping product here at the house, I don't think. Our old hiding spot is empty except the money. He won't let me use the money he earned to get him out. He said for me and Toni to split it and to stay clean," Javie finishes.

"And what about me?" squeaks out as tears fill my eyes. Of course he would take care of those two, but knowing he didn't even give me a second thought is a punch to the gut. I stand, ready to walk away, unsure what my next step should be. Pregnant with the child of a man who does not want me.

"Lola. Stop." Javie stands, quickly maneuvering me back into the chair. "He wanted me to tell you to find someone better and that he was sorry."

"I guess that's it." My hands are shaking, and I feel sick. I pop out of my chair and run to the fence, vomiting.

Toni is by my side, holding my hair and rubbing my back. What am I going to do? Can I raise this baby on my own? What happens when he realizes I'm carrying his child?

"I'm pregnant." The words slip out, and I regret them as soon as they do.

"What?" she exclaims loudly.

"Nothing. Never mind." I straighten up, building the courage to... To what? I'm so lost right now, I'm not sure.

"Did you just say what I think you did?" she whispers.

I nod, not wanting to say any more.

"Does Alex know?"

I shake my head. I don't have anything to say.

She grabs my hand, pulling me back to the chair and sitting me down. I will not cry again. I refuse to. How will tears help?

"Why is he doing this?"

"Because he's a stubborn bastard. I don't know why. It's like he feels he doesn't deserve the life he wants us to strive for," Toni answers. "We're getting him out," she turns and says to Javie.

"No, we're not. He told me not to tell you about the money. Just to help you out until you finish grad school."

"What the actual FUCK!" Garrett finally explodes. His usual quiet demeanor, and his practice of letting them handle their own family issues, has finally reached a tipping point. Everyone turns to face him. "Why the hell would Toni need assistance when she has me? I'm sick and tired of sitting around and letting y'all scramble. I've kept my mouth shut for long enough. If you all need to move out of this area to avoid your past, sell the house. I know y'all grew up in it, and it has memories. But maybe getting away from this place is what you need."

Toni and Javie do not say anything in return, but Garrett has lit a fire in me.

"I'm getting Alex out." I turn to Garrett since I figure he would be my best ally to help. "How do I do that?"

"We don't even know what his bail is yet," Javie chimes in.

Garrett ignores Javie. "We will have to wait until they arraign him. Since it's Friday, it won't happen until Monday. He's stuck there for the weekend."

"I don't care what the bail is, I'm getting him out. If he wants to be mad at me, then so be it." I'm tired of following what they say. For once, I'm going to let the money do the talking. "Can you or your parents find me a lawyer too?" I ask Garrett.

"Sure. I got you."

"How are you going to pay for all this? Ask Daddy?" Toni wonders out loud.

I guess it's time to come clean.

"I have money. I never use it. My mom left me her estate. I have never really touched it for anything because my dad supports me, but it's there. It's mine."

"It's yours? How about your dad?" she inquires.

"My mom left me everything. It's my maternal family inheritance. My dad has no say about how I spend it. Although I do have to request it. How much should I withdraw?"

"Are you kidding me?" Toni exclaims. "How in the hell have you kept this from me? Especially after the shock of finding out who Garrett was."

"That's especially why. I didn't want it to change anything

between us. And I knew Alex would freak out if he knew. He never would have given me the chance if he knew who I was. My mom fought hard to marry my dad. He wasn't who my grandmother had in mind for her daughter. My grandmother wanted her to marry money. My mom married for love. My dad does very well for himself and proved himself to my grandparents after a while."

"Your dad is not like Alex at all. Your dad is going to flip when he finds out who you're dating. Or were dating," Javie declares.

"My dad is not going to flip because my dad already knows. I told him already."

"Told him what?" Toni asks.

"Told him everything I suspected minus him being arrested since it happened today. He knows everything." I shrug.

"WHAT?!" she exclaims. "Why would you tell him?"

"Because the one friend I trust, I couldn't really talk to." I look at her sadly.

They all look at me with concern written all over their faces, no one knowing what to say.

Toni finally breaks the silence, "I'm sorry I wasn't there for you."

"It's okay. Everything is just so fucked up." I take a breath.

"Who are you?" Javie asks.

A small smile pulls at my lips. "No one famous like Garrett. My maternal last name is Morgan. But that would only mean something to you if you know old oil money. My mother's family has built a small empire with it."

"Did you know who she was?" Toni asks Garrett.

He nods his head. I'm surprised he knows.

"And you didn't tell me either?" Her frustration shows.

"I just found out a few months ago. That's why Jared is

pursuing her. He thinks her old money name and status can help him. The house is talking."

"I have never used my mother's name. How did he find out?" I ask Garrett.

He shrugs and shakes his head. I know he doesn't hang at the house often, and I'm surprised he knew that much.

"So you have money. Lots of money?" Javie says.

I nod.

"And you have Daddy's approval to be with Alex?" he continues.

I nod.

A full-bellied laugh escapes his lips. As he catches his breath he says, "Alex is going to lose his shit when he finds out." He continues laughing, and Toni joins him.

Once they compose themselves, Toni says, "The house isn't going to clean itself."

She stands, and we all follow her back in. A couple of hours pass, and the house is back in order.

"I don't want to go home. Can I stay here?" I ask Javie.

"Of course." He sits on the couch and places his feet on the cooler Garrett and Toni were sitting on outside. He was creative, using this as a make-shift coffee table since theirs was somehow broken. He pats the couch next to him, and I sit down curling into him.

"We are heading out. Garrett has some things to do at the ranch. We'll be back Sunday night," Toni informs us.

"I just sent you a text with the name and number of a lawyer. He's available to meet with you tomorrow after lunch. Call him in the morning to confirm. He'll handle everything for you," Garrett tells me.

"Thank you."

They walk out of the house, leaving Javie and I to drown in our thoughts. I know he doesn't like going against Alex's wishes but is secretly relieved I'm doing it anyway. He's flipping through channels, and I'm imagining every possible scenario that could possibly happen on Monday.

"Why don't you go to bed?" Javie shakes me awake. I fell asleep on the couch.

In Alex's room, I look around. I cleaned it earlier and wanted so desperately to get in bed and feel him around me. I refused to let myself earlier, but now I indulge my senses. Stripping down, I pick up a shirt that was thrown on the floor earlier and slide it over me. I can still smell him on the shirt. I crawl into his bed and let the mental and physical exhaustion from the day take me under.

ALEX

I HAVE ENDED up exactly where I believed I would. I can't blame anyone. I knew what I was doing. My lips are sealed, doing my time to avoid bringing revenge onto Toni or Javie. Hector may have been arrested with me, but I doubt he'll stay that way. I'm sure Jefe has someone on the payroll to get him out.

Time here runs slowly. Minutes seem to turn into hours. Not sure why I want time to pick up. I'll only be moved to county after my arraignment, where I'll no doubt spend years.

I'll be the sacrificial lamb out for slaughter to ensure Jefe and Hector stay clean. Now I understand why they didn't deliver or pick up at the tire shop. They knew something was up and let me continue working. They left me out to hang. Which is usual, and I wouldn't have expected any less. I have seen this game played way too long. It just sucks when it's you.

. . .

Monday finally arrives, and we can get this show on the road. I will get my court-appointed lawyer and be moved to county to await my bogus trial. I'll do my time and probably end up back in anyway. No reason to think I'll be any different than Jefe's other minions.

I watch as each person who has been arrested over the weekend takes their turn. Some are let out on their own recognizance and others with a small bail. The same court-appointed lawyer stands with each of them, whispers a couple of words, and announces the plea; the judge makes his decision, and they are whisked away for release.

My name and docket are called, and I am escorted to the front with the same lawyer until I hear "James Madison, legal counsel for Alejandro Martinez."

The court -appointed lawyer steps away as Mr. Madison stands next to me.

"Plead not guilty when asked. I will handle the bail," he instructs me before I can formulate a question.

"I don't have money to pay you" finally comes out.

"I've already been paid. Face front." He demands. Is Jefe helping me? This would be a first.

"On the charge of drug distribution, how do you plead?" the judge directs at me.

"Not guilty," I answer quickly, not that I would have answered any other way.

"Bail is set at ten thousand dollars." The judge orders.

"Your honor. This is a first offense. We request leniency in the amount," Mr. Madison intervenes.

"Fine. Bail is set at five thousand dollars," the judge agrees.

Mr. Madison nods his head to the judge then turns to me, "We will have you out in a bit."

Who's the "we" that will have me out, I wonder.

Walking out into the sun after being locked up this whole

weekend felt surreal. I can't imagine what it will feel like after years. My eyes adjust to the brightness, and that's when I notice Lola standing near Mr. Madison. Did she do this?

Mr. Madison extends his hand to me, so I take it and shake. "Thank you." I am at a loss of words, and that was the only thing that I could think of.

"Sure. Okay. I'll leave you two, but before I do, some guidance. Don't go to work in the club. Stay away from there. Actually, stay away from anywhere they could try tie you to selling. Talk to no one who is tied to this. I'm going to figure out what information they have and where the charges stemmed from. I'll call you later this week when I have more information, and we can move forward." He tips his head and walks away.

I finally look down at the woman who owns my soul, angry she did this. Why would she place herself in the middle of a mess she has no business being a part of?

"I told Javie to tell you to stay away." I begin walking away from her again. It hurts just as badly as the first time, but I will not drag her down with me.

She grabs my arm quickly. "He did, and I refused to listen. And you are not walking away from me. Let's go home, and you can shower the stink off you." Her voice is angry and hurt simultaneously.

Not having the energy to fight with her, I concede to her wishes. We drive to my house in silence. Neither of us is willing to enter this battle yet. She parks and exits the truck, walking to the front door. After treating her the way I have, I wasn't sure whether she would stay or go.

I hesitantly follow her in. Looking around, I notice they cleaned up the destruction the cops left behind. She sits on the couch and stares at her phone, refusing to look at me. I look, feel, and smell awful, so I head straight for the shower. It will give me time to think of how to make Lola understand she needs to leave me. I am not the person for her.

I take my time, not wanting to confront her, not wanting to see the hurt in her eyes I saw when I broke things off. Not knowing if I can be strong enough a second time. I dress in jeans and T-shirt. Seeing her has awoken my dick, and I can't be thinking with him. Straining in the jeans will help me remember what I need to do.

Back in the living room, she is still scrolling on her phone and will not look up. I clear my throat, trying to get her attention. Her eyes remain glued to whatever is on that small screen.

"Why are you here if you're going to ignore me?" I finally ask, agitated.

She slowly brings her gaze to me, her lips pulled down and brows pulled together. I wait as she stares a hole right through me.

"I'm here to talk to you. But I will not engage with you if all you are going to do is tell me to leave. When you can remove that statement from what you are going to say, then we can talk. Until then, I will be here waiting." She looks back down to her phone.

"Lola, what part of 'I'm a piece of shit' don't you understand? You are too good for me. You need someone who can take care of you. You need someone who won't place your life in danger." I plead with her to listen.

She begins looking through her purse. She pulls out her AirPods and places them in her ears, never once looking at me. I do notice her eyes begin to collect tears. It feels like someone is squeezing the shit out of my heart. The scale is beginning to tip; knowing her leaving is best but wanting to wrap her in my arms to feel her is weighing more heavily on me.

I sit next to her on the couch, waiting to see if she will

look at me. When she continues to ignore me, I run my fingers down her arm, her soft skin calling me. A trail of goose bumps follow.

"Fine. I won't tell you to go, even though that's what's best for you. Talk to me." I fall to her stubbornness.

She finally pulls her gaze away from the phone to look at me.

"There are so many questions I have, but Mr. Madison has told me not to ask them. If you are honest with me and disclose any information, I could be called to testify. I can figure out enough for myself. At least for now," she tells me.

"If that is the case, why in the hell would you want you be with me?" Frustration sets in quickly. If she knows I'm guilty, why is she here?

"Because I love you. You don't just walk away from someone you love."

"People fall in and out of love all the time. People walk away. People leave. Couples destroy each other. Love isn't enough." I told myself no one would ever have control of my heart. I didn't need or want that type of drama in my life. But I was dumb and gave her my heart anyway. I gave it away, knowing I would be hurt in the end. She is the only one who deserves it, but I'm not worthy to keep her. I will destroy her if I insist.

"You're right. They do," she agrees with me, and now I'm waiting for her to wake up and leave. "But sometimes they don't. Sometimes it's for a lifetime. Sometimes couples walk through hell together and come out the other end, unscathed and stronger for their journey."

I don't have any words to disagree with her. I have told her time and time again I'm nothing but trouble, and each time she has fought me on it. The love she has for me blinds her to all of my many faults. I can't let her believe in us.

I need to veer the conversation away from us and on to

something else. "Okay, but Mr. Madison, I can't afford him. You need to call him and tell him to stop."

"You don't need to afford him. I already paid his retainer fee."

"How can you afford that? Did Javie give you the money to bail me out?" My mind needs to come back to the problems at hand, and a girlfriend, or lack thereof, should not be what I'm concentrating on.

"No. Javie did not give me money. I paid your bail too."

Shocked I ask, "What the fuck have you done?"

"I used my money. That's what I did." Her voice raises in anger.

"What money?"

"I used my trust fund. I'm one of those people." She rolls her eyes at me, picking up her phone and staring at it again. She begins blasting music loudly, I can hear it from her AirPods.

Trust fund? What does that mean? Is she another Garrett?

I tap her arm to get her attention. The music stops as she looks at me.

"What does that mean?"

"It means I'm wealthy. It means I have more money in my name than I know what to do with. It means I have the power to pay for a lawyer and bail in cash with a few hours notice. It means even if I didn't work a day in my life, I would still have money to leave my kids." Her eyes widen and roll in as she turns back to her phone, starting the music again.

"Wait, what?" Is she being serious?

Her focus is on the phone, so I tap her again. She pulls an AirPod out of her ear.

"You're rich?" leaves my mouth because I don't know what I'm asking.

"You can say that."

"Why didn't you tell me?"

"What would you have done if I told you? Push me away or take a chance with dating me?"

"Push you away" flies out of my mouth before I can stop it.

"Exactly. You were already pushing me away, and you didn't even know that part. I didn't want that to become the reason we couldn't try being us."

"We are from two separate worlds. We don't belong together. Never have." I try to reason with her.

"Why can't our worlds coexist?" she pushes back.

I don't have an answer except that I don't want to fill her lightness with my darkness. "It's not just two separate worlds. My world is filled with despicable actions. Things that should never see the light of day. Things I don't want touching you."

"Answer me this?" She waits for me to agree. I nod. "Would you have done these despicable things if you didn't have to?"

"I did them. That's all you need to know," I counter.

"Yes. I know you did. But here's the thing. You, at your core, are a good person. You only did these things to keep your family safe. I don't believe you would have if you weren't pushed into becoming the man of the house. Taking care of Toni and Javie." She pauses, and when I don't fight her, she continues. "I realized when you fall, you crash. There has never been a safety net to catch you. I'm your safety net this time."

"I can't let you do it."

"I know you don't want me to, but I'm still going to. I'm not sure why you won't accept help. Accepting help won't make you look weak. We all need help sometime. You give and give and give and expect nothing in return. You're now going to accept help from me."

I know I have done nothing in life to deserve this girl, but she insists on me. On us.

"I can't." How could I ever repay this debt? The price is too high.

"You can, and you will. End of story." She is about to stick the AirPod back in her ear, so I place my hand on her arm, stopping her.

How do I make her understand she doesn't need to do this? That she needs to take her money and walk away from the hellhole that is my life. "I know I can, but I won't. How will I ever repay you? I don't have the ability to."

"You will because it has already been done. Fire Mr. Madison if you want. I don't care. He has been paid in advance. I knew you would pull this shit, so I figured if everything was paid up front, you would have to take it." She shrugs and looks away from me.

"Why are you fighting me on this? You deserve the sun and the moon, and I will never have the ability to give that to you."

"I am not accepting your excuse on why we can't be us. I can buy the sun and moon if I want. I don't need a man to do that for me. I do, though, need a man to love me. To protect me. To cherish me. To believe in me. And I do know you are the man that can." She's getting frustrated. "I haven't touched my trust fund until today. It sat there because I learned the hard way, money does not buy my happiness. It does make life easier, but not happier. I have never had to fall and catch myself. You, on the other hand, have never had someone look out for you. To make sure you never have to do things out of desperation. You have been in survival mode since you were a child. I want you to relax and turn that off for a moment. I will catch you, just like I know if I ever needed to be caught, you would be there for me. The short and simple reason is I love you. I want to be with you."

She declares this with such conviction, I am tongue tied. "I...uh..."

"Do you love me?" she asks.

"You know I do. I told you, *ya tienes mi corazon*, and I never want it back." I do not deserve her, but damnit, I can't fight this any longer.

Relief washes over her. "Our story is not a fairy tale. It never will be, and as much as I always thought that's what I would have, I don't want it anymore. I want us. Our story will not only be sunshine and rainbows, because life isn't either. Life is filled with just as much sadness and anger as happiness. Happiness wouldn't be as sweet if we didn't know the opposite." She pauses, then asks, "All I want to know is, have you been with anyone else since me?" She stares into my eyes.

"No. There has only been you."

A small smile appears.

"When we look back, all we will see is a tragically beautiful beginning to our love story." She's watching me.

I extend my arms to her, not able to fight her any longer. She comes to me, wrapping her arms around my neck, clutching me tightly.

CHAPTER 25

LOLA

IT'S FELT LIKE A LIFETIME SINCE I WAS IN HIS ARMS. I PULL back to look at him. The strong, powerful man I fell in love with is shrouded in worry. Bags under his eyes and an overgrown five o'clock shadow show his exhaustion. I bring my lips to his, gently at first, nervous, but the need for him quickly takes over. I kiss him greedily, eager for more. I bring my leg over to straddle him, his bulge contained in the jeans he's wearing. My hands move quickly to unbutton them. He pulls my shirt and I bring my arms up, helping him. His lips find my neck, and I want nothing more than for him to fill me.

He pushes himself off the couch, standing with me in his arms. I hold on to him tightly, scared if I let go, he'll disappear. He enters his room and places me on the bed gently, his take-charge attitude subdued.

"Are you sure?" His face is pained.

"I'm positive. Make love to me." I grab his face bringing it down, our lips meeting in a rushed kiss.

Our hands are stripping each other of the clothes between us. The desperation we felt when we were apart controls our frenzied actions. Each article that falls away leads us to the place we are so urgently working towards.

Once I feel him enter me, everything slows. He stays buried deep, bringing one hand to my cheek rubbing it softly with is thumb.

"Don't ever push me away again," I whisper to him. "We are doing this life together."

"You don't let me, even when I try." His lips touch mine; his tongue runs along mine, requesting permission.

He begins to rock into me, and I am lost in him. I wrap my arms around his back trying to pull him closer, scared what will happen after my announcement. We come together quickly, both of us soothing the ache of being apart. His body falls to the side as he quickly pulls me closer to his side.

I can't wait any longer. I overcame one battle, but I'm terrified to drop the next bomb. He's quiet as I listen to his deep breaths. I should let him sleep, knowing how much he has been through, but I can't sit on this information any longer. He needs to know.

"I don't want to push you away, but what happens if I'm locked up? I can't ask you to wait for me." Pain carries each one of those words.

"Mr. Madison said there is a great chance of getting you off. He did not seem worried about the arrest." I prop myself up on my arm to look down at him.

"And if he's wrong? I'm being selfish keeping you with me. You don't need to be saddled down with a convict." Tears begin to collect in his eyes. He's terrified.

"We will fight it. I have the resources to continue fighting, and that's what we will do." I need to carry the burden for him right now. He has carried so much for so long, he needs a break.

"Why would you want to do that?" He shakes his head in resignation.

He has just opened the door. "Two reasons. One, because I love you. Two, because my baby needs their father."

His eyes widen in surprise. He's quiet. I'm waiting, and no words are leaving his mouth. None from anger, surprise, or denial. I need to know what he's thinking. Finally, his eyes leave mine and travel down my naked body, landing on my stomach. His hand comes up slowly and gently strokes my stomach.

When his eyes finally come back to mine, he asks, "Are you sure?"

I nod, smiling.

"You want to have a child? With me?" Apprehension fills each word.

"Yes. I want to have this child, and I want to have it with you."

"You know my life. What if I'm an awful dad? Look at mine."

"Shhhh." I cover his lips with my finger. "You are going to be a wonderful father. You have taken care of Javie and Toni since you were a child yourself. You ensure the ones you love are safe. You push them to be more than you want for yourself. From what I've seen, you are going to be the perfect father."

I kiss him, hoping he listened, truly listened, to those words. He separates us, and his hand finds my stomach again.

Cautiously he asks, "Are you sure you want to do this with me?"

"I'm positive. Now sleep. You look exhausted." He closes his eyes, and I lay my head on his chest. The tension-filled past couple of days have caught up with me too. Once my eyes close, I don't remember anything else.

. . .

VOICES in another room wake me. Alex's fingers are travelling up and down my side. I look up at him.

"How long have you been awake?"

"Not too long."

"Why didn't you wake me?" He was the one in jail, the who probably did not sleep much, but I'm the one who's sleeping like the dead.

"You need your rest." He kisses the top on my head.

Here he is again, becoming the protector. It is engrained in him.

"We need to get up before they begin knocking on the door. They have started talking louder, the longer we have stayed in the room." He smiles, the first real smile since we arrived home.

Sitting up, I watch him get out of bed and dress. I quickly follow, sliding shorts on and grabbing one of his shirts. I grab my hair and tie it up in a messy bun before we walk out to explain everything to the others.

A deep sigh escapes Javie's lips when he sees us walk hand in hand into the kitchen.

"I'm so happy you didn't kill each other." Worry melts from his face.

"You thought we would?" Alex asks.

"I did think it was a possibility, as stubborn as you are and with Lola digging her heels in, insistent she was getting you out. Either that or you would come home and kill me for not following instructions."

Toni laughs out loud, "He's not wrong, you know."

Alex shakes his head, rolling his eyes. "Fine. No one is getting killed, and now we wait."

"Wait for?" Javie asks.

"Mr. Madison, the lawyer Lola hired. He said he would call later in the week when he knew more."

"Why did you get involved with Hector again?" Toni asks.

"Nope. You are not answering that," I pipe in, directed at Alex. Then I turn to Toni. "He can't talk about anything to any of us. We can't ask anything until after the trial, if there is one. Mr. Madison made it very clear that if the prosecution thinks we know anything, they will call us up as witnesses against him. The only person he would be able to talk to is a spouse, and since he's not married, he can't say anything."

"Like we would ever testify against Alex?" Toni responds.

"I don't care. I'm not chancing anything when it comes to him. He will not say anything." I glance up at Alex, and he's looking down at me, smiling.

He shrugs his shoulders, "I guess I'm not answering any questions." He squeezes my hand, and I know he will follow Mr. Madison's directions.

He pulls me with him to one of the chairs and sits down bringing me to his lap. He whispers in my ear, "Can I tell them the news?"

I nod, worried Toni will reveal she already knew. And I wonder if she told anyone else.

"Lola and I are having a baby." His smile is big and genuine.

"What the actual fuck?" spills from Javie's mouth as Toni's eyes widen in disbelief. "Seriously?"

"Yes. Seriously. That is why I will do anything and everything Mr. Madison says. I will not risk being away from Lola or the baby."

"Congratulations," Garrett says politely since Javie and Toni still seem to be shocked.

Toni walks over to me and brings me in for a tight hug. "Congratulations," she says out loud, then whispers, "I'm glad he took it well." She kisses my cheek and lets me go.

Every bad scenario I had dreamed up has vanished with his joy at the news.

Chapter 26

ALEX

The meeting with Mr. Madison went well. From what he could gather, my arrest was based on an anonymous tip. He is waiting to see why the charges have not been dropped since no drugs were found in the house. He believes there is more because he has had to pry information from the DA's office.

He has not asked me for any information, which I find odd. When I tried to tell him some things, he stopped me and told me to wait until more information was released from the DA. No one from the SEV has tried to contact me, and I don't know if Hector is out. I feel like I'm sitting on a ticking time bomb.

My drive home is quiet. Lola has been going to her classes each day, and Javie has his job. I have been left home alone with my thoughts and regrets. I pray all this will be soon forgotten. I don't want my child to see me like I am, weak and vulnerable. I need to be a better, stronger man for them. I don't want them exposed to this life. They are going to be better than me. They are going to have every advantage I never had.

Not wanting to sit around and let life happen to me, I begin driving to the ranch. I'm not sure if Garrett has mentioned anything to his parents, but I need to find something for me.

Coming up to the big house, I know Mr. Anders will not be there; he is up working every day in the field. I drive through to the workers house close to the barn, hoping to find him there.

Walking into the barn, the familiar smell of animals hits me. I hated the smell while I was here but have come to miss it. Mr. Anders is unsaddling a horse.

"Hi, sir. I was wondering if you had a minute to talk?" I ask, unsure of his reply.

"Sure. Come on and help me brush him down."

I pick up one of the brushes and begin to brush the horse like I was taught all those many months ago. Life has changed too many times in less than a year. If I'm going to be a father, I need to find stability.

"I'm not sure if Garrett has mentioned anything that's going on with me, but I am here to ask for advice." This is the only man I have ever known who is respectable.

"No, he hasn't. What's going on?" He answers in his gruff rancher voice.

"I was arrested for selling drugs. According to my attorney I'm not to talk about that, but I need to leave the life I've lived behind. There are only two roads for me if I continue on that path. Jail or dead. I don't like either of those choices. You are the only man I know who I can go to for advice and help. I need to find a job in town. Lola is going to have my baby. I need to be a better man for her and the baby. Will you help?"

He has not looked at me as we have continued brushing

the horse. I know he listened to every word. I know he is choosing his words wisely.

"Were you doing any of that crap while you were here at the ranch?"

"No, sir." I answer quickly and honestly.

"Can you tell me why you were mixed up in it? Without details."

"My past came back to haunt me. When the boss of the neighborhood asks you to do something, you do it, or there are consequences."

"Fair enough. Are you sure you are out for good?" He wants a guarantee I'm going to walk the straight line.

"Yes sir. Because I do not want to raise a child in that life."

He nods his head to me. "Stay for dinner. I'll make some calls. I can't say they will be the best jobs, but I'm sure you can work your way up." He claps my shoulder walking past.

"I would love to stay for dinner, but I didn't tell anyone I was coming out here. Lola will be expecting me back home."

"Okay. Come out this weekend to get away from town. The house will be empty. The boys are heading to Mexico for a few days."

"Thank you."

On the drive home, I feel better than I have since before Hector came to drag me back in. The weight I knew I was carrying, but was too ashamed to admit was heavier than I could bear, is slowly lifting.

Turning the corner, I see Lola and Javie are home, their cars in the front. All of a sudden, the car coming towards me opens fire on the house. I brake as the sound of bullets pierces me. The rounds continue, never seeming to stop. Once the sound stops, I hit the gas, knowing Lola is in the house. The car peels out, passing me, but my only thought is getting to Lola.

I park the car, running into the house scared of what I may find. Javie is yelling for Lola from the kitchen.

"Lola, *amor*. Where are you?" I yell, straining to listen for her.

"Alex!" I hear her.

"Call the cops." I yell to Javie as I run towards Lola's voice.

She is laying down in the fetal position in my closet. I sit on the floor on the outside of the closet to coax her out.

"*Amor, vente.*" I place my hand around hers, which is clutching her knees tightly. Her body is trembling. I gently pull her arm away from her legs, and she slowly eases her way out, coming to sit on me, crying into my chest.

"*Nada te va pasar.*" (Nothing is going to happen to you.) I'm rocking her, clutching her to me tightly, making a promise I don't know if I can keep. "Shhh. Shhh."

Javie comes to the door, his phone to his ear, answering questions from the person on the other end. Sirens in the distance coming closer announces a quick response. We were probably not the only ones to call.

I motion for Javie to meet them at the front door, not wanting to move Lola yet. A couple of minutes pass before officers enter my bedroom and find me on the floor holding Lola to me.

"Sir, we need you to exit the premises," one officer announces.

"Can you help me?" I whisper and point to Lola.

"Miss, are you hurt?" he asks her.

She continues crying, not answering. He grabs her elbow and begins to try and lift her. She grips my shirt tighter, refusing to move.

"Is she hurt?" the officer asks me.

"No. She wasn't hit. She's in shock I think," I inform him.

He speaks into his radio.

"*Amor*, look at me."

She pushes herself into me again.

"It's over, baby. I need you to look at me." I can feel her trying to take deeper breaths.

She finally pulls back a bit, and I bring my hands to her face. Her mascara has run down her face and is smeared from rubbing against my shirt.

"I need you to stand up."

She nods slightly as she continues taking deep breaths, slowly moving to stand. I jump up quickly to hold her. I guide her out as the officer follows us. I look back at him, wondering where he wants us to go. He points to the front door. As soon as we exit, Javie rushes to us, taking Lola from me. He sits down, bringing her down with him. Her head is leaning on his shoulder, eyes closed. I stand, observing everything unfolding.

I watch as officers enter and exit the house. They work for several minutes before asking us to come in to answer some questions. As soon as he mentions this, I remember I should call Mr. Madison. I do not want to inadvertently say something I shouldn't. I pull the phone from my pocket and dial his number. I leave a message with his receptionist, as he was with a client. I worry as I make my way into the house.

An officer asks us just a few generic questions. This wasn't the first drive-by shooting in the neighborhood, and it won't be the last. I wonder whether their lack of questions had to do with their "it's just another shooting in the hood" attitude or if they know my link to Jefe. By the time Mr. Madison calls back, all the cops have left. I relay the couple of minor questions they asked and how we answered. He suggested we do not stay at the house for now.

"Javie, I need you to pack. We are going out to the ranch for the weekend. Go ahead and pack for next week too."

"Why?" His brows pull in.

"I don't think it's safe here. Not now. I can't stand not knowing what the hell is going on with the SEV, but I can't risk poking around. I don't know who set up my fall. I—"

Lola interrupts me. "Enough. You are about to say too much. Stop talking." She turns to Javie, "Please, just pack. You will stay at my apartment if necessary."

Javie looks at her and nods.

"I'm going to pack." I extend my hand to Lola. She stands up, grabbing mine and following. I don't want to be away from her right now.

I quickly throw clothes in a bag, wanting to leave this place as quickly as I can. Nailing a large board to the front of the house to cover the front window took longer than I wanted, but if I hadn't, we would have come back to an empty house. The money in the shed is the last thing I grab.

We each drive away in our own vehicle, not wanting to risk anything happening to our vehicles while we are away. Lola drives off first, with Javie close behind. I take the tail, making sure we aren't being followed. I may be paranoid, but I can't take any chances with Lola and my unborn child.

We meet at Lola's, and before we enter her apartment, Javie announces he has some errands to run, being vague on his whereabouts. I wonder what he's up to, but my mind is focused on Lola and her safety. I know he can take care of himself.

CHAPTER 27

LOLA

Sitting on the back porch of the ranch with only the sounds of nature surrounding me, the day's turmoil finally begins to melt away. I have never felt as scared as I did today. The sound of bullets and glass shattering was something I never thought I would ever hear, much less be in the middle of. Falling to the floor and crawling back to Alex's room, I didn't know if one would strike me. Going through this has given me yet another insight into how he grew up. A drive-by shooting was and is unheard of in the neighborhood I grew up in. This is only something you witness on TV and is dramatized for ratings. But it isn't. It is terrifying and nerve-wracking when you are present.

Trying to snap out of the fear that paralyzed me earlier, I made myself numb, until now. Now all the feelings I bottled tightly have come back and tears begin to slide down my cheeks. I'm able to hide right now, gather myself together before facing Alex. If he knew I was out here crying alone, he would want to fix it, and this is something that can't be fixed. I have to work through these feelings.

He is inside cooking, and Javie should be on his way. Alex told him to stay away from the neighborhood, and Javie promised he wouldn't be anywhere near there.

The door opening breaks me from all the thoughts floating. "Dinner is ready. Do you want to eat inside or out here?"

"Out here." I answer. I don't turn to see him, instead facing out, waiting for him to close the door.

"Look at me."

Shit, I thought he would go in and bring everything out without seeing me in distress. Knowing I won't be able to hide it with the steps coming toward me, I wipe my face quickly.

"*Amor*, you can't be keeping things from me." He crouches in front of me.

"I'm not," I lie.

"Then why are you crying?" he pushes.

I drop my gaze to my hands, not wanting to answer.

"Talk to me."

"It's nothing." Nervous I'll break down again if I speak about today, I try and deflect.

"It's something. Talk." I have watched him go from scared and broken back to domineering in a matter of days.

"I'm scared. I don't want you back at that house. What if they come back? And what about Javie? It's not safe for him either."

"I know. And I don't expect you to feel anything other than scared and pissed. You should be pissed at me for putting us in this situation. But instead, you are still with me." He grabs my hand tightly.

"I don't want to be anywhere without you. Did you hear me? I don't want you back in that house."

"I know, because all I've thought about is you in that house. Watching it all play out in front of me. I have never been more scared in my life than I was at that very moment.

I don't think my heart began beating again until I heard your voice. I can't lose you, and now my life's mission is to keep you safe and away from that shit."

"What are you going to do?"

"Sell that damn house. Pay off Toni's school and get Javie set up somewhere else, I guess. I don't know. I can't do anything without discussing it with them. They own it also." He comes up, kissing me softly. "Let me get you fed and relaxed first. I will figure everything else out later."

"Okay."

He stands up, walking back inside. How did I fall in love with a reformed gang member? Was he a gang member? I don't even know, and I may not ever know the extent of what he has done. I just have to trust he's out now.

Dinner was, of course, delicious, and even though I thought I wouldn't eat much, I devoured a full plate. We are rocking on the bench, waiting on everyone else to arrive. I'm leaning into him; his physical strength, one of the first things I was attracted to, is providing me comfort.

The rumble of cars driving up breaks through the silence.

"Quiet night?" Toni comes out the patio door, beer in hand.

"After today, that is the only thing I want." I answer her.

Garret and Javie follow her out each with their own drinks.

"Want one?" Javie asks Alex.

"Yeah. Grab me one, please." He answers then looks at me, "Do you want anything?"

I shake my head. With my nerves rattled, I wish I could have something to take the edge off, but I'll just have to handle it sans alcohol.

"Do you know who it was?" Toni is the first to ask about the day.

"I didn't recognize the car or the guys in the car. But I'll admit I didn't really look hard. I was too worried about Lola and Javie in the house."

"Sure, you were worried about me. You had Lola on the brain." Javie snorts as he hands Alex a beer.

"If we are talking about this, let's do it now because I invited someone up here." Javie says, then looks at Toni, "And you need to play nice."

"You invited a girl here. After everything?" Alex says harshly.

"Yes. I had plans already. I didn't want to cancel, so I invited her here. Garrett said it was fine." Javie says, unaffected, not cowering beneath Alex's death glare.

"Be nice. Let Javie have his fun too." I squeeze Alex's leg.

"Fine. Then let's talk." Alex says gruffly. "I think we need to sell the house and move. I can't go groveling back to Jefe. I don't know what's happening. There is no way for me to figure out if it's a SEV or a random hit. I'm flying blind." I hear the frustration in his voice.

"Where would I live?" Javie wonders out loud. "You have Lola's apartment and Toni and Garrett have theirs. I'm the homeless one in this equation."

"You would not be homeless. I will find you something temporary until you decide what you want. I haven't thought that far ahead. All I know is, it's not safe there anymore. I wouldn't want you back there next week either," Alex tells him.

"You will have an apartment, ASAP." I announce. "Movers will come by, pack up the house, and it will go on the market. Javie, you will have an apartment of your own. No need to worry. I got it covered, at least to start off." I announce proudly to all. I will not have the people I love in danger or floundering when I have the means to support them.

"I can't let you do that," Alex, of course, jumps in, hating to depend on anyone but himself.

"You can and you will. Javie will not go back there except to pack and be out. I will make calls tomorrow and have something ready this coming week." I push back. I look at Javie, "What part of town do you want to live? Where should I ask them to look?"

"Uh..." He looks to Alex.

"Babe. I've got it," I reassure them both. "Don't worry about it. I will get him set up, then y'all can take over the monthly payments. I just want this done quickly and quick sometimes takes money."

He lets out a frustrated sigh before bringing the beer to his lips taking a long pull. He's quiet, and everyone is watching him for direction. This man, born into a life of poverty and hardship, is the cornerstone of his family. While Toni and Javie love to test him, they depend on him more.

"Javie, if it makes you feel better to take your time, why don't you stay out here? There is space and dinner every night. This way you can take your time and really figure out what you want to do," Garrett offers.

"Actually, I like that idea more. Sorry, Lola." A small frown appears as he answers.

"Are y'all really ready to sell? That is a big decision to make in one night, especially when emotions are still high," Garrett questions.

"No. But with everything going on, no one can be there. At least not right away," Alex answers him.

"Lola, I can only imagine what it was like for you in that house today. It was awful, I'm sure, but you are leading with fear right now, and Alex would move heaven and earth to keep you safe. He's only agreeing to make you happy," Garrett says softly. "Pack up the valuables in the house and store them or bring them to our apartments or the ranch. Lock up the house and wait. If and when you truly feel you are ready to sell, after this has passed, then go for it. There is no need to rush," Garrett says to the cousins.

"I agree. I'm not ready." Toni's eyes water. "As much as we are all trying to get away from that place, I'm not quite ready to say goodbye to it yet."

"I can look for someplace cheap for six months to a year. A dump, until I decide what I want to do and see if my dream job comes calling." Javie says with more confidence than he had before.

"Then it's agreed. We pack up the house, then no one is allowed to go back into the neighborhood," Alex stresses.

"Why?" Toni asks. "Not that I want to or am going to, but you know something."

"I don't. Not for sure anyway. But the day I was busted when I was talking to Hector—" Alex begins.

"Stop. You can't talk about that." I interrupt again. I hate being this person, scared and helpless, but my heart drops every time I think he could go to jail.

"Why don't y'all just get married, and Lola can stop worrying about what you say," Javie jokes.

"Way to put pressure on them." Garrett laughs.

I look to Alex, and I can't tell what he's thinking because he has his game face on. I had thought about it but didn't want to say anything if he's not ready. I just got him back and don't want to lose him over marriage pressure.

Ignoring Javie's joke of a comment, he begins again, "Back to what I was saying." His words are firm. "It's no secret because you heard the conversation at the house that day." He looks at me sternly. "Hector threatened to bring the neighborhood down on me, and I welcomed it. I welcomed it... *on me*. But he saw I was protecting Lola, trying to get her out of the house. He saw me with her several times. He knew what she drove. If it was SEV, they were sending me a message. The car drove right past me *after* shooting at the house. They could have taken me out easily but didn't even try."

ALEX

LOLA'S EYES WIDEN. I've scared her even more than she was already.

"They are going after the people who I care for unless it was truly random. But not taking me out when they had a clear shot? Jefe wants me to come back groveling. Wants me to pledge allegiance. Ensure I'm not the leak."

"Makes sense," Javie agrees, nodding his head. "When do we go back to the house and pack, then?"

"I'll do it on Monday. Rent a truck and get it all out. I'll have someone come out and fix the window so we can lock up for now."

"You can't go back to the house alone." Lola is quick to respond.

"I can, and I will. No one will be getting hurt on my account."

I know she's nervous, but her safety is my only concern. I can't believe Javie would throw out marrying her. I would marry her in a heartbeat, but is that what she wants? There are too many unknowns in my life, and I can't bring her down that path with me.

"I'll go with you. We can knock it out faster if it's the two of us." Garrett volunteers.

Toni goes in for a quick kiss, thanking him. He did it to temper Lola's fear, and Toni can stay with her while we are at the house.

A car driving up breaks the conversation.

"She's here," Javie exclaims, standing up quickly smiling.

As soon as he walks around the house to meet her, Toni asks, her eyes wide with wonder. "Who is she?"

Everyone shrugs and shakes their head. He has kept this mystery girl a secret from everyone.

He's gone for a few minutes as we wait in suspense for his return. No one says anything. He finally opens the patio door, and he is followed out by a petite brunette.

"Hi!" She says smiling brightly. "I'm Maritza. Sorry to crash your party."

Her smile is covering the nerves, as I notice her clutching Javie's hand tightly. I wonder what he has told her about us.

"Ritza, this is my brother Alex and his girlfriend, Lola." He points in our direction.

Lola speaks for us, sitting up. "Hi, welcome." A new person to take in gives Lola a break from everything she is currently worried about.

"And that's my cousin Toni and her boyfriend, Garrett. This is his ranch we're crashing." Javie continues the introductions.

Garrett smiles shaking his head.

"Hello. Not crashing, definitely invited. Did you find it okay?" Garrett speaks, full of his usual charming manners. We are complete opposites.

I sneak a peek at Lola and she is smiling brightly, in her element, befriending yet another new person. She has a way of collecting all us strays. I guess I shouldn't be assuming anything about Javie's girl since he has kept her a secret.

"Are you in school?" Lola, of course, begins the questioning, but with her, it doesn't sound intrusive.

"I was, but then my brother needed me full time at the garage, so now I'm just working."

"Garage?" Lola is trying to keep the conversation going.

"Yes, the body shop he owns and is trying to build up." Maritza smiles brightly.

"That's how you met Javie!" Toni exclaims loudly. "Is that the shop you want to work in full time?" She turns to Javie.

Shit! Way to bust his balls if she didn't already know. A laugh escapes me.

"Way to play it cool, Toni. Thanks. But yes. That is the shop I want to work at."

Maritza plays it off very well, kissing Javie's cheek.

"My brother only has a couple of friends who work for him full time. He wants to get a bit more established before he takes on any more. He contracts out right now for the things he can't do like interior seat work and welding. But he is very impressed with Javie's work. He just doesn't know about us." Her mouth is still pulled in a smile, but it has left her eyes. There is more to this story, and now I can see why he has kept her a secret. He may be in for an ass kicking for messing with her, or he might be jeopardizing his dream job for this.

I stay quiet, just listening to their discussions, letting Lola relax and enjoy her element. She becomes the lively and chatty girl I met all those months ago. The girl who stole my heart doing nothing but being so different from any girl I have ever met. Her persistent nature when she wants something. The smile that lights up her face. The gentleness she exudes, ensuring those around her are comfortable. A guy like me has no business with a girl like her, but I got her anyway.

Lola slowly begins to lean on me again as the conversation continues until I hear her deep breaths. I look down to find her asleep on my shoulder. After everything today, I know she is worn out.

"Looks like I need to tuck her in." I grab her knees to bring them over me so I can pick her up and place her in bed without waking her.

But I wasn't as smooth as thought, and she grumbles, "What are you doing?"

"Taking you to bed. You fell asleep, *amor*," I whisper to her.

"I can walk." She shakes her head, smiling at me.

"Good night, all," she says as I grab her hand, pulling her behind me.

Her back is curled into my chest in bed. When I walked out on her a few weeks ago, I never thought I would have this again. She is so much stronger than I gave her credit for. She fought for us. She is going to have my child. With or without me, she was going to take on that responsibility. My hand slides to her stomach, and I splay my fingers out, holding her.

Chapter 28

LOLA

"We are having a baby," I whisper as I feel his fingers rubbing my stomach. I wonder if he's scared.

"I know," is all he says.

"Scared?"

"Terrified," he says.

"Why?"

"For one, I never thought about having a child. It never crossed my mind. If I didn't like any girl enough to commit to, why would it? And everything I've done in life. How can I tell my child to be an upstanding citizen if I wasn't one? What if I'm in jail? What if I miss out on them growing up because I'm locked up? If that happens, you have to promise me to not bring them. I will not have them see me as a fucking inmate." His words are full of anguish.

"Babe." I stop him from continuing. "I've told you, you are going to be a wonderful father. You are caring and loving." I turn around to face him, my eyelids heavy, but I want to make sure he stops this worry. "Yes, you have done bad things, but we talked about it. You didn't have choices. And jail...I don't know yet, but I do know I will burn through every dollar I have to keep you with me. You are the only one I want to do this life with." I place my hand on his scruffy cheek, which needs a trim.

"*Te amo*." He places a soft kiss on my nose. "Sleep."

"I love you." My eyes close, not able to fight the extreme exhaustion.

MONEY ALWAYS MAKES THINGS EASIER. I was able to get the window fixed in a day, and Alex and Garrett packed up essentials and any things of value to store. Javie still refuses to get a place in town, saying he's going to stay at the workhouse on the ranch for at least a week or two before making any decisions. I wonder if his hesitation over where to live has something to do with Ritza. She was interesting, but I wonder why they have kept their relationship a secret. Javie is too sweet for some girl to toy with his feelings.

Not my business, I know, but I can't help but worry for him too.

Back at my apartment we are trying to get back to life as usual. But what is usual? All I know is, I need to graduate this year.

"I'm headed to class." I announce to Alex. I hear his phone ring before I walk out the door.

I pause at the door, wondering who is calling him.

"Mr. Madison, hello," Alex says, phone to his ear.

He is listening to whatever Mr. Madison is telling him. I close the door, waiting to hear whatever news he is getting. As I stand there, waiting for Alex to get off the phone, my phone chimes. I pull it out of my pocket to find a text from Toni.

Why is Alex not answering me? Amelia my friend in the hood just said there was a major bust!

He's on the phone with the lawyer. Hold on. I type out quickly and send.

Alex hangs up the phone and looks at me.

"I have to go. Mr. Madison wants me in his office." He sits on the couch, slipping his shoes on.

"Can I go with you?" I hesitantly ask.

"You have class," he responds.

"I know, but this is more important." The need to go with him uncontrollable.

"Okay." He stands up, coming to me, wrapping me in his strong arms. He holds me for several seconds before he pulls back, looking down at me. "I know Javie joked about it, and now there is a big, fat elephant in the room."

He takes a long breath, and I wait for him to continue.

"I want you to know I've thought about marrying you. I thought you needed someone better, but now I know you need me as much as I need you. You bring light to my darkness." He places his lips on mine gently. "I hate that you are paying to solve my problems, but I will not fight you any further. I want to be a part of my child's life, and if letting you help me does that, then I will not fight you any further. I don't have a ring. I don't have anything to offer you except my love. I want to be able to give you everything, but right now, I don't have the means. But I will work at it, and you will have the man you deserve."

"You are already the man I want and deserve. I would marry you today if I could." He pulls me in again, and I place my head on his chest, listening to his heartbeat. This is the safest place I know.

"Come on, then. Mr. Madison is waiting." He lets me go, grabbing my hand firmly.

. . .

Sitting and waiting for Mr. Madison to enter his office, I can tell Alex is nervous. I completely forgot about Toni's text when he brought up marriage.

"Hey, I forgot to tell you that Toni texted while you were on the phone. She said something about a bust in the neighborhood. Did you see it?" I feel guilty for focusing on me and us and not giving him the message.

"Shit. I didn't look at them." He pulls his phone out. "Fuck," he says out loud.

"What?" His reaction worries me.

"I wonder if Jefe was raided and busted? She said Amelia mentioned it was a big bust, and only he would make that kind of news, for the neighborhood to be talking."

"You won't call anyone there to find out, will you?" My heart drops.

"No. I promised you, I'm done. I will not stick my nose out there. I am doing everything Mr. Madison says." He reassures me, just as the lawyer walks in.

"Hello, Alex." He extends his hand out to shake, then greets me.

"We have some things to discuss." Mr. Madison hesitates, looking at me.

"Does it make a difference if we are engaged?" Alex asks. I look at him in shock.

"It's up to you what she knows," he responds.

"Lola will stay," he says firmly.

He nods his head. "Okay. Then I'll begin." He takes out a legal pad and scans the page. "Hector Gomez was arrested at the same time you were, correct?"

"Yes. He was at my house at the time."

"He had been released without bail. But he was arrested again this morning. His father, Angel Gomez, was also arrested on multiple charges. It seems like there was a mole in their organization. An unnamed source so far and they are not releasing much more information than that. But I spoke with the DA, and it looks like they will not need you anymore. From what I gather, they have enough evidence without your testimony."

"Wait, what?" Alex asks confused.

"You were arrested for the sole purpose of corroborating the unknown source. They thought they were going to be able to find something on you to hold over your head and get information on Angel and his organization. They wanted to use you. Instead they found nothing and had no other evidence on you except parking in front of a random house to allegedly make a sale."

"David set me up?" Alex says under his breath.

I look to him as Mr. Madison says, "Don't say anymore."

Alex nods his head.

"As I was saying, since they have nothing on you, the DA has dropped all charges." His facial expression relaxes, and he cracks a small smile.

"Seriously." Doubt fills the one word which escapes Alex's mouth.

"Yes. All charges have been dropped. But I suggest you continue to avoid all relations with anyone who could tie you to Angel or Hector Gomez. If anything goes wrong, or if their witness falls through, they will come looking for you again. And for that reason, I suggest not speaking to anyone about anything," he warns.

"Yes, sir."

Alex's head drops into his hands, his breathing long and deep.

"It's over," I whisper to him placing my hand on his leg.

He takes a moment, but then looks up at me with tear-filled eyes and a sad smile, which breaks my heart.

"It's over," I repeat.

"Thank you." He sits up straight again, my bad boy too proud to show weakness for long.

"I'll be in touch if I hear anything else, but for now, you are free." Mr. Madison stands, extending his hand to Alex again.

Alex takes it, shaking firmly, then grabbing my hand and squeezing it.

"I wonder who shot the house," he says as we get in the car to leave.

"I don't know if we'll ever know. But that's behind us, and I would like to leave it there," I answer him.

EPILOGUE

ALEX

CRYING. A BABY'S CRY IS THE SWEETEST SOUND.

"Congratulations, it's a girl!" the doctor exclaims.

The nurse takes her from him and brings her to Lola, placing the baby in her arms. She's small but so beautiful. I can't believe this tiny little human is my daughter. She has my dark hair. Lola kisses her face, and I watch them in awe.

"We'll clean her right up and give her back to you." The nurse reaches out for the baby.

"You did it, *amor*." I kiss her forehead. It was getting a little dicey there for a bit with the contractions and pain.

She smiles, her gaze watching the nurses as they weigh, measure, and clean up the baby.

The nurse walks back, about to place her in Lola's arms again, when Lola stops her. "Her daddy wants to hold her."

"Ready?" The nurse looks at me, probably wondering how a guy like me won a girl like her.

I extend my arms. The nurse tucks her into my arms, and

I'm in awe. I sit in the chair by the bed, placing her on my lap. My heart feels like it will burst with pride. I unwrap the blanket to check her feet and hands. Ten toes and ten fingers. As I touch her tiny hand with my index finger, she grabs it. Tears collect instantly.

"*Tu siempre seras mi muñiquita,*" I whisper to her.

"I love you speaking Spanish, but I'm still not fluent enough to know what you just whispered to her."

I snort. Lola has been trying to learn Spanish with an online program she purchased.

"I just told her she will always be my baby doll," I answer Lola as I wrap her up again. I pick her up and stand to hand her over to her mom. I place her down, and Lola grabs my hand.

"I've already lost my place with you?" She teases me as she swirls my wedding band.

I, Alejandro Martinez, am wearing a fucking wedding ring and am also damn proud of it. I wanted to be married before the baby came. A bastard baby would be expected of me, and I didn't want to be a cliché. Lola wasn't so keen on the shotgun wedding because she didn't want to be "big," her words, not mine, in the pictures. So we compromised, as I've come to learn to do being with her. We got married at the courthouse and will renew our vows as soon as she fits into the dress she wants.

Her dad was not thrilled with Lola's choice in a man but has slowly come to accept me into his family. I hope to show him each and every day how much I love his daughter and that I will do everything in my power to take care of her. I never want him to think I am after her money. I would want her even if she was as poor as me.

"Never. You just have to share now." I kiss her deeply. This woman has given me everything I never knew I wanted.

"Good." She smiles knowingly. "I can't believe we are here."

"You are the reason we are here. *Soy el desastre que mas te adora*." I wink at her knowing her next question.

She gives me an exaggerated frown at me.

"I'm just the disaster that adores you the most."

She is the only reason we are ready for our baby. She insisted on buying a house for our family. I am nowhere near being financially able to help purchase, but again, she has taken over. I did insist that we should start in a modest home. I need to be able to contribute to our family. She listened, and we have a small home in a safe neighborhood. I would like to say she is the one who went crazy in the baby's room, but I didn't even try and stop her each time she showed me another "cute" necessity. I want my daughter to have all the love, stability, and comfort I never had.

Lola has given me a life I never dreamt possible. A life full of love. A life full of family. My childhood may have been turbulent, but I will not have that for my daughter. I will continue to grow into the man worthy of my girls, appreciating everything that has come into my life.

The nurses finish cleaning up the room and walk out. As soon as they are gone, there is a knock on the door. It opens slowly and Toni sticks her head in. "Can we come in yet?"

I look to Lola for guidance. She nods at me, smiling brightly.

My family and her dad walk into the room, congregating around the bed, all congratulating us.

"Can I hold her?" Toni asks as she grabs the bundle out of Lola's arms, not waiting for an answer.

"Sure, since you've taken her already," Lola teases her.

"She's beautiful." Toni whispers, fixated on the tiny person in her arms.

"What are you naming her?" Lola's dad asks.

We have tossed names around not settling on one. There were the few too-common names Lola threw out: Allison, Paige, and Taylor. I didn't know what name my daughter needed, but I knew it must fit her. Then she suggested Alexandria, after me, and I had to veto that idea. We decided to wait until she was born to see what name fit her. We have another few in our pockets we haven't shared with the others. Now to figure out which it was.

Lola nods her head at me.

"Let's see," she answers her dad. "Bring her to me, Toni."

Toni places her back in Lola's arms, and I crouch down to look closer at her.

"What do you want your name to be little one?" Lola speaks to our daughter. "Do you like the name, Anabel?"

Baby stays still.

"Anabel." Lola says a little louder.

Baby still does nothing.

"How about Gabriela? Do you like that?" Lola begins asking again. "Baby Gabriela?" She repeats. When baby stays still, she turns to me. "You ask her those names now."

"Hello, beautiful Anabel." I say to the baby, and she stays quiet. I look to Lola, and she nods.

"Hello, beautiful Gabriela." I try the next name, and baby still does not respond.

"You don't like those names I see. What about my sweet Madeline?" I say to baby.

She gurgles and squirms a bit. Our eyes widen. Did we find the name?

Lola asks, "Do you want to be our sweet Madeline?" Baby makes a tiny noise, eyes opening.

Not believing she was going to pick her own name, I decide to try calling her one of the previous names.

"Baby Gabriela?" And she is quiet again.

"Baby Madeline?" She moves, freeing her tiny arm from the blanket.

"Looks like we found her name." Lola says to everyone in the room. "Meet Madeline Martinez, a beauty born from a tragically beautiful love story."

ACKNOWLEDGMENTS

Time for all my THANK YOUS!

First and foremost I need to thank my family. To my husband who supports this BIG dream of mine and all that goes into it; all the endless time in front of the computer & money. To my teen who may not understand why I'm doing what I'm doing, but hopefully she will see later on, she can do anything she sets her heart to. To my dad who continues to push me in the author direction even if he doesn't enjoy my genre.

To my sister, Marisa, and sister friends, Susan & Stephanie, who are always willing to listen to my writer life struggles, read my books, and cheer me on.

A HUGE thank you to my author friends, Melissa Frey, Andrea Nourse & Melanie A Smith, for beta reading my work. With your help I was able to make this a much stronger story. Your feedback helped me grow. You will also want to pick up one of their books. They are amazing writers as well.

And here's to Maria Ann Green for always being patient when I decide to tweak the cover! I may or may not have done that again with this book. I also have to thank her for introducing me to the next person, my new editor.

Thank you Jackie for editing my book. I loved our conversations and your help in fine tuning everything. I'm truly grateful to have met you!

I need to mention the Bad Ass Book Babes! This amazing group of indie authors are relentless in their help & support.

They will lend an ear, answer a question or many, make you laugh, and pick you up when you are down. Thank you.

And lastly to all the readers and bookstagrammers. Your support of sharing, reading and reviewing keeps me typing the words.

ALSO BY TORI ALVAREZ

Graffiti Hearts Series

Beautiful Collision

Book 1

Beautiful Serenity

Book 3

Stand Alone

Naive in Love

Steamy Novella

Love's Influence

About Tori Alvarez

Tori Alvarez is an educator by day and author by night. She spent many days and nights daydreaming different stories and scenes, so she finally took the plunge and began putting them down on paper.

Tori writes real, honest romance with a hint of steam. She is a sucker for happily ever afters, so you will always find them in her books too.

Tori is a Texas girl, born and raised. She lives in South Central Texas with her husband, teen daughter, dog & cat.

You can follow her at:
Website & Newsletter Sign up:
http://www.torialvarez.com

facebook.com/tori.alvarez.3551

twitter.com/MsToriAlvarez

instagram.com/mstorialvarez

amazon.com/author/torialvarez

bookbub.com/profile/tori-alvarez

goodreads.com/torialvarez

tiktok.com/@mstorialvarez

A Texas sized Thank you!

Thank you for spending time with Alex and Lola. I hope you enjoyed their story as much as I loved writing it.

Love the book? Please review!

As a small indie author, I appreciate any reviews. Reviews help future readers decide on the next book they will be picking up. Please take a couple of minutes to drop your review. Please visit Goodreads, Bookbub, and/or Amazon to leave your review.

If you post on social media, please tag me. I LOVE to see all the beautiful pictures and mentions.

Thank you, Thank you, Thank you!
 Tori